FAULT LINES

FAULT LINES

STORIES BY NORTHERN CALIFORNIA CRIME WRITERS

EDITED BY MARGARET LUCKE

SISTERS IN CRIME
NORTHERN CALIFORNIA CHAPTER

ISBN (Print): 978-1-7336942-0-9
ISBN (Ebook): 978-1-7336942-1-6

This book is a work of fiction. Names, characters, places, and incidents are either the products of the author's imagination or used in a fictitious manner. Any resemblance to actual persons, living or dead, events, or locales is purely coincidental.

Cover design: Miguel Ortuno of PR Chicago/Cover Story Design
Interior design and formatting: Sue Trowbridge

Sisters in Crime Northern California Chapter
PO Box 1093
Penngrove, California 94951
www.sincnorcal.org

*With thanks and appreciation
to the founders of the Northern California Chapter
of Sisters in Crime, who brought us all together.*

Contents

Foreword

The Northern California Chapter of Sisters in Crime is a dynamic and gifted group of women and men—or as we say, sisters and misters—who have a common passion for mysteries and crime fiction. For many years we've been intrigued by the idea of publishing a short story anthology, both as a way to share our love for this genre with readers and as an opportunity to showcase some of the many writers that we are proud to count among our 150 members.

We knew that we had plenty of talent to draw from, but also that any new venture can a challenge. The question was who had the skills and chops to manage the project? How fortunate we were that Margaret (Peggy) Lucke generously offered her services, proving herself to be the perfect person for the job. Organized, experienced, and a skilled editor, she kept the anthology committee on task, and what you have in your hands is the result of her vision and hard work.

The title, *Fault Lines,* was a natural for an anthology produced in the San Francisco Bay Area, with its crisscross of geological fault lines and its seismic activity. But the word *fault* can have many meanings and nuances. The stories we received made liberal use of fault in the sense of blame, guilt, weakness, imperfection, flaws, sin, divorce, and other meanings. Our authors also took up the concept of *lines,* as in cracks, family and community connections (or disconnects!), lines drawn in the sand, and other subtleties.

What is it about fault that is so fascinating? For the concept of fault lies at the heart of mysteries and crime fiction and is central to its appeal. It's not just a matter of whodunit—which person is responsible for a wrong that has been done to another individual or to the community or to social norms. We also want answers to the questions of how it was done, and why, and what can be done to achieve justice and restore balance.

Collectively, the stories in *Fault Lines* explore all of these angles. Some follow a detective through the course of an investigation. Others look at what happens from a victim's perspective, while several examine the perpetrator's take on his or her misdeeds. That is only one aspect of the variety you will find in this anthology. These stories take you from the California coast to distant Zanzibar. There are tales rooted in the here and now, those that dip into the past, and a couple that have a touch of fantasy.

In addition to the meanings mentioned above, the word lines can refer to the lines that a writer puts on the page. The lines in *Fault Lines* will entertain you, intrigue you, mystify you, and make you think.

The committee was delighted with the quality of the stories we received. We think readers will be, too.

Diana Chambers
President
Sisters in Crime
Northern California Chapter

Terry Shames
Immediate Past President
Sisters in Crime
Northern California Chapter

March 2019

SEGFAULT

Robin C. Stuart

My phone buzzed with a text alert while I waited for a latte at Caffe Acri. The first of the midday ferries to San Francisco pulled away from the Tiburon pier. I had an hour or so until the next boat arrived. More text alerts came in as fast as I could read them.

I took my coffee to one of the outdoor tables, my phone buzzing nonstop. It was tempting to ditch my late breakfast and go next door to Guaymas for a margarita. I checked my watch. Cue a phone call from the boss in five ... four ...

The phone rang. Caller ID announced the computer systems engineering manager. I took a sip of my latte before answering.

"What's going on?" I said.

"Are you seeing this?" Cassie said.

Nothing like an emergency to make both of us forget

professional pleasantries. No "hello," or "how are you today." Just straight to the point.

"My phone's being flooded with network errors," I said. "I stopped for coffee on my way in. What happened? A patch gone awry?"

"I wish."

In the background I heard voices raised over the buzz of alarms in the operations center of the San Francisco Municipal Transit Agency.

"There's been a glitch," Cassie said. "Traffic lights, Muni light rail, BART, and buses are all affected."

I set my cup down. "Glitch? What kind of glitch?"

"That's why I'm calling you. No one can figure it out. Where are you?"

"Waiting on the pier for the next ferry."

"Dammit," she said.

A moment later I heard a rustling, followed by Cassie's voice saying, "I've got him on the line." I figured she meant me. The rest of what she said was too muffled to understand, but I heard her yell something at whoever happened to be closest. She must have a hand over the phone's mic. Another round of rustling, then the sound cleared up again.

"Do you have your laptop with you?" she asked me.

"Yeah, hang on." I hefted my backpack to my lap with my free hand.

"Call me back when you figure it out." Cassie clicked off before I could respond.

It seemed like a shitshow had erupted in the city since my shift the previous night. I set my laptop on the table and logged into the SFMTA VPN—its virtual private network.

Within minutes, my screen filled with mayhem. Traffic lights at every intersection up and down Market Street were green. In both directions. Electric buses had rammed into each other at street crossings.

Underground wasn't any better. Lights at every underground BART and Muni station within San Francisco's city limits were green. Trains rear-ended each other as they barreled through tunnels, their controls believing the coast was clear.

I checked the SFPD public website. Their Twitter feed announced dispatched officers to so many accident scenes, I lost count. The chaos had brought the city to a standstill. The EMT and hospital websites encouraged visitors to sign up for text updates to keep phone lines clear.

My office had a side channel into the 911 call centers around the city. I checked the morning's logs. Multiple injuries reported from the Ferry Building to Van Ness Avenue. No fatalities yet, thank God.

While I kept one eye on the computer screen, watching more alerts scroll into the MTA's security monitoring database, my thumb scrolled the contacts on my cell phone. I found Cassie's number.

"Hey, Cassie, it's me," I said when the boss clicked on. "Who's on point?"

"Adam B. is running the incident. I'll text you the Slack channel where the first responders are working through this. I need a grownup in the room to give me info to feed up the chain. Everyone from the mayor to the governor is demanding updates."

"On it." I clicked to end the call. This was a full-blown crisis.

As promised, Cassie texted me a link to join the agency's computer security incident response team chat.

"Welcome to the party," Adam typed.

"'Sup?" I answered.

One of the computer engineers piped in. "Memory leak in the control system software. Everything's crashing."

"Failing open, I gather," I typed.

Error conditions typically caused software or systems to shut down. By failing open, the computers essentially told traffic control systems that everyone had the right of way. At the same time.

"Seemed like a good idea when we set it all up," the lead engineer said. "I mean, when these systems crash we didn't, like, want trains to literally crash because the third rail loses power."

"I remember." I nodded, even though I was in a text chat, thus no one could see me. "No one thought about the repercussions of all the signals going green."

"Yeah, I thought we were buying time for SFPD to get traffic cops in place," Adam said.

"Shit," another network engineer chimed in.

"Anyone from SFPD here?" I asked.

Someone with the screen name BlueBlood415 answered with a hand-wave emoji. I waited to see if he or she offered a status report or if they'd make me ask. After a couple of seconds, the chat app showed *BlueBlood415 is typing*.

I took a sip of my latte. The patio tables had filled up around me with locals and tourists savoring gourmet sandwiches and sustainably grown, fresh-roasted coffee. I closed my eyes and let my head fall back to enjoy the warmth of the sun on my face. Listening to the waves lap against the rocky shore half a block away gave me a momentary respite from the insanity erupting across the bay.

I returned my attention to the screen. BlueBlood415 had finished his/her comment.

"We're overwhelmed. Evacuating subways, working with you guys to stop BART trains from coming into the city, stopping street traffic in a perimeter around Market Street, coordinating EMTs to triage the worst injuries and get them out. Thousands of people are pouring from the hotels and office buildings to see what's going on. It's a nightmare."

"Why don't we cut power?" someone asked.

A chorus of "No" responded. A blackout would only add to the pandemonium. Emergency response teams needed the lights on to get people out from the underground Muni and BART stations.

"Has anyone tried rebooting the systems?" I asked.

"Yep, we tested one offline and it came back healthy," Adam said. "We're just waiting for the rest of them to come back from reboots now."

I checked my watch, then scrolled backwards through my email inbox. The first alerts had begun a little over fifteen minutes ago.

"What about ferries?" I typed.

While I waited for a reply I opened the application that let me monitor the status of the systems on the SFMTA network. All of them showed spinning wheels in primary colors of the rainbow with same message overlaid on the center of the screen. "Gathering info ..."

"Still running," BlueBlood415 answered. "Outbound only. We've stopped service inbound to the terminals at Ferry Plaza and Fisherman's Wharf."

Seemed reasonable. Although that meant I couldn't get to the office now if I wanted to.

"Cable cars are still running," Adam said. "Those are manual so they're not impacted."

"Let's hear it for historical preservation," another person said.

"FFS," someone typed. For fuck's sake. "Alarms are going off at businesses up and down Market Street. The looters are showing up."

"At the banks, too," Adam said.

"They'll have to wait," BlueBlood415 typed. "SFPD's stretched to the limit. We're waiting on reinforcements. All time off's been cancelled for the day."

"Any idea why this happened?" I recognized Cassie's username. As I was the senior network engineer on call, the question was meant for me.

"Still reviewing logs," I said. "Gotta head back home. No way I'll be able to get into the office in a reasonable amount of time. There's only so much I can do sitting here on the dock for a ferry that's not coming."

I watched the SFMTA's network error logs fill with rows and rows of data from the multiple segment faults. SegFaults, we called them.

"Heading back home to my own lab/network," I typed. "I'll be back online in 15-20 min."

I sat back in my chair and finished the last of my latte. The sun would cast the patio in shadows in another few minutes. I took a couple of deep breaths. The scent of fresh-mown grass from Shoreline Park carried over to the cafe. Deep breathing helped slow my rising heart rate. I inhaled deeply as I laid my hand over the top of my laptop. Exhale, close the laptop.

A long shadow began to stretch over the table. The sun had nudged farther west. In ten minutes, the lunchers would move inside the restaurant to escape the chill. I tucked my laptop back in my bag. Time to go.

I headed for the public parking lot across Main Street. My pride and joy, an early nineties model Toyota pickup truck, faced the bay. I tossed my backpack onto the passenger side of the bench seat as I slid behind the wheel. And then I waited.

My phone chimed with an incoming text. I retrieved the phone from my jacket pocket. Cassie's name showed on the caller ID.

"Hurry home. Just found malware."

The back of my hands tingled with a rush of adrenaline. To be on the safe side, I used the voice-to-text feature to make it look like I was already driving.

"Malware? Where?" I said out loud. The text sent itself a moment later.

The script I planted during last night's shift resided in computer memory only. There should have been no trace left on any system after the reboots. My heartbeat thudded against my eardrums while I stared at my phone, waiting for Cassie's answer.

"One of the backup servers. Robert unplugged it from the network as soon as he spotted a weird service running. Need your help to figure out how it got there."

I covered my eyes with my free hand.

Shit.

I totally forgot about backups. They ran every night. Of course, they picked up my script. I had obfuscated the code, so it should take them at least a couple of hours to decipher. Not that it was complicated. Just a simple timer that launched a memory leak. I copied the script onto all of the control computers. The leaks were timed to synchronize across the transit systems to create a massive systemwide failure.

A bleating horn sounded. From my vantage point in the

public parking lot I watched a ferry maneuver its way to the dock in front of Guaymas.

"C'mon, c'mon," I muttered.

My phone chimed again.

"Where r u?"

I breathed a sigh of relief. The text was identified by a phone number. It didn't map to any of my contacts, but I'd committed the burner cell's number to memory.

"First row, facing the bay," I typed. "I'll flash the headlights when I see you."

The crowd of people spilling out of the ferry was as dense as a normal five o'clock commute. As the cop in the chat indicated, the ferry operators turned away anyone attempting to board.

I flicked the high beams on and off when I saw the first person carrying a large black duffel bag. Headlights at noon may be noticed by a keen observer so I only did it once. The man nodded, then glanced backwards. Behind him, a woman pushed a bicycle; she had a duffel bag slung over her shoulder. Another man with a black duffel bag walked alongside her. The only one I recognized was Jacob, the first guy. He led the others to my truck.

I heard another incoming text. Cassie again.

"Urgent — call me."

I set the phone on "do not disturb" as Jacob and his team surrounded my truck. I rolled down the window.

"Hop in the back. We need to go," I said.

They hefted their duffels into the bed. The woman struggled to fit her bike in.

"Dammit," I said under my breath. I got out to help her.

"Three people, three bags, and a bike aren't going to fit," Jacob said.

"Here, let me put one of these in the cab," I said, grabbing the closest bag.

I nearly fell over. The weight surprised me.

"Jesus, what did you put in here?"

Jacob grunted as he tried to maneuver the bike while his hand-picked accomplices clambered into the truck bed.

"The bank had gold bars in their vault," he said. "The hell with this, it stays."

Jacob tossed the bike. It landed with a clatter in the empty parking space next to me. He hopped into the bed while I threw the duffel in the cab, onto the passenger side of the bench seat. For the hundredth time since owning the truck, I wished I'd bought a king cab.

I unzipped the bag enough to see clumps of cash and a glint of gold. I moved a bundle of cash to reveal several gold bars. Jacob wasn't lying. What were gold bars worth these days?

When I answered his post on a dark web forum, we agreed on an even split. He was looking to bribe an insider at SFMTA to help pull off a colossal heist. While I created the traffic diversion, Jacob's team robbed banks up and down Market Street, then blended in with the crowds of looky-loos. They escaped by hopping on the Powell Street cable car to the wharf where they caught the ferry.

Jacob pounded on the roof. "Let's go."

I zipped the bag back up, then started the engine. Before I put the truck in gear I turned to confirm that everyone had settled in. Jacob and his friends sat alongside the two other duffels in the bed.

I backed out and headed out of Tiburon. I checked my speed as we passed the police station. Several glances at the rearview mirror assured me we weren't being followed. Yet. I gradually accelerated as I wound through town to the freeway.

It was just a matter of time before my radio silence would tip off Cassie that I had something to do with the day's transit chaos. I intended to put as much distance as possible between myself and my overpriced apartment in Mill Valley by the time the police came looking for me.

A tap on the rear window interrupted my reverie. Jacob sat hunched, waiting. Keeping my eyes on the road as I navigated around the other cars on 101, I slid the window open. It felt like Jacob reached in and stuck his finger in my ear.

"Hey, what're—" I turned. The muzzle of a gun nearly poked my eye.

"Pull over," Jacob said. "You're getting out."

So much for our partnership.

My eyes darted around the traffic lanes while my brain kicked into high gear. I hit the gas pedal and turned the wheel abruptly. The sharp lane change threw Jacob off balance. I darted in the other direction for good measure. The gun landed on my bench seat while Jacob flailed around in the bed of the truck. I watched him in the rearview mirror, clambering for something to hold on to. The other guy and the girl collided with each other.

Jacob got a grip on the threshold of the open rear window. I hit the accelerator.

"You motherf—" he yelled as he fell backwards.

The speedometer nudged the 100-mph mark. At this point, I welcomed the prospect of being pulled over. A cop scared me less than a thug with a gun. The steering wheel shuddered in my hands as I wove in and out among other cars on the freeway.

"What are you doing?" Jacob hollered from somewhere behind me.

"You're going to get us all killed," the girl said.

Someone reached into the window and tugged on the back of my hair.

"Hold on tight," I said.

I slammed a foot on the brake pedal. A body smacked against the cab with a thump. The hand let go of me. I stomped on the gas pedal, threw the truck sideways, and barreled to the right across two lanes. I swung the wheel in the other direction, straightening out again, seconds before hitting a retaining wall holding a hillside back from the freeway.

More thumps behind me told me my passengers weren't enjoying the ride. They'd stopped yelling.

I risked another glance in the mirror. Jacob was on all fours, trying to brace a foot against one of the duffel bags while crawling forward. His eyes blazed with pure hatred. A familiar building caught my attention. The Marin Civic Center. Home of the local Superior Court and the Sheriff's Office. Surely, other drivers had called 911 by this point. To keep Jacob and his cohorts off balance, I stomped the brake pedal before punching the gas again.

Red and blue lights flickered behind me.

Finally.

The motorcycle cop was joined by two Marin County Sheriff's cruisers by the time I pulled off at the Civic Center exit. The minute the truck slowed down, Jacob hopped out of the back with one of the duffel bags strapped across his back. The second guy jumped out and ran in the opposite direction. The girl waited until I stopped in the middle of the road to try to lift the second bag. She gave up and ran off when the motorcycle cop dismounted.

I grabbed my phone. A Lyft was four minutes away. I opened the door and slid out. My hands were up so the cops could see I was unarmed.

"Thank God," I said. "There's a gun on the seat. That guy with the bag pulled it on me."

"This your truck?" the cop said.

"No, it's his."

"What his name?"

I gave the cop mine. It just slipped out. I hoped a plan would bubble up from the same place in my subconscious. One of the two cruisers peeled off to pursue Jacob. I was committed now.

"Why were you driving?" the motorcycle cop said.

"I was on the Tiburon ferry and going to my own car." I nodded at the open door. "They were on the ferry, too. I noticed the girl. I didn't realize the three of them were together until I got to the parking lot across the street. That guy pulled a gun on me and told me to drive."

Shut up. I heard myself babbling. The cop took her glasses off to look me up and down. Maybe she thought I was rattled from being carjacked.

"If you were driving, how did you get the gun away from him?" she asked.

Or maybe not. I forced a smile. "Did you see the way I was driving?"

"You have ID?" she said.

"He took my wallet," I said. My hands were still in the air so I pointed in the direction Jacob had run.

"What's your name?"

"Jacob," I lied. "Is it okay if I put my hands down? My fingers are getting numb."

The cop nodded and turned away from me. She sauntered over to the remaining cruiser. The sheriff had been leaning against the fender of his car, watching us.

The two of them talked briefly. They were too far away

for me to hear but the motorcycle cop gestured in my direction. The sheriff never took his eyes off me.

Until he did. The woman continued to talk while the sheriff looked away and put his sunglasses back on. Then he got back in his car and got on his radio.

I'd told more lies in the last five minutes than I had in the previous five years. Sweat rolled down my back. The sheriff just sat there in his car. That could be good, or I could be carted off in handcuffs in the next few minutes. What if he had a screen and pulled up my driver's license while calling in the name I gave them for Jacob?

The motorcycle cop headed back to me. I relaxed my facial muscles. The picture of an innocent victim. I hoped.

"The sheriff is impounding the truck. He'll get your statement," she said. She pointed her chin in the direction of the cruiser.

"Can I go pick up my kid from school?" I said. The lies kept rolling off my tongue with ease.

She straddled the CHP motorcycle while she snapped the strap on her helmet.

"Of course. You're free to go after talking to the sheriff." She nodded in the direction of the sheriff. "But how are you getting there?"

My Lyft car pulled up behind the cruiser. The whites of the driver's widened eyes were visible from here as he took in the scene. I pointed to the car.

"I called a friend."

The cop pressed the button to start the motorcycle. The sun reflected off her helmet as she gave me a brief half-nod. "That was smart, you know," she said. "Crazy driving to get our attention? Stupid. But smart."

I gave her an aw-shucks smile. She revved the engine. The tires squealed along the pavement on her way back out to 101.

When I turned my attention back to the cruiser, I saw the sheriff had gotten out. I forced myself to keep my stride casual as I walked over to him. A tow truck rolled slowly toward my pickup. I turned to bid a silent farewell to the Toyota and pretended not to notice the bag in the bed.

What a waste.

After giving the sheriff Jacob's burner phone number as my own, I blurted out a semblance of events that heightened my role as an innocent bystander who got carjacked. I promised to be available for further questioning, then got into the waiting Lyft. The driver said nothing. His eyes were still wide as he pulled onto the freeway and headed north.

I settled back in the seat. The bundles of cash dug into the small of my back. I'd snatched during my examination of the duffel bag in the cab and tucked them into my waistband. It wasn't as much as I'd hoped to get, but it was more than enough to buy a fresh start.

This time around went better than the last one. I learned new lessons I'd take with me to the next town, the next identity, the next computer job at a high-value target. Next time would be even better.

———————

When I heard the theme for this anthology, the first word that popped in my head was "segfault," techie shorthand for "segmentation fault," which is an error condition that causes a process or system to fail. I knew then I wanted to write a good, old-fashioned caper with a cyber spin. Part of the story was inspired by an element from an investigation early in my crime-fighting career. Another part incorporates (and embellishes) a situation that happened to someone I know. While noodling around with how to tie it all together, I was on my way to a meeting in San Francisco. The meeting got postponed because of a power outage that shut down a significant portion of downtown, including BART and Muni stations. That gave me the idea for the inciting incident. The cause of the real outage was a fire in a power substation, but not in *my* story.

—Robin C. Stuart

A NO-FAULT MURDER

Susan Kuchinskas

He was a bad boy, with a record—internet fraud, drugs—and a worse reputation. She was a good girl. College degree, nice job as an accountant, friends. So why was she the one who ended up dead? That's what her sister wanted me to find out.

I call my agency Woman's Eye. The idea is to let clients know up front they're getting a woman detective, with hopefully a little edge. Even today, in this age of female empowerment, you'd be surprised how many people don't think a woman can handle the ugly jobs.

And the jobs are ugly. Deadbeat dads, rent skippers, the occasional lost dog.

The one thing I didn't do was divorce.

And the one thing I'd never done was murder. Not that I was averse. It's just that most people are content to let the cops sort that out.

So, when my first big case involved divorce *and* murder, yeah, it got my juices going. This could be the big time.

• • •

The sister, Emily Melendez, seemed like a very nice girl. I know, I'm supposed to say *woman*, but when you hit fifty, the young ones start to look really young. She came to our meeting at WeWork in a skinny pantsuit. She had a trendy, shaggy haircut and cool shoes. I pegged her for one of the tech elites, and it gave me a little twist of pleasure that she was coming to see me. There are some things you still can't just google.

"They said it was an accident," she told me. "She slipped and fell down the stairs." Her green eyes flashed.

"But you don't think so. Why not?"

"Rosie was so careful. She was, like, the most organized person I know."

"Accidents happen." I was playing devil's advocate and also trying to gauge how tenacious she might be as a client.

"Not to my sister."

I had to laugh a little, although I tried not to. "Really? No broken bones? No skinned knees? No fender benders?"

She flushed. "You know what I mean. A scraped knee, sure. But plunging down a flight of stairs? No way."

"So, what do you think happened?"

"I think Eddie Litz murdered her."

There it was, bare and bold. It would be my first murder

case—even if it probably wasn't murder. How could I say no?

• • •

Emily gave me the goods on her sister, showed me a photo of Rosie and Eddie Litz on her phone. Eddie was blond and a bit pudgy, in a good way. He looked like he liked his beer and would be fun to drink with. His fair skin and blue eyes contrasted with the jail tattoos all over his arms, which were twined around Rosie in the photo. She looked like she liked it. She was laughing, big white teeth like seashells, long dark hair curling down one shoulder.

They seemed like a happy couple. But then, things change, don't they?

Rosie and Eddie had been separated for a couple of months, figuring out how much they wanted to spend to get a divorce. It's easy enough in California, which is a no-fault divorce state. You can do it yourself with a book from Nolo Press, or you can spend many thousands of dollars on fancy lawyers.

Emily gave me a check for $1,000. That was just to ask some questions, scope it out. I started, of course, with Eddie.

According to Emily, he was camping in his art studio in West Oakland. He wasn't too hard to reach. I texted him a couple of times with no response, so I called him at 7:00 a.m. on Monday. Ever since menopause, I'm up before daylight, which is a bitch but gives me an advantage over normal sleepers.

"Wha ...?" he answered.

"I'm calling on behalf of Emily Melendez. We need to talk."

"Arrggh." The groan could have been at the name or just the time of day. "What does she want? I gave her back the cat."

"I need to find out some details, that's all. When can we meet?"

"Um, Friday?"

"Today, Eddie."

"Uhhhh."

"I'll be over in an hour. With bagels. What's your address?"

"Fuck off." He hung up.

No worries.

• • •

The ramshackle warehouse where Eddie lived was in an ungentrified part of West Oakland. Next door, garbage drifted against broken bleachers in a battered playing field.

The dented metal door had a small window fortified with thick mesh, a single doorbell marked doom. The guy who opened the door was elaborately tattooed and pierced. A bloody-looking rose covered the left side of his neck, and his shaved head was covered with a Celtic symbol. His earlobes gaped where large plugs had been removed, but the thick ring under his nose remained. Three stainless steel bars twinkled along his left eyebrow.

I'm always conflicted in these situations. My mom taught me not to stare, but I assume these decorations are meant to be stared at. He watched me calmly, obviously used to the effect.

"I'm looking for Eddie."

"He's in back." The Illustrated Man led me in with no apparent interest in what a middle-aged woman wearing mom jeans wanted with his friend.

We went through a narrow hall cluttered with bikes and the carcass of a motorcycle, out into a large, high-ceilinged room. Machine shop tools hulked on carts. Industrial shelving lined the walls, holding a clutter of equipment and parts.

I almost tripped on something, a tangle of machinery stretching along the floor.

"That's Star Roller," he said.

"Oh." It didn't look like anything to me.

"My Burning Man project." He tapped a piece of it with his foot, and it skidded a few feet along a curved track. "That will all be on fire."

"Nice," I muttered, just to be polite.

We wove among worktables and piles of deconstructed machinery to a fire door. He opened it, and the chill of the main room was replaced by the old-gym-socks smell of male habitation.

It was a man cave for the kind of man who loves the dark—all kinds of dark.

The air was thick and steamy, soaked with the tang of testosterone. The walls were unfinished drywall stained with traces of mildew and marked with the relentless prints of dirty hands. The light was cool blue, thanks to a huge flat-screen TV playing a YouTube of jellyfish.

A poster on the wall showed a snarling, yellow-eyed wolf with the words: *You can't throw me to the wolves. They come when I call.*

In the center of the room was a double mattress, saggy and tangled with sheets. In the center of the bed was Eddie Litz, looking like a beached fish, the soft, pink body sprawled out, the cupid's lips gaping. As we stood there, a wet, snorting snore jerked his body.

"Eddie," said my guide. "You have company."

Eddie thrashed and snorted again. The Illustrated Man had a smirk on his face and I understood the game—humiliate the roommate.

"Dude. Wake up."

Like many big men, Eddie was slow to rouse. Blue eyes opened, closed, and opened again. He groaned, rolled his head, and finally got up on one elbow and saw me.

"What the fuck?" he said, with not a lot of emotion. It was literally just a question.

The roommate smiled as though the whole thing had given him some kind of satisfaction and left us there.

I pushed a wadded-up hoodie off a dissolute armchair and sat. I put the bag of bagels on the floor in front of him.

Eddie did not look good. His nails were grimy and bitten ragged. The knuckles on his left hand were battered. He stared back with eyes that could sparkle, but they were dead now. His face was puffy, with sunken eye sockets and lips that dragged down. His hair clung to his head in oily locks, like a mess of discarded french fries.

He didn't seem to question who I was or why I was there; he just returned my gaze, breathing through his half-open mouth. I noticed a mummified dog's head on a shelf behind him.

Finally, he produced a croak of a voice that seemed to belch from his belly. "Who are you?"

"My name is Carla Strong, and I'm investigating Rosie's death."

He stared at me, mouth hanging open. The damp heat of the room settled on me like a dirty duvet. I pushed the bag of bagels a bit with my foot.

"Have a bagel."

He ignored the food. "Why is she torturing me?"

"Who? Emily? It's hardly torture to want to find out how her sister died."

"It was an accident," he moaned. "The police said so."

He thrashed, tearing himself loose from the fusty blankets, and swung his legs over the side of the mattress, head in hands. "That bitch. That fucking bitch."

"Rosie?"

"Emily. She's hounding me. She won't leave me alone."

I put some sympathy into my voice. "What's she done?"

He was practically spitting. "She got me fired from my job. And now you." He pushed off the bed and began pacing.

"Calm down," I said, knowing that this is the best way to egg someone on. I wanted him off balance.

"Fuck off! I loved Rosie, and she loved me. And now she's dead."

"But you were getting divorced."

"It was all a big misunderstanding. We were going to work it out. Until Emily stuck her nose in."

"I'm just trying to get some more information."

"No, you're not. You're trying to fuck with me. Like Emily did. Like they all do." He whirled and hit the wall with his fist. The drywall stood up to the blow. It must have really hurt him.

"Well," I said. "Let me know if you change your mind. Here's my card, and my number's on your phone."

I left him the bagels.

• • •

Eddie was an interesting character, and I like that. I'm a people person. My shaking his tree might or might not bear fruit. Is that a mixed metaphor? In any case, it was time to get a fuller picture of Rosie and the rest of the cast of characters.

She'd worked as an accountant at Oregano, one of those

concrete-and-steel restaurants with a wood-burning pizza oven and a crew of hipster cooks working the line in an open kitchen. I stopped in on Tuesday afternoon and caught the owner, Pierpaulo Castelli.

He was huddling over salads with his sous-chef when I pushed open the heavy glass door. "We're closed. Sorry."

He was lithe and dark and made me wish I was in my thirties. I introduced myself and said, "I just need ten minutes of your time. It's about Rosie Melendez."

"Of course." He put down the chef's knife and came toward me, indicating an aisle table. "Sit down. Can I get you a glass of wine? An espresso?"

"Nothing but your time. What can you tell me about Rosie in the days before her death? Was she anxious or fearful about anything?"

"I wouldn't know."

"You wouldn't know. She worked here four nights a week."

"She was on her way out. In a sense, she was already gone."

"You were going to fire her?"

He leaned back, giving me a view of his fine nostrils. "Fired, quitting, whatever. She was unhappy here. She thought she wasn't being treated well."

"And was she?"

He leaned toward me. "You know how it is. There's lots of pressure in our industry. We like to let off steam. It's playful. We tease and fool around."

I could feel the sexual heat coming off him. "But she didn't like that."

He shrugged. "Rosie was a beautiful girl. I let her know that. It's the most natural thing in the world. But she took offense."

"How far did that go?"

His eyes got sharp as one of his knives, and the heat looked more like rage than sex. "She was a—" He swallowed, got control of himself. "People beg me to work here. They understand it's a privilege. And you know what they say"—leaning in to me again, so I felt the intensity of his emotion—"if you can't stand the heat, get out of the kitchen."

• • •

I took a stroll through Rosie's social media. Her Facebook profile was still up. It was the usual Millennial mix of selfies, travel photos, and inspirational memes. She and Eddie looked like they had a lot of fun. Of course, that was her public face. Anything revealing would be in Messenger.

I paused on a group shot of Rosie and coworkers, all decked out in chef's whites except for Rosie, who was in a tailored shirt and jeans, and Pierpaolo, dressed in a blue oxford shirt. They were a diverse and attractive bunch. Pierpaolo was in the second row, and maybe it was chance, but he seemed to be looming over Rosie, who stood in front of him. His lean, dark jaw looked ready to bite her ear.

Rosie's tweets had been hitting #MeToo hard, mostly retweets but a few of her own, also hashtagged #restaurants. I knew the restaurant business was hard on women, and a lecherous boss made it a lot worse. Rejecting someone's advances didn't seem like cause for murder. But you never know about people.

• • •

Tavia Brewer was Rosie's best friend, according to Emily. She suggested we meet on Tuesday evening at Club Mallard, a bar in El Cerrito that looked like a duck-hunters' lodge. Tavia ordered a complicated tequila cocktail off the drinks menu; I got one called Death and Taxes. The bartender looked annoyed. We took our drinks to a pair of red leather club chairs in front of the gas fire, where we could ponder the eighteen-point rack of moose antlers above the fieldstone fireplace.

Tavia was butch-lite, on the androgynous side, with short auburn hair, a tailored jacket and motorcycle boots, but with cat-eye glasses to take the edge off. Her handshake was warm and firm, and her gaze was open.

"I miss her every day," she told me.

"Let me just ask you straight out. Emily thinks Eddie killed her. What do you think?"

She stared down into her cocktail. "Eddie can be a dick."

"A murderous dick?"

"Good question. But really, how would I know, right?"

"Intuition?"

She looked up at me. "Women's intuition?"

"It's a real thing, intuition. Things we notice that don't quite make it up into the conscious mind, but we file them away. And women may be better at it. Sometimes."

She smiled slowly. "Is that your detective secret weapon?"

I smiled back, enjoying her. "Maybe."

She stretched her long legs out toward the fire. "I don't know," she sighed.

"Why were they getting divorced?"

"She liked Eddie because he was, you know, kind of an outlaw. But he wasn't really her style."

"How so?"

"He was a big fuckup. He'd been in jail."

"I know."

"At first, Rosie thought it was cool. But it was a symptom, you know?"

"A symptom."

"Of general fuckedupedness. He just couldn't keep it together. He always had these big schemes but they never worked out." She ruffled her hair with her fingers. "They were saving to buy a house. Then Eddie lost the money in some deal to import organic, loose-leaf green tea. I mean, really?"

"Wow." I swallowed some beer. "So Rosie decided to dump him."

She threw her head back and laughed. "Not even! Rosie made excuses for him, like she always did."

"Then why the divorce?"

Tavia banged her glass on the table. "Because he didn't understand her! He didn't understand her." She looked at me, eyes wide in exaggerated disbelief.

"Well," I said, "he probably didn't."

She snorted, and we both burst out laughing, sharing a moment. She was a strong, competent woman, and I wondered if Rosie might have been better off with her instead of Eddie.

• • •

On Wednesday I was kicked back on my couch, savoring a scandalously early Manhattan and thinking about Eddie Litz. I could see the attraction—even the fuckedupedness part. There's something about a sweet loser. And I felt a lot of sympathy for him. I know what it's like to reach for something better and come up short.

The decision to divorce Eddie probably came from Rosie's accountant brain rather than her heart. Could I see the man throwing her down the stairs in a rage? No, but it didn't matter. I'm not psychic.

My phone buzzed and I swiped. "Woman's Eye."

"It's Neal Steiner."

"Okay."

"Ed's studio mate."

"Eddie Litz's?"

"Yeah."

The Illustrated Man. "What's up?"

"I need to talk to you. About Rosie."

"Okay."

"No, in person. Can you come to the warehouse?"

I didn't relish trekking back down to that dank and deserted place. While I can take care of myself, there were too many items that could deliver a killing blow just lying around in there. On the other hand, my office is wherever there's wi-fi.

"I have a lot of appointments, today, Neal, and I'm up in Piedmont. Can we meet halfway?"

• • •

Neal was wearing the same greasy black pants, and ripped T-shirt as the last time I'd seen him, or maybe different ones. He didn't draw any stares in Hella Vegan Eats, and neither did I in my black jeans, white silk top, and ankle boots. Yes, I had dressed up for the occasion, not sure why.

We sat down with a couple Novel Plotline IPAs; I'd paid. Neal dug into his front pocket and brought out a wad of crumpled bills, dirty tissues, and a couple of greasy ball bearings. "Here's for my beer."

"That's all right," I said, suppressing a shudder at the grease and grime. "My pleasure. Now, what did you want to tell me about Rosie?"

He'd put the plugs in his ear piercings, and he fingered one of the polished black stones. "She wasn't like everyone thinks."

"And what do they think?"

"Rosie was the nice one, the smart one, the good one."

"But she wasn't?"

One side of his lip curled up in a tiny sneer. "She was a bitch. She ran Ed like a train. She ran him right into the wall, until he couldn't take it anymore."

I raised an eyebrow. "Are you implicating your friend in murder?"

"He's not my friend."

I winced at the venom. "Okay, whatever. But let's be clear. Are you saying you think Eddie killed Rosie and made it look like an accident?"

He stuck out his lower lip in a way that made him look, despite all his modifications, like a sulky three-year-old. "I'm just saying."

• • •

Neal and I had gone round and round, but he hadn't given me anything more concrete. I finished my beer and headed home for an early night with Netflix.

The next morning, I didn't check my phone until I was sitting down with coffee and an English muffin. Yes, I'm old-school. I don't sleep with my phone.

I had seven texts from Emily. The first one said: *I finally got Verizon to unlock Rosie's phone. Look at these.*

The other six were forwarded texts from Eddie, sent to her over a period of five days, getting more and more desperate. The first said, simply, *Pls call me.*

The last was troubling, obviously a voice-to-text from someone who was losing it. *You cannot do this I'm not going to let you do this to me you can't know I got Rosie please listen I just please no no.*

Despite my misgivings about the place, I was at Eddie's warehouse in fifteen minutes flat. Again, it was Neal, the Illustrated Man, who answered the door. In the vast shop, his angular machine was growing, spiky arms like swords sprouting from the Star Roller.

Again, Eddie was laid out in bed, looking like he hadn't moved since the last time I'd been there. He looked up at me with the miserable eyes of a refugee. Nowhere to go.

I wanted to view him with a cool eye and a clear head, but all I felt was compassion. I flashed back to the days after my husband left. It had been all Ménage à Trois Merlot and binge-watching Jessica Jones. If someone had shown up on one of my worst days, I might have looked just like Eddie. Sans the stubble.

"Eddie, you have to talk to me."

He just groaned. Neal was lurking ghoulishly in the doorway. "Help me get him up."

Eddie stank. Beer, pot, dehydration, and BO. We walked him into the bathroom. I turned on the shower, nice and hot. "Come on, Eddie, you'll feel better if you get clean." I turned away while he got naked and into the shower stall, then I used the tip of my shoe to put down the toilet lid and sat.

I heard more groans, the sounds of Eddie giving it up to the heat.

"Eddie."

A sob. "I just want it to end."

"You can end it right now, Eddie. Just tell me the truth."

He muttered something, too low for me to hear through the running water.

"What?"

"She was seeing someone else."

Poor Eddie. I tamped down that compassionate impulse fast and tried to summon some killer instinct. This was motive for real, one of the oldest in the book. I took a deep breath. "That must have hurt."

"It killed me."

Interesting choice of words. The shower stopped, and the shower door opened. I hastily thrust a towel into the hand that emerged. The rest of Eddie followed, modestly wrapped, skin glowing like a baby's against the muddled dark-blue tattoos. He looked at me hopelessly.

"Did you kill her?"

"No!" he howled. "I would never. I loved her."

I had to look away. His tears undid me.

• • •

So, I had a distraught, soon-to-be ex-husband, a lecherous rageaholic restaurateur who might have pressed Rosie too far, and the muttered innuendo of a roommate with some axe to grind—no pun intended. I had nothing.

What makes someone snap hard enough to overcome one of civilization's deepest strictures? What does it take to drive a person to that kind of violence? I had no clue. Eddie Litz was a lovable bumbler. Could he commit a passion crime? Pierpaulo Castelli was an asshole, but why murder Rosie when he could get rid of her by firing her?

But what did I know? I was so-so at tracking down deadbeat dads. My big success had been recovering Bumpus, the stolen fox terrier. I wasn't a real detective, just a middle-aged ex-insurance agent with delusions of grandeur.

I hated to give Emily the news, but I didn't want to keep taking her money. We agreed to meet at Rosie and Eddie's apartment. She was cleaning it out.

It was a sweet little upstairs flat in a North Oakland duplex, behind a wrought-iron fence and the de rigueur butterfly garden. The stairs were steep, and highly trippable. I felt a pang for both of them, imagining how pleased they must have been to be starting life together.

Emily was kneeling on the floor of the living room, putting books into a cardboard box. The place was half packed up; a rolled rug leaned against the wall, the bookcases were empty, and the curtains were folded on a table.

She rose onto her knees when she saw me, hopeful. "Did you find something?"

"Emily, I'm sorry."

"What about those crazy texts? They're evidence, aren't they?"

"You should take them to the police."

She slumped back down, fat tears dripping off her chin. So much crying. I wondered if Rosie cried before she dumped Eddie.

"They don't give a shit," she wailed. "You were my only hope."

I didn't want to say all the things I was thinking. Maybe it really was an accident. Maybe it didn't matter exactly what happened—Rosie was still dead. Maybe you should have placed your hope somewhere better.

I moved toward the kitchen to get her a drink of water, and my foot skidded out from under me. As I fell to one knee, I heard a metallic noise and put a hand out. It was a ball bearing, its greasy surface coated lightly with dust.

• • •

We were sitting on the deck at Julie's Café, Emily, Eddie and me. Sun filtered through potted palms onto our wrought-iron table. At the next one over, a golden lab snuffled for crumbs under its owner's chair. It was a lovely setting for a sad scene.

Emily stared moodily into her chai. "I still think Neal pushed her," she said.

When I brought what I'd found to the lead investigator on Rosie's case, the detective wanted to shrug me off. I mean, one ball bearing? Really? But she was smart and committed, so she'd checked it out. It hadn't taken much for Neal to break. He admitted most of it.

He and Rosie had hooked up, but she wasn't that into it. That night, they argued, he tried to kiss her, she'd pushed him away. Somehow, they both ended up at the bottom of the stairs, him on top, her not moving. He panicked and ran.

Who knew? Maybe she slipped on another of those goddamn ball bearings. They might charge Neal with something, but it wouldn't be murder.

Still, I was thrilled. I'd solved the case.

Eddie's head was hanging, though. "I can understand her not wanting to be with me. I fucked up. Again. But her and Neal?"

Emily gave him a dirty look. "She had terrible taste in men. Obviously."

"Aw, fuck you." But his heart wasn't in it. They'd both loved Rosie. They'd do better if they could lean on each other while they mourned.

"Maybe she was planning on coming back?" I said tentatively.

And then, Eddie lost it. His fist slammed the table, and he bawled. Tears spurted, and soon Emily's followed. My own eyes were wet, as their grief reignited mine.

"It's my fault," Eddie kept saying. "I should have been a better husband. I should have taken care of her. It's all my fault."

"It's not your fault, Eddie," I told him. But I couldn't help thinking it kind of was.

———————

W hen I heard the theme *Fault Lines,* my mind went to *no-fault divorce* and, from there, to contemplating how, in relationships, we often do our best but make mistakes anyway. I enjoy fiction that takes me into new places, so I decided to set the story in San Francisco's underground art scene. From there, this was one of those rare times when the characters introduced themselves to me and took the story away.

—Susan Kuchinskas

TWO-BUCK HITCH

J.J. Lamb

Clearwater, Florida—1951

"Where you goin'?" asked the blonde, leaning across the seatback of a faded, cream-colored '48 Ford convertible.

"North," I said. "Gainesville. Tallahassee. Pensacola. Anyplace."

"Yeah, me, too. Jump in."

I tossed my duffel bag into the backseat and watched while she cleared clothes, newspapers, and take-out food debris off the passenger seat and tossed it all behind the seat.

She was older than me, maybe ten years more than my twenty; attractive, in an I-don't-give-a-damn way—no makeup, hair wind-tossed, bosom-tight T-shirt, and tan, wrinkled and food-stained short-shorts. But mainly, she was offering me a ride.

I avoided a couple of broken seat springs sticking up through the cracked brown leather upholstery. The rest of the three-year-old drop-top was in the same ratty condition.

"Gonna need some gas," she said. "Can you chip in?"

I didn't like the sound of that. I'd been standing alongside U.S. 19-Alt in Clearwater with my thumb out since around 8:00 a.m. This was my first ride offer in close to three and a half hours. But ...

The $200 I'd left home with almost a month earlier was close to becoming just a memory, despite my staying in YMCAs and very cheap hotels, and, for the past two weeks, with friends of my parents. During numerous rides that got me from Fort Wayne to Tampa, no one ever asked me for gas money.

The friendly ex-Hoosiers drove me to the highway earlier in the morning, not only to help me get a start on the day's hitchhiking, but also, I think, to get me off their screened-in back porch.

I'd wanted to stick around, but work was scarce. Despite my impressive experience as soda jerk, grocery clerk, movie usher, gas station attendant, backyard mechanic, apprentice butcher, and factory assembly line worker, no one offered me a job. I even had union cards for a couple of those humble skills, but I stopped showing them after a few interviewers threatened me and chased me out of their offices.

Two weeks of looking and the only thing I'd found was

busing tables in a cafeteria for one dollar and one meal a day, seven days a week.

It was time to move on.

"I can come up with a buck," I told the blonde, not wanting to lose the ride. That would be good for five gallons.

"Double that and we can make it to Gainesville for sure. Maybe even Tallahassee, if we're lucky."

I stared at her too-small T-shirt, fantasized, and nodded in agreement.

"Okay!" She banged a fist on the steering wheel. "You had breakfast?"

"Yes."

"Well, I need something to get me started."

I looked at my watch, then at her. It was almost noon.

"So I got up a little late this morning." She ground the gears shifting into first, pulled away from the curb, and held out her right hand, palm up. She snatched up my two one-dollar bills without comment or change of expression.

A few blocks down the street, she pulled into a gas station–café, parked by the pumps, and told the attendant to fill the tank.

"Come on in," she said. "It's getting hot out here."

"No, thanks. I'll stick by the car."

"Up to you, kid. But it's fifty miles between here and the next decent place to stop. You might wanna use the potty while we're here."

She was right about that.

I got out of the car and started toward the café, then looked back at my duffel lying across the back seat of the open car.

"Hey!" she shouted from the doorway. "No one's gonna bother your lousy stuff." When I didn't move, she shrugged. "If you're that worried, bring the damn bag in with you."

She was already seated at the lunch counter when I entered. I motioned that I was going to the men's room and dropped the duffel bag beside her. She nodded.

Fact was, I really needed the john for more than a simple stand-up pause. With each passing minute I became more anxious, certain that when I came out, she, the convertible, my two bucks, and my duffel would be gone.

But she was still there, shoveling heaping spoonfuls of sugar into a steaming cup of coffee.

"My God!" she said. "I thought you'd moved in." She picked up a piece of dry toast and bit off one corner.

"Sorry."

"You finally ready?"

"Yes."

"Good!" She put money on the counter, gulped down the coffee, and headed for the door, still nibbling at the toast.

• • •

"How long you been on the road?" she asked after we were clear of town.

"Almost a month."

"Couldn't stomach your mommy and the old man anymore, huh?"

"Just wanted to get away for a while," I said. "Couldn't get any of my friends to come with me."

"Yeah, people are like that."

"You live around here?"

"Just travelin'," she said. "Gettin' from here to there." She turned on the radio, found a country music station, and tapped her fingertips on the rim of the steering wheel, not quite in rhythm.

With the sun and hot air beating at me, I soon fell asleep.

• • •

Someone shook me.

I forced open my gritty eyes to find my blonde chauffeur pulling on my arm.

"This is it," she said.

"This is what?"

"Where I turn off."

"But ..."

"Out. You and your duffel bag."

"But ..."

"Don't give me a rasher of shit." She pointed a small, chrome semi-automatic at me.

"I thought ..."

"I don't give a crap what you thought, buster. Now get out!"

I reached into the back seat and grabbed my duffel, afraid if I got out first she'd drive off with it. In the process, I wedged the bag in the too-narrow space between the seatback and the doorpost. Caught there for a moment, I held on tight to my bag while I twisted around enough to get the door open.

"Move it!"

I lifted the duffel up and out of the car and plopped it down in the dirt at my feet. "Where are we?"

The rear tires spun as she did a left turn across the highway and headed off down a dirt road. I watched dumbfounded as the convertible disappeared, leaving behind a lazy cloud of brown dust.

She'd dumped me in a desolate stretch of wind-whipped sand and scraggly, unidentifiable-to-me vegetation. There wasn't so much as a tree, let alone a building, within sight in any direction.

During the next several hours, none of the infrequent northbound drivers even slowed, let alone stopped to offer a ride. One couple actually sped up, and another pulled so far over to the left that the car's tires dropped off the two-lane asphalt road. A few people actually smiled and waved.

I thought about how my parents and friends tried to talk me out of dropping out of college after only one semester to hitchhike through the South. They were certain I would end up on a chain gang.

But I was adamant. I was tired of snow, sleet, and slush; I

wanted to see something other than Indiana before Uncle Sam nabbed me for Korea.

Now, I was tired, hungry, disgusted with myself, and considering how I might have to sleep alongside the road. My spirits picked up a bit when I heard the faint roar of a truck in the distance. Even though I knew no trucker with his rig up to speed was going to stop for a hitchhiker, I stuck out my thumb anyway. I watched him whiz past, and then sat back down on the duffel bag.

The hiss of air brakes spun my head around. The tractor-flatbed was pulling off onto the berm. An arm waved from the driver's window.

I hoisted the duffel onto one shoulder and walked toward the semi, half expecting the rig to accelerate away and the friendly hand to turn into a middle-finger salute.

The passenger door swung open.

"Going as far as Tallahassee, if you don't mind ridin' with me," said the Negro driver, his expression solemn.

"Sounds good to me," I said. "Where should I put my bag?"

"Latch it down on the trailer, with my stuff."

I used a couple of tie-downs to make the bag secure. Next to it were an old leather suitcase and a twine-tied cardboard box. The rest of the trailer was empty.

"Carter!" he said, offering a hand to help me up into the sharp-as-new International Harvester tractor. Despite the heat, he was wearing a necktie, beige twill jacket, and sharply creased pants of the same material.

"Earl," I said, shaking his hand.

"From up north?"

"Indiana."

"Uh-huh! Army sent me to Fort Benjamin Harrison, near Indianapolis."

"Never been there," I said. "I live farther north, Fort Wayne."

He nodded, concentrating on going through the gears to get the truck back up to speed. "Have to make a stop a few miles up the road."

"Long stop?" I asked.

"Huh-uh! Just gonna pick up my wife. Movin' to Pensacola."

"Oh!"

"Probably wondering why I said Tallahassee, huh?"

I nodded.

"Figurin' that for a stopover. Can't make Pensacola without a little sleep." He was quiet for a moment. "You can come with us, though, if you want."

I was up for the ride, but not for getting trapped into spending money on a motel room.

"Can you drive a rig like this?" he asked.

"Have a chauffeur's license," I said. It was Indiana's version of a commercial driver's license, but I'd never driven a semi.

"Well, to tell the truth, we could make it to Pensacola by drivin' straight through the night, providin' you could swap off at the wheel."

"I could do that." I pulled out my wallet and showed him my driver's license.

"Looks good," he said. "I'd sure enough appreciate the help. Sometimes it's real difficult finding a place to stay overnight."

I leaned back and relaxed.

"Your truck?" I asked.

"Yes, sir! Saved my money while I was in the army. Didn't gamble it away like some fellers. GI Bill helped, too."

He pulled off the road just after dark and stopped at a dimly lighted, clapboard gas station–café–grocery.

"Truck and I need fuel," he said wearily. "You hungry?"

"Maybe a sandwich or something," I said, not wanting to admit I hadn't eaten since breakfast. "Food good here?"

"Nothin' fancy, but it'll stick to your ribs." Once we were on the ground, he added, "You go on in and order while I fill the tanks."

"Want me to order for you, too?"

"No, just get for yourself."

"I'll wait for you."

"No, go ahead on in." He started filling one of the truck's two saddle tanks. When I didn't move, he looked at me, frowned, and said, "Don't give me no grief here, Earl. I know you mean well, but ways here are different than in Indiana."

"You're not going to eat?"

"Yes. Out back with the cook."

"Doesn't seem right."

"Maybe, maybe not." He nodded, more to himself than to me. "Won't do either of us any good to make trouble over it, though." His worried expression told me not to push it.

The white and colored signs on restrooms, water fountains, and other facilities hadn't surprised me when I crossed into Kentucky from Indiana, but I had a hard time accepting it as a reality. I was used to a more passive, seldom-mentioned kind of segregation back home.

Now, I was frustrated, angry, and ashamed.

What was happening was wrong. But I didn't know how to make it right.

I had no personal experience with Negroes beyond playing football against a few in high school; there were none on our team. The only colored people I knew by name were either in sports or entertainment. I didn't know a single colored person in my hometown. I'd never shaken hands or spoken to a Negro before Carter stopped to pick me up.

And I was going to be his champion?

I went inside, found a seat at a small, chrome-edged Formica counter across from the pass-through window to the kitchen. Almost got into trouble anyway by insisting that I didn't want any grits on my plate.

After a few minutes, I saw Carter enter the kitchen and greet the Negro cook. He looked out and gave me the briefest nod. The cook scowled.

• • •

"Need a favor, Earl," Carter said when we met at the truck again.

"Sure."

"See, my wife's momma always expects a pint of whiskey when I drop by. Part payment, I reckon, for taking away her youngest."

I reached for my billfold, assuming he wanted me to pay for the booze.

"No, no, Earl. Put your money away." He pulled a chained wallet from the back pocket of his pants and took out a crisp five-dollar bill. "See, the thing is, the man won't sell whiskey to colored folks."

"May not sell it to me, either, Carter. I'm not twenty-one."

"Whoo-ee, Earl, don't you worry 'bout that. He'd sell you whiskey even if you were still in diapers, long as you're not colored."

"Any special brand?" I said.

"No, no. Just a pint of somethin' cheap. Oh, yes, and a bag of lemon drops, please."

As I walked back to the café, I worried about my duffel on the back of the truck, but there was nothing I could do about it.

I bought the lemon drops and a pint of Three Feathers without a problem; Carter and the truck were waiting and we were on our way again.

We'd gone only a few more miles when Carter slowed and pointed ahead.

"My wife's momma's place is off down that road up there a ways."

I looked where he pointed, but all I could see was coastal fog.

"You're welcome to come along, if you like ... or you can wait here and we'll pick you up on the way out 'cause I'd really like to hold you to that drivin' offer."

It was a moonless, black night and I had no idea how far we were from anywhere. "Okay, I'll go with you." I hoped he didn't hear the lack of assurance in my voice.

He nodded and made the left turn, dropping down onto an asphalt secondary road. After a while, the pavement ended and we were on a relatively smooth two-lane marl road, which eventually narrowed to one lane. Carter drove as if he were waiting for something to happen, then stopped when a bump jolted the front suspension.

"Gets pretty tight up ahead," he said, reaching out to fold the outside rearview mirror back against the side of the cab. "Mind gettin' the mirror on your side?"

I peered out through the windshield and could see a sandy wagon path ahead that disappeared into the fog and underbrush.

"Best keep your arms inside the truck," he said, using only the lower gears to move ahead slowly. "Some of the scrub along here is prickly and downright mean."

Limbs, stalks, and brush slapped at the sides of the truck

without let-up, occasionally flicking in through the open side windows. Carter said nothing, intent on maneuvering the big rig through the dense vegetation. I knew we'd started out driving west, but I had no idea now in which direction we were headed. My vision was limited to ghostly images pulled out of the fog by the headlights.

It took forever before we bumped into a clearing. Off to one side was a tiny house on stilts, light filtering through small windows and vertical slits between the weather-shrunk siding.

As Carter did a half-circle with the truck, the headlights flashed on several old pickups and sedans parked near the house.

"Looks like lots of folks here tonight," Carter said in response to my unasked question. "Might be best if you stayed here while I go get my wife." He turned off the engine and lights. "Never know who all might be in that ol' house."

Which I took to mean that I'd be the only white person there if I did go in.

"Shouldn't take long," he said. "Maybe ten, fifteen minutes." He saluted me with the bottle of whiskey and grabbed the lemon drops as he climbed down out of the cab. I caught a glimpse of my watch before the dome light went out: 9:25.

Carter was engulfed by the blackness, then the house door opened and I saw him in silhouette before the door closed behind him.

I rolled up both windows to protect me from the squadrons of buzzing and biting insects that wanted to share the cab with me. But the air in the cramped space quickly became heavy, difficult to breathe. And even with the windows closed, I could still hear a symphony of unfamiliar night sounds.

All I could do was sit in the cab and stare at the house. Blurs of light at the windows, yellow streaks between boards, and occasional formless shadows told me nothing about who was in the house or what they were doing.

I searched the glove box and interior of the cab for a flashlight, thinking I might be able to hike my way back to the highway.

Nothing.

Besides, how many miles was it? How many lurking alligators between here and there?

Carter had left the keys in the ignition. I flicked them with my index finger and fantasized about making a run for it with the truck.

Yeah? What then?

My chances of getting the big rig away from the house and back to the main road without getting stuck, or caught, were slim to none.

And if I did get there, every one of those jalopies would be right behind me.

My mind was a movie screen filled with images of Carter's friends and relatives beating me unconscious, tossing my limp body into the swamp.

I'm going to die. Here and now. No one is ever going know what happened to me.

I thought about all the things I would never get to do, and then I was crying.

The house door opened and a splotch of light broke through the darkness.

A short, heavyset man stepped onto the porch.

I flipped up both door handles to set the locks.

Another man, tall and skinny, moved through the doorway. I pressed back into the seat as far as I could. Both men picked up long guns that were leaning against the porch railing. I closed my eyes.

Would they dare shoot through the window, damage Carter's truck? Cold sweat trickled across my ribs.

The cab of the truck filled with blinding light. Then I was sitting in darkness again, watching an old car swing around and drive out of the clearing.

I held my breath as two more men came out of the house, picked up weapons, went down the steps.

I couldn't swallow.

Again headlights bounced off the fog and two more vehicles drove away—in opposite directions. Then a steady stream of men and women left the house, most with guns. They seemed to scatter in various directions.

Were they going to surround me?

It wasn't my fault I'd had to usher Negroes to the balcony and rear seats in the movie theater where I'd worked.

It wasn't my fault Negroes were forced to live in only one area of my hometown.

It wasn't my fault Negroes were told which schools they could and couldn't attend.

It wasn't my fault my dad used the word *nigger*.

Everything was quiet now, too quiet.

The door to the house opened again and a single figure moved through the light, followed the path the others had taken across the porch, and down the steps. The person was carrying something—an axe to kill me, to cut me into small pieces for the alligators?

I cringed, I shook.

The door handle jiggled on the passenger side. I slapped a hand across my mouth to keep from crying out and scrabbled across the seat to get as far away as possible from that door. One foot got tangled in the pedals and I couldn't move.

There was a sharp rap on the driver's side window. I almost wet my pants.

"Earl!" said a voice on the other side of the door.

I opened my mouth but nothing came out.

"Open the door, Earl. It's me, Carter."

I began to tremble.

"Must be asleep," he mumbled and inserted a key into the door lock.

"Sorry it took so long," Carter said, looking up at me. "Must be terrible hot in there with the windows all rolled up like that."

"I was, uh, trying to keep the mosquitoes out."

He nodded, but his expression said he didn't believe me.

"Lots of peoples here tonight to see my momma-in-law," he said. "She has the gift. Sees the future." He tossed a cardboard suitcase up onto the trailer. He reached into the cab, slapped the seat, and laughed. "Wife's still saying her goodbyes. I'll go hurry her along."

I scooted back to my side of the seat to wait for whatever was coming.

When light again filled the doorway to the shack, two people came out. One looked like Carter, but the door closed too quickly for me to see who was with him. Then the blackness sucked them up.

"Open the door," Carter called out as they drew close. His voice sounded different; I hesitated.

"It's time to go, Earl," he said, more an order than a request.

I slowly turned the door handle, pushed outward.

Carter was standing there, but not the same Carter who had gone into the house. A thong-strung amulet rested on his bare chest, and a minimal loincloth hung low beneath his belly.

Next to him, naked as the day she was born, was the blonde from the Ford convertible, her hair in row-upon-row of tight braids. She was holding the bag of lemon drops.

The clearing suddenly was ablaze with light from a circle of headlights.

"Told you I'd find you a good one, didn't I, Carter?" said the blonde.

"Two-Buck Hitch" is based on an actual solo hitchhiking trip I took many years ago. The route was from Indiana, through Kentucky, Tennessee, and Georgia to Florida, then across the deep South to Texas, followed by a jaunt north through Oklahoma, Kansas, and Nebraska, before heading home via Iowa and Illinois. The situation, characters, and incidents mentioned in this segment are essentially real; most of the story, however, is pure fiction.

—J.J. Lamb

GET A LIFE

Judith Janeway

My name is Nadine Gale. At least, that's the name I've used for the past three months. Before that I went by ... well, let's say quite a few other names. No need to go into specifics because there are warrants out for some of those names, even for my real one, which by now doesn't feel any more real than the other names I've used.

I'm not the only Nadine Gale in the world, and one of them is pissed off at me because she thinks I've stolen her identity. She's right. I have.

When I first moved to Berkeley, I scoped out the local restaurants. A holiday weekend rolled around, and I walked into Alessandro's because I knew it would be jammed and understaffed. I showed up dressed like the servers—black pants and black T-shirt but with some modifications. Baggy pants instead of skin-tight jeans. The T-shirt had long sleeves. And I covered my hair with a black scarf. An ambiguous look that could signal a religious affiliation or a fashion preference. An ambiguity that would make describing me later difficult.

I fast-talked the harried manager into letting me jump right in with a promise to fill out paperwork at the end of shift. He assigned me a neglected corner of the room, nicely situated out of the pay station's line of sight. I hurried to soothe the disgruntled diners who had drawn the short straw for customer service.

As long as the manager kept an eye on me, I focused only on the customers' needs, moving with unobtrusive efficiency. I have moves. Useful ones like waiting tables. Dumb ones like pulling a quarter from behind someone's ear. And smart ones like palming credit cards and swiping the mag strips through the skimmer in my pants pocket.

With certain customers, when the manager wasn't at the pay station, I'd return to the table and apologetically ask to see the customer's driver's license. "That card issuer requires additional identification," I'd explain, and the customers would hand over their licenses. Those mag strips got swiped too.

By the end of the shift I had eight credit cards but only two driver's licenses on my skimmer and one table of six to go. I waved off the server assigned to take over my tables, insisting I'd finish dealing with the boisterous group celebrating a birthday. One woman stood out—a blonde wearing an off-the-shoulder blouse. She really pulled off the look. Not slutty. Not boho. Elegant. She also wore a possessive boyfriend who kept one arm draped over her shoulders and whispered in her ear when she paid too much attention to someone else.

After the cake and the song and some more wine, she was the one who signaled for the check. When I brought it, a few others at the table reached for their wallets. Not the boyfriend, of course. She laughingly waved them off and handed me her credit card. I glanced at it. *Nadine Gale.* I asked for her driver's license. She gave it to me. I smiled. One more square and I'd have bingo three times over.

Twenty-nine states still put a Social Security number on a driver's license. California isn't one of them. But with all the other information a license gives you, it isn't hard to track down a Social. When you have a Social, mag strip info, and friends in low places, you can get a counterfeit driver's license. And counterfeit plastic off the skimmed numbers. I couldn't afford to get as many of those as I'd have liked.

With a little more effort and time, I could get legitimate driver's licenses with scrutiny-passing holograms, but time had become an issue when I used up my savings posting bail in Omaha. Usually I work one month out of four and always keep a cash reserve. But after an expensive stay in Florida, I set myself up in Omaha and, ignoring my own good advice, I got in with a bad crowd. Enough said.

Within days of my Berkeley restaurant gig I'd acquired Stephanie Klein's, Jennifer Williams', and Nadine Gale's identities. I went online and put a one-month's vacation hold on their mail. Credit card security codes aren't on the mag strips, but I'd memorized those when I'd skimmed the cards. I hoped to be named an authorized user on those cards. I even went to the trouble of finding mothers' maiden names on a genealogy site. Paid for with their credit cards, of course.

Not all credit card companies require mother's maiden name, but some do, and I needed to get as many cards as possible. That became more imperative when Jennifer Williams was turned down everywhere because of her bad FICO score. I couldn't get anything for Stephanie Klein either, because she'd subscribed to a credit-tracking service that blocked all my applications. Almost by default I ended up being just one person—Nadine Gale. Like it was meant to be.

The credit cards I'd skimmed and the ones coming in the mail would contribute a lot to my financial stability. But I'd arrived in Berkeley close to penniless. I hadn't been this broke since I'd walked off a Harris County jail work detail five years ago. To become solvent I had to use all my skills, including going old school and raiding trash cans.

Lucky for me recycling is like a religion in Berkeley, and everyone is strictly observant. And none of that single-streaming stuff for this city. Paper goes into one barrel and bottles and cans into another. Anything food-related goes into a wheeled cart for composting. What's left over, which sometimes isn't very much, goes into the trash barrel. It makes my work easier. No more digging through disgusting layers of rotting food and stinking disposable diapers.

I'm not a master of disguise, but I'm very good at a few. White-faced Goth before it went out of fashion. Spaced-out heroin addict, which has come back into fashion. Christian-sect wife in a *Little House on the Prairie* calico dress. For trash sorting, I put on a frowsy gray wig, a wide-brimmed hat, some wrecked clothes, and dirty white gardening gloves. I make sure to talk to myself, shouting "Fuck!" frequently, and I haul along a garbage bag with some soda cans in it. I look just like a familiar local—either a crazy lady who makes a few cents for every aluminum can she acquires, or a crazy lady who takes trash home to keep. Either way, people don't want to mess with me.

When no one's watching I drop the can-quest act and sift through paper trash looking for credit card bills. A few banks still put the entire card number on the bill. And since most people are lazy about shredding their bills, they pay the price. Literally. Then there are the card companies that try to get customers to transfer their balances and send them checks to make it convenient. I appreciate their thoughtfulness.

Last Monday was a good day because I found two new credit cards in the box I rent at Mail and More. I'd collected my mail and headed for the door, not looking where I was going because I was more interested in my credit cards, and I nearly bumped into Nadine Gale.

I have to admit that I was curious about her, which was

totally out of character for me. I'd even been to her house and gone through her trash—I was that curious. She had sort of the same idea, only she had confrontation and not curiosity in mind.

She must have staked out the business where I rented a mailbox. How long had she been waiting for someone to go to that box? She had to have a lot of determination. That fit with how I thought of her.

After nearly crashing into her, I took a step back. She wore a black-and-white striped maxi dress with a neon green scarf tossed over her shoulders in just the right way. How did she pull off that artfully negligent thing? She looked great—except for the bruise on her left cheekbone and a split bottom lip.

She waved a piece of paper in my face. "Not so smart after all, are you? You tried to defraud me by putting a hold on my mail. But my credit card company emailed me about your trying to get on my account using this address."

"No, not me. You've made a mistake."

"I'm Nadine Gale and you're committing a crime using my identity."

"I'm Nadine Gale, too. I imagine there are even more Nadine Gales around than just you and me. Are you going to accuse them of committing a crime, too?"

"Of course not. They haven't stolen my identity. You have."

"You sound very certain about that."

"I'm certain that you're going to jail."

I didn't want to break it to her that fewer than one percent of identity thieves are ever prosecuted—the main reason I went into the business in the first place after my other efforts earned me a police record in several states. Besides, she wasn't in the mood to chat. She headed out the door and returned immediately with a cop in tow. She must have called the cops ahead of time. Like I said—determined.

She pointed to me. "That's the woman I told you about."

He approached me and held out his hand. "Identification please."

I handed over my Nadine Gale driver's license. He inspected it, but, lucky for me, he didn't hold it up to the light to verify the hologram.

When he gave it back to me, I made a show of peering closely at his face even though I'd recognized him as soon as he walked in the door. "You're Officer Wong, aren't you? I remember you from the shooting last week. The one up the street at the Alta Apartments? That was scary. I've gotten used to hearing gunfire at night, but a shooting in broad daylight made me think twice about leaving my apartment."

He didn't react overtly to my words, but I noted an almost imperceptible lessening of body tension. "We already have a suspect in custody for that shooting." That's the way cops who're trained in community policing talk. They're supposed to reassure fearful citizens.

"That's good news." I gave him the grateful smile of a reassured citizen.

The other Nadine looked from Officer Wong to me and back to him again. "You're here to arrest her, not chat about crime in her neighborhood. She's the crime in her neighborhood."

Officer Wong nodded. "How long have you lived at your current address?"

It was an easy enough question, but I knew better than to answer even one question from a cop. He could legally ask to see my identification, but that was it. I took a step back. "I have to go to work now."

"I have a few questions for you."

"Am I being detained?"

Any rapport I might have established with Officer Wong vanished when I said those words. They identified me as someone familiar with police procedures from the other side of the badge. Oh well. I turned to leave.

"Ms. Gale?" Officer Wong said. "We'll talk later."

That's what he thought. I headed for the door.

"You're going to let her walk away?"

"I don't have a basis for detaining her."

"I gave you a basis!"

Funny, but I felt bad that she was so frustrated. She didn't know that she'd never get anywhere with the legal system. I turned around in the doorway and met her gaze. I wanted to signal that I sympathized. I tilted my head to one side, lifted my hands palms up, and shrugged.

She glared at me. I hoped she didn't get stuck in the anger stage. It went much easier for people if they could move on to acceptance.

I'd made a mistake mentioning the Alta Apartments. Now the other Nadine knew where I lived. I couldn't do anything about it except move, and I didn't have the ready cash for that. I'd better get to work and fix my money problem.

Cell phone minutes are a quick source of cash. I buy them online with a stolen credit card, get the codes that will load the minutes on a cell phone, and sell the codes at a discount through Craigslist or on the street. As I peddled minutes on Telegraph Avenue, the other Nadine stayed on my mind. All I could think when I saw those marks on her face was what a shame. In every other respect she had her life together. She lived in North Berkeley in an old house with tons of character like all the houses in that area. I knew from the pay stub in her trash that she had a well-paying job at the University. And I also knew from seeing her at the restaurant that she had friends who liked her. But even with all that, she was in a relationship with a guy who hit her.

Me, I lived by myself in a miniscule studio apartment in West Berkeley. Not the part of West Berkeley with chic boutiques housed in former warehouses, but the part where you pay your landlord in cash by the week. He collects it personally and carries a gun in his jacket pocket in case someone gives him trouble.

I occasionally do favors for him. No, not that kind. The kind that involve handing him a credit card and telling him to use it once and lose it. In return he makes sure that his eyes and ears on the block look out for me. It's not a guarantee of safety, but it helps when you live in a place where your landlord isn't the only one around with a gun.

Even with these precautions, no one gave me a heads-up that the other Nadine's boyfriend was stalking me. Not long after the face-to-face meeting with her, I walked out of my apartment, and the boyfriend came up to me. "Hey. You."

I gave him a brief once-over. I remembered him from the restaurant. Short and stocky. Sort of nerdy-looking, but a nerd who spent regular time at the gym. I moved to walk past him.

He stepped sideways and blocked my path.

I turned around to go the other way and he grabbed my arm.

I jerked free. "Get your hands off me!"

He didn't grab my arm again, but he stepped in close, challenging ownership of my personal space.

"Or what? You'll call the cops? I doubt that."

I didn't want to give away that I knew who he was. "What do you want?"

"The better question is—who are you? Really?" He looked me up and down. "You're some sicko, aren't you? Stealing her identity and trying to look like her, too."

My hand went to my hair before I could interrupt the

gesture. True, I'd gone blond. But it wasn't anything new. I'd been all shades of the rainbow in the past, though I did think that blond was my best look. And I'd snagged a neon green scarf recently, but so what? Neon green looked good with my complexion and current hair color. "I'm not 'trying' anything. I am who I am."

"Which is nothing." He spat out the last word.

A woman called to me from the second floor walkway. "Hey, girlfriend. You okay?"

I looked up. DeeDee, one of my landlord's lookouts, rested her forearms and her ample bosom on the walkway railing and leaned forward to see better. Some other neighbors peered out their windows. Nadine's boyfriend and I hadn't been yelling, but we'd definitely raised our voices.

"I'm fine, DeeDee. Or at least I will be as soon as this asshole leaves."

"Who're you calling an asshole?"

"I would've called you an anus aperture, but I know you wouldn't have understood what it meant."

He lashed out before I could duck. His fist landed on my cheekbone with a thud. My head jerked backward and forward like a bobblehead doll and my vision filled with flashes of light. I staggered but managed to keep my balance.

Damn, that hurt.

"Girlfriend?" DeeDee called to me. "I'm calling Raymond."

Raymond, my landlord, had zero tolerance for any bad behavior that might bring the cops to his door. Perpetrator or victim didn't matter to him. If he heard about what had just happened, I'd be out on the street.

"Please don't, DeeDee. This … this"—I wanted to call him names but didn't want to experience close contact of the bruising kind again—"guy is just leaving. Aren't you?"

Boyfriend held his ground.

"If you don't leave now, Raymond will be here before you can blink. And FYI, he carries a gun at all times."

He took a step backward. "You got my message. If you keep messing with Nadine's identity, I'll be back with a longer message. I'm not afraid of your friend Raymond."

Of course he wasn't afraid. He was too stupid. Had Nadine sent him? I couldn't believe she had. But then, I couldn't believe she'd have anything to do with him in the first place. I watched him back away a few more steps before he turned and crossed the street to his car.

After he drove away, I looked up at DeeDee.

"Hang on a minute, DeeDee. I have something for you." I climbed the stairs to her landing and gave her a sizeable number of minutes.

"What's this for?"

"For looking out for me. I appreciate it."

"And not calling Raymond. Right?"

"That guy won't be back, so Raymond doesn't have to hear about it."

"If you say so. Cuz next time I don't call him, he be putting my butt out on the street."

"I understand." I turned to go with a "You take care now."

"Me?" she laughed. "You the one got hit. You oughta put some ice on that."

"I will."

I gave her a wave and went back to my apartment. I applied the ice for a bit but didn't have time to hang around icing my cheekbone. I was going to have an ugly black eye, but I needed to go to work. I put on sunglasses and headed out a second time. I had fewer minutes to sell after buying off DeeDee and that worried me. I had enough to live on but not enough to leave with.

The following week, I doubled the number of recycling bins I searched. I mailed half of the credit information to a box I kept in Reno to help me get started wherever I landed after here. I used my current credit cards to buy minutes online and to get cash advances from ATMs. Ever since the banks cracked down, going to an ATM was more like playing a slot machine. Now ATMs spat out twenties on only a small percentage of my cards and ate the rest.

The battering boyfriend didn't show up again. I had a replacement debit card and new pin all ready to go for the day I left town. I held off making my last move on the other Nadine—emptying her bank account.

I'd actually debated with myself about this final step, like I'd gone soft. A black eye cured me of that. She'd sicced the boyfriend on me knowing he would hit me. That was just pure mean. What I did wasn't personal, not like punching someone in the face.

When I got back from my ATM tour, I checked my apartment mailbox like I did every week. I never used it for my personal mail. But the mail carrier stuffed it full of catalogs and flyers mostly meant for someone named Resident, and he got mad if I didn't empty it out when it was full. I stood over the paper recycling bin and thumbed through everything before dumping it, in case something looked interesting.

During the time I'd lived here, I'd scored two credit card applications meant for previous renters. But this time I had a letter addressed to me personally. I tore it open and found a California Handgun Safety Certificate awarded to Nadine Gale.

I dropped everything else in the bin and hurried to my apartment. The other Nadine had completed the training and made sure that the certificate came to my address. Talk about sending a message. She had a gun and she intended to use it. Or have the boyfriend use it. Either way, she'd make sure I could no longer be Nadine Gale because I would no longer exist.

I had a hard time packing. A new experience for me. My lifestyle required me to have one foot out the door at all times, and I knew how to pack and leave in bare minutes. This time I had hours to triage my possessions into take or leave. It was early evening, and I needed to wait until only the dope sellers and buyers were on the streets. Best if no one noticed I'd left until rent day. I probably could have acted more quickly with a tighter deadline. I debated for a long time over the green scarf. I should trash it, but I liked how it looked on me.

Without meaning to, I fell asleep on the 600-thread-count sheets I would have to leave behind. The sound of gunshots woke me. I looked at my watch.

Two A.M. Hell. I'd planned on going at three, but if someone had been shot, the cops would be here longer than that doing what they called investigating. A process that amounted to getting someone to point a finger at the shooter. They never did the fingerprints-hair-fiber-DNA thing the cops did on TV.

Several cop cars pulled up in front of the apartment complex. Their flashing lights bounced off my walls like multicolored strobes in a club. I waited until they'd turned off their sirens before I went to the window. Nothing much to see from the angle of my window, so I sat down and distracted myself by repeatedly unpacking and repacking my bag. If only those cops would finish up and leave. It might be full daylight before I could get out of here.

A knock came at my door accompanied by a loud, "Police. Open up." I didn't jump up and run to answer. I knew that by rights I didn't have to. Besides, I hadn't seen anything anyway.

The second knock was more peremptory and the

command an adrenaline trigger. "Nadine Gale, we know you're in there. Open the door."

I stood up, but still didn't move to let them in. I heard muffled voices, a key in the lock, and the door opened. Raymond had used his master key. Two cops, guns drawn, pushed past Raymond.

"Put your hands where I can see them," the cop in the lead said.

I raised my hands slowly, and from that action on, I did only as ordered. My questions went unanswered. Requests unheeded. Handcuffs clicked around my wrists to the narrative that I was under arrest for the murder of Lance Newell.

"Who? I don't know Lance Newell."

"Quite a few of your neighbors say you do. They also say they saw you walking away from the body."

They gave me the Miranda recitation and marched me outside into the wincingly bright glare of the LED street lights. Occupants of Alta Apartments as well as neighboring complexes crowded the street and sidewalk, but they were observing the thin barrier of yellow police tape. I saw DeeDee, but she averted her gaze when I looked at her.

On the sidewalk, a man's body lay in a sprawl. Blood had seeped out from under him and stained the sidewalk. When we approached, the cop blocking my view of the man's face stepped aside. I stopped in my tracks and stared. Lance Newell was the boyfriend.

The cop who had me by the arm led me to one of the police cars and shoved me into the backseat.

I'd started shaking when the cops had come in with guns pointed. And I thought I'd faint when I saw Lance Newell's body.

Sure, I had felony arrests on my record, but only for larceny. They'd have to see that I wouldn't hurt, much less kill someone. That just wasn't me. I had to think. I needed a plan, but I was still shaking, and my brain had gone numb.

I sat hunched forward. The cuffs pinched my wrists and put painful pressure on my shoulders when I leaned back. I shifted sideways in the seat to get more room.

That's when I saw Nadine Gale in a car parked across the street. She'd cut her hair short and dyed it brown, but I still recognized her. She met my gaze and held up a blond wig with one hand and a green scarf with the other. She'd set me up. The handgun certificate wasn't a warning. It was evidence against me.

"Hey!" I yelled to get the attention of the closest cop. "That's her. That's Nadine Gale."

The cop turned and looked at me.

"She did it." With my hands cuffed behind my back I couldn't point, so I jerked my head in her direction. But the cop and another one near him eyed me and didn't turn around.

I jerked my head toward her again. "Over there. That's

Nadine Gale. She did it. You have to arrest her. Over there."

Frantic, I turned my head as far as I could either way to see if I could get someone else to look at Nadine. All eyes were focused on me.

I slammed my head and shoulder against the window. "Listen to me! She set me up!"

A cop came to my side of the car. "Quiet down in there."

I kept banging my shoulder against the door. It was like once I'd started, I couldn't stop. "She's right there! Across the street! She did it!"

The cop put one hand on his taser and the other on the door handle. "I said, quiet down."

The taser threat stopped me from thrashing around but not from talking. "Listen to me."

The cop kept his hand on his taser. "No. You listen to me. You have the right to remain silent. I suggest you use your right and zip it." He waited to see if I would take his advice. I held still and kept quiet. He moved away.

I locked gazes with Nadine. When the cop moved away from the car, I screamed at her, "You won't get away with this!"

She tilted her head to one side, lifted her hands palms up, and shrugged.

I have always had a fascination with the idea of telling a

story from the point of view of an unlikable character. The goal is to create a narrative that leads the reader to take the character's side despite her being unsympathetic. When the idea of a character who was an identity thief came to me, I knew I had the perfect setup for this challenge.

—Judith Janeway

IF, IF, IF

Nancy Tingley

He leaned into the mirror, pulled out another one. IF, IF, IF. He'd thought that word, over and over, written it, the F capped like the I, and he liked the way the two letters looked together, the hard edges, the straight lines, the finality. That F stopped you in your tracks. Or did it point you forward?

The doorbell rang and he ignored it, turned sideways to the mirror, unable to grasp the long strand of hair that shot forth, an announcement. Unable to find it in the reflection, though he could see it, his hand moving too far forward, too far back. And maybe that's what had happened. Maybe that was what had gone wrong with that slut. Maybe he'd intended a backward movement, like a film run in reverse, rather than ...

Now they were leaning on it. He pressed down the hairs at the nape of his neck and headed for the door.

There were two of them, one in uniform, one in a sloppy

trench coat straight from the wardrobe department of the local community theater.

He put on his puzzled look. "Can I help you?"

Raincoat hesitated. "Is your father in?"

He frowned. "My father? No, he went out. Said he was going to visit a friend."

"What friend?" asked the uniform, the woman, taking her notebook from her pocket.

She was attractive, or would have been if she wasn't dressed in a man's uniform—the pants, the shirt, a belt that weighed her down and added at least six inches to her hips, lowering her height and broadening her, giving her the profile of a pyramid.

"He didn't say. He's a gregarious guy." Lie, he thought, then mentally spelled it in caps, LIE. LIE, unlike IF, was mutable, angular but liquid. It was a word that gave you latitude. "He has a lot of friends."

"Locally?" asked the little tank. Rebecca, he saw on her chest. Becky. He knew a Becky once. Boy, did he know a Becky.

"What is your name, sir?" she asked, pencil poised.

Why did they carry pencils and not pens? But he knew the answer. So they could change the evidence. "Myron Woods."

"With an 's'?"

What was she, stupid? "Yes."

"Does he have a car?" asked Raincoat.

He turned his gaze from her chest to the man. "Yes. Down in the garage, space 1-D. Unless he drove."

"I'll go check it out," said Raincoat.

She looked surprised. Becky was the one to run the errands, get the tea, do the shit jobs. Then she shifted her expression, took it in stride.

They both watched him go.

"Would you like to come in?"

She stepped through without a moment's hesitation. Wants to case the joint, he thought, and laughed. You can case my joint.

"Did you say something?" she asked.

"Nah." He watched her glance down at the coffee table, the two empty mugs, the sports section, a full ashtray. She swiped at her nose, pushing away the smell of cigarettes.

"You smoke?" she asked.

"Nah, my father." He smiled at his little tableau as he ran his finger along the back of the blade in his pocket, that little indentation to pull it out. A different knife, not the knife he'd given the girl. A similar knife, but with an ivory handle. Old. Worn. Used. No, not the new knife he'd given the girl, and he tried not to think about it, looking at Becky's ass, the way that equipment weighted it down.

He walked up behind her, flipped open the knife, slid the blade down the middle of her back, up into her kidney. He couldn't see her face—her bulging eyes, her open mouth which he covered before she could scream. He pressed his joint against her.

And opened his eyes. DREAM, he thought, in caps. And he spelled it out. DREAM. "Would you like some tea?" he asked.

"No, thanks," she said, looking at his bookshelf. "Who's the reader?"

"My father," he said, wondering why he'd let her in, but knowing it was the adrenaline. "He likes to read mysteries." LIE, he thought.

"Thrillers," she said, leaning in to look at the titles.

They were on the same wavelength, he and Becky. "Do you read thrillers?"

"Sometimes," she said, wandering away from the books, heading for the kitchen. She stopped at the door. "Do you have coffee?"

"Yes." But he didn't make any move to get it. He liked women who liked tea. "Is he your boss?"

"Not exactly. He's a detective."

"Doesn't that make him your boss?"

"I guess." She came back into the living room and he could tell she was debating sitting down.

He wondered how she smelled. Sweat, perfume, deodorant, maybe shampoo or rinse. He moved towards her.

The front door opened and he stopped.

"Rebecca?" said Raincoat.

"In here," she said, watching him.

"No car there. What does he drive?"

"Prius," Myron said, which was ridiculous. His father

cared about the environment as much as he cared about ... but he couldn't think of a comparison. "Silver."

The cop grimaced. Silver was the most popular color Prius in California.

"License plate number?" Becky asked, holding up the notebook that she hadn't put away, which was just as well because it made her ass bulge more than it was already bulging.

"I have no idea," he said.

"Your father's papers?" asked Raincoat.

"Why exactly do you want my father?" He realized as he asked that he should have asked the question earlier. When he'd told them where his father parked his car. LIE. When he'd invited her in.

"We just need to ask him a few questions regarding a case," she said.

"What case?" he asked.

They looked at each other. "It's not important," said Raincoat.

"What case?" he asked again, digging in his heels, something he should have done already. And he heard the edge in his voice, the anger.

"A suspicious death," said Raincoat. "A witness saw him near the scene and followed him to this"—he hesitated—"this neighborhood."

"Saw my father?"

"Saw an older man. Thanks for your help," Raincoat said dismissively.

He felt the same anger he'd felt toward the girl, that smarmy know-it-all girl. Treating him like trash, ridiculing his accent. People from the South got it all the time. The lengthened vowels drawled over their tongues made people think they were lowlifes.

And that bitch had shown it in the way she looked at him, the way she put the plate in front of him, refilled his ice tea. Haughty as hell.

"When your father comes home, would you have him call us?" said Becky. She and Raincoat headed towards the door.

"Yup," he answered.

She turned back, reaching out to hand him her card, and he met her halfway, close enough that he could smell her shampoo. "Here you go. This number, the bottom one."

He leaned towards her. Like a vanilla milkshake.

Startled, she pulled back. "Thanks," she said and followed Raincoat out the door.

Women sent out signals, like Becky giving him her card, telling him what she wanted. He wondered why they all liked to smell like fruit juice, milkshakes.

The waitress had smelled like strawberry.

He remembered the way she slapped down his burger, slopped the ice tea over the edge of the glass, didn't thank him when she gave him the bill.

He hadn't had a choice, so he'd waited. A long time. A long time out behind that crap restaurant until she came out. From behind the dumpster, he watched her flirt with the dishwasher. The fucking dishwasher. They stood outside smoking their cigarettes, until the boss, irritated, told the guy to get his ass inside. And he did, turning back to give the boss a dirty look as he took the dishwasher's place, to chat, flirt, give her ass a slap before he went back in.

It wasn't his fault; he didn't have a choice. When they'd left her alone, she walked towards him, cigarette in one hand, looking at her nails. Ignoring him, as if he wasn't there. Looking at her damn nails as if he didn't exist, picking, picking at the thumb, so that he walked right up to her and even then she didn't look up. Even when he slid the knife in, her eyes stayed down, the blood spreading, her mouth an O but silent.

Such a sharp knife, such thin flesh. He never liked girls like that. Thin girls, girls like blades in bed and in speech. Now Becky, she wasn't a thin girl, those hips, luscious and wide. The breasts—even her arms—had weight. But she was a cop.

He didn't like cops.

Back in front of the mirror, he tried again for that gray hair that had escaped the dye.

• • •

In the car Rebecca said, "Earl, that guy is weird."

"That's not an offense we can arrest him for. Got to

track down his father." The car phone beeped and Earl picked it up. "They got him."

"Who?"

"The boss did it."

"The boss?"

"Yeah, the dishwasher said he went out for a flirt. Said he had it in for her."

"I don't know," she said, arranging the belt on her hips. "This guy made me very uncomfortable."

"Well, couldn't be him. Witness said it was an old guy with gray hair, like the boss."

She looked up at the apartment. "The witness also said that the man came here."

Earl shrugged and started the car.

———————

I began this story in my writers group with the prompt "narration, looking back, recreating the moment," though I think what engaged me was the framework of our work that day, which was Sudden Violent Events. Like many of the short pieces that I write, it arose unplanned from some dark place in my brain. After submitting the story, I decided it was a good starting point for a thriller, most of which I wrote in November during NaNoWriMo. So "IF, IF, IF" will shortly be a novel.

—Nancy Tingley

KATE CHOPIN TUSSLES WITH A NOVEL ENDING

Ana Brazil

October 1899

"Madame Chopin! Madame Chopin!" The plump landlady huffed into the screened summer parlor. She anchored her hand heavily on the doorframe and announced, "You have a visitor. From Chicago."

Kate finished her paragraph before lifting her fingers from the typewriter keyboard. Her focus on writing was legendary amongst her large family; she was known to craft an entire short story while hurricane winds whipped the Louisiana gulf coast or to edit an essay while her grandchildren screamed for their supper.

Kate followed her landlady through the narrow hallways until they arrived at the front gallery. The landlady nodded her head in the direction of the gulf waters before returning inside. Kate examined the back of the dark figure standing on the walkway leading to the water. When the stranger did not turn around, Kate stepped down toward her.

"Hello?"

The woman turned slowly toward Kate, as if released from an unexpected reverie. She bounced a thin indigo-and-crimson carpetbag against her knee before saying, "It's not quite how I expected it. Louisiana and Grand Isle ... the beach ... the ocean beyond. It's all so vast. Like an eternity."

The stranger inspected Kate from scalp to shoe and then scanned the building behind Kate. "Your boarding house is smaller than I expected. And you're smaller than I expected, too." She extended her ungloved hand. "You *are* Kate Chopin, aren't you? The author of *The Awakening*? I'm Theodora Jensen, secretary to Clifford K. Reese, your publisher."

"You're Theo Jensen?" Kate recalled the cramped signature at the bottom of all of the typed correspondence from the Clifford K. Reese Publishing Company. "I thought that ... that—"

"That I was a man. Yes, I've heard that before."

"You do sign your letters *Theo*." Kate had mused once or twice about the almost-unreadable signature at the bottom of the publishing-house letters. Did it belong to an overworked mouse-man who obeyed Clifford's every command? Or was it the signature of a nearsighted dragon who protected the publisher from all unsolicited parcels?

Neither, Kate now realized. Theo Jensen appeared to be a woman between thirty and forty years of age, as un-ironed and un-corseted as Kate, but blond of hair and blue of eyes. Not a Chicago native, Kate thought, but a woman from somewhere higher up river. Minnesota, perhaps?

Despite the harsh autumn heat and humidity, the woman was dressed entirely in black. So black that Kate searched her visitor for clues of mourning—a broach or ring containing braided hair. She saw instead the twist of reddened skin on the ring finger on the woman's left hand. There had been a wedding or an engagement ring there, Kate was sure of it. And it had been recently removed.

Kate instinctively felt for her own wedding ring, which, despite having been widowed over fifteen years ago, she continued to wear. Yes, it still clung to her finger.

Kate did not care what the woman's name was, not really. She only hoped to God that there was a check in the woman's carpetbag. All of Kate's recent short stories had been rejected, and although most of her children were settled, they all depended upon her for something. Kate's rent had been due four weeks ago and once again this morning, she had not joined the other autumn boarders at *le petit dejeuner*.

"You've brought papers for me to sign? A check from Clifford?"

"May I visit to your privy first, Mrs. Chopin?" asked Theo.

"Around back, but watch your step; we had a hard rain last night."

Kate watched Theodora Jensen—Kate could not continue to think of a woman as *Theo*—set her carpetbag on the bottom step and pick her way around the house. Kate listened for the swing of the privy door before she clicked open the carpetbag.

It was empty. Or almost. No papers to sign, certainly, and no checks from Clifford K. Reese inside the first pocket. Kate retrieved Theodora's gloves from the second pocket and found the small hard circle of a wedding band inside. Kate dug deeper inside the bag as she listened for the next bang of the privy door, but she came up empty.

Had the woman been carrying a purse? A check could fit there; papers—the number of papers that Kate had been told she would have to sign—might not. And who arrives at the coast with nothing in her carpetbag? Just where did the woman think she would sleep tonight? Kate certainly could not afford to host her at the boarding house.

Kate set down the carpetbag on the step, unsure what to do next. She wanted answers about the stranger as much as she wanted the check. Then Kate remembered the warning she had received from Clifford K. Reese: that the bold actions taken by Edna Pontellier—Kate's protagonist in *The Awakening*, the novel she was eager for Clifford K. Reese to publish—would shock and disgust many people.

"Men," Clifford had warned in one of the few letters that his secretary Theodora had not typed and signed, "will be alarmed at how your heroine rejects her husband and takes a lover. And women"—Clifford had underlined the word twice—"will be both appalled and inspired by Edna's adultery and actions, especially the ending of the novel. You must be aware and alert, my dear Kate, that everyone will conclude that Edna's infidelity is based on your own."

Was Clifford's secretary—if Theodora was Clifford's secretary, a fact for which Kate realized that she had no actual proof—the very first of those women? And if so, was she appalled or inspired by Edna's infidelity?

"Would you like refreshment?" asked Kate when Theodora returned from the privy. Kate noted that the woman now held a bulging envelope in her hand; an envelope that appeared large enough to contain both a check and papers. Perhaps she had secured the envelope on her person as she traveled from Chicago? And perhaps she had traveled down just for the day and would return north or to New Orleans after everything was signed?

Kate moved toward the boarding house steps. "There's a desk inside with fresh ink. I'm sure I could get you a glass of lemonade."

"The gulf breeze is refreshment enough, isn't it?" Theodora dropped the envelope into her carpetbag, which she clutched in her right hand. "Would you walk with me?"

Kate would walk. She would skip, hop, run, or even attempt to fly if it secured her check. "There's the pier, if you're interested. It's your best view of the shore, unless you go out in a boat."

"A walk along your beach. That's what I want."

Kate grabbed her hat and two large umbrellas, but did not pause to put on her stockings. As she offered an umbrella to Theodora, she noted that her blond hair was shot through with gray strands and her blue eyes were lustrous, but only from tears. Kate would have offered a handkerchief from her own pocket, but she had not been able to afford the services of a laundress for the last two weeks.

It was Kate's beach and she took the lead. After all of her summers on the Louisiana coast, she was still fascinated by the salty waters that rolled so faithfully in and out. The sun shone hard and stark—it was almost midday—yet the visitor from Chicago plowed through the soft sand as though she were late for a business appointment. Did Theodora even notice the seductive pull of the tide or smell the brine of the sea? Did she not marvel that the breeze had dried her tears?

Kate watched the carpetbag swing at Theodora's side, calculating how to convince her landlady that a check from Chicago would soon mean money in the bank. And a place for Kate at the breakfast and supper table. "Do you know"—Kate attempted to settle her anticipation with light conversation—"that we both have a Densmore typewriting machine? I admired how clearly your letters were typed and Clifford sent me a Densmore for my birthday. *'Lightest Touch. Fastest Work. Numerous Handy Features.'* So says the advertisement."

But Theodora continued her deliberate walk without response. The sun was directly above them and despite the shade of her umbrella, Kate cringed; it had been years since she had been in the midday sun. Theodora had not even opened her umbrella.

After a mile of walking, the women reached the row of elevated changing houses. Kate looked at her regular changing house, not at all alarmed to see a pelican carcass floating in an isolated pool of water. She relished everything about the strong gulf tides, including the exotic sea creatures that landed at her doorstep. Death was a natural part of the ocean's rhythms and Kate knew that the next high tide would roll the carcass back into the gulf.

Theodora studied the changing house and then the waves that foamed inches from her boots before declaring, "This is where you murdered her."

Kate stepped back as if assaulted, but Theodora grabbed Kate's arm and pulled her close. "You murdered Edna right here!" Theodora's voice swelled with emotion. "There's the changing house that she used. I can even see the peg where she kept her bathing suit. This is the very spot. The place where you murdered her!"

"I didn't murder Edna!" Kate pulled away and raised her own voice. "This is the spot where Edna swam out, but I didn't murder her!"

"'*The foamy wavelets curled up to her white feet, and coiled like serpents about her ankles,'"* Theodora's voice calmed as she quoted from the final scene of Kate's manuscript. "'*She walked out. The water was chill, but she walked on.*' And then she drowned."

"She did." Kate fell silent for a few moments, remembering the hot afternoon when she had decided Edna's fate. "Edna was a selfish woman, but she had young children and she would not let her infidelity taint them. An accidental drowning would insure that the children would carry no blame. You understand that, don't you? That was the only ending possible for her story."

"I have young children also!" Theodora let her umbrella drop to the sand. She opened the indigo-and-crimson carpetbag as suddenly as if her children were hiding inside and would pop out for pleasure. She removed the large envelope and let the bag drop into the sand. She tore open the envelope and pulled out what Kate realized from the stiff brown boards were studio photographs. Kate could only imagine the images on those boards. Two children? Four or five children? Or perhaps six children, just like Kate?

Theodora hugged the photographs to her chest and looked directly at Kate. "'*The water was deep, but she lifted her white body and reached out with a long, sweeping stroke.*'" Theodora took a quiet breath. "And now you know, Mrs. Chopin. I haven't come here on business. I've come to take my place with Edna."

"No, you don't mean that!" Kate rushed toward

Theodora, all of her mothering instincts alert to the woman's pain, yet something kept Kate from physically reaching out. "I won't let you!"

Kate took her eyes off Theodora and glanced along the shoreline toward her boarding house. She could barely make out the roofline of the house and saw no one else on the beach. There was not even a solitary fisherman on the pier or out on a boat. Still, she waved her umbrella over her head, hoping that someone would take notice of her actions and come to her assistance. Someone must help her keep Theodora from drowning herself.

"Don't be alarmed, Mrs. Chopin. Edna did not leave a note and neither did I." Theodora carefully set the photographs back in her carpetbag. "No one will ever know that my drowning is your fault. Although *you'll* always know it was, won't you?"

"My fault?" Kate's umbrella dropped to her side. "What are you talking about?"

"I never would have abandoned my husband and children if I hadn't read your manuscript!" Once she finished spitting out her sorrow, Theodora stood silent and still, as if waiting for her words to echo in the breeze. Then she said calmly, "I read it before Clifford did, did he tell you that? I was the first person to read your manuscript and take it seriously. I understood it. I *lived* it. And I convinced Clifford to read it. I had to tell him that your heroine gives into sexual pleasure because he wouldn't have read it otherwise."

Kate swallowed slowly. She was not at fault. She was not to blame. She was guilty of nothing. She was a writer, and Edna and her lovers and husband and children were not real. Kate was proud of writing Edna's story and would be even more proud of the paycheck for it, but she could not let a woman commit suicide because of something she'd written. Once more Kate searched the shoreline. She must find someone, something to help her keep Theodora away from the water.

But Theodora turned from Kate and approached the shoreline. Kate put herself protectively between Theodora and the waves, feeling a tingle of cool water run into her shoes and circle up to her ankles. "Why come here? Why come to me?"

"I want you to remember what you've done; what *your* words did to me."

"I could—" Kate took a solid breath before lying as boldly as she knew how. "I could change the ending."

"But you won't. I already suggested that to Clifford. And he suggested it to you and you refused."

Kate stabbed her umbrella into the wet sand, infuriated by Theodora's petulance. "You're right, I won't change the ending." But she still had to put an end to Theodora's childish behavior. If a lie would not work, what about a threat? "Theodora Jensen, if you even go into that water I will type up a suicide note for you. On my Densmore. Which is just like your Densmore. And I'll sign your name to it." Kate could even imagine her right hand clutching

96

the pen and see the thick ink clump as she replicated Theodora's cramped signature. "Your children will know that you killed yourself. And *that* shame will be all your fault."

Theodora swore something under her breath and lurched forward, swinging her carpetbag wildly at Kate and hitting her squarely in the chest.

Kate landed hard on her rump and sat stunned as the waves rushed up to her waist. She dug her fingers into the sand but it gave way beneath her and the tide pulled her slowly into the gulf. Kate rolled with the water as best she could, choking back mouthfuls of saltwater.

Theodora kept swinging her carpet bag in Kate's direction, back and forth, back and forth, like the heavy pendulum of a clock, each swing arcing closer and closer toward Kate's head.

Finally Kate was able to command her limbs to swim out a dozen strokes, well beyond Theodora's reach. She caught her breath, pushed her sopping hair from her face, and surveyed the shore. Theodora stood in front of Kate's changing house, clutching the carpetbag to her chest.

Kate treaded water, watching to see what Theodora would do next.

Theodora began to remove her clothing. Quickly she stripped down to nothing except her black hat, as though sunbathing had been her plan all along.

Kate gasped and gulped salty water. "' ... *for the first time in her life she stood naked in the open air, at the mercy of the sun,*

the breeze that beat upon her, and the waves that invited her.'"
As Kate recited her own words, she imagined that she saw
Theodora's lips mouthing the same sentence.

Buffeted by the waves, Kate felt her muscles grow tired.
She raised her head above the foam to search the
shoreline, this time looking for someone, anyone, who
could rescue *her*, if she needed it. She tore at her
shirtwaist, which was sodden with seawater and
encumbered by two dozen buttons. But the fabric bound
tightly across her strong shoulders and she could not
release herself.

Theodora placed her pile of black clothing on the top
step of Kate's changing house. With carpetbag in hand,
she walked toward the water.

Kate's breath steadied as she rode the water. She had
not swum for a week and despite the terror of Theodora's
sudden insanity, she was thrilled to be back in the water.
This was *her* shore and these were *her* waves. She knew
every rock and ledge and fault beneath the shoreline. She
knew just where to swim out and just where to swim in.
She also knew where not to swim, for three summers ago
she had watched a new swimmer—an overconfident
salesman from St. Louis—drown in these very waters.

Kate knew that there was a sharp underwater ledge
located twenty-eight paces from her changing house. As
Theodora walked toward the water, Kate counted each
pace, knowing exactly when Theodora would drop off that
ledge and crumble into the water.

Twenty-six. Twenty-seven. Now!

Theodora sank swiftly. Her black hat floated off along a foamy wave.

Kate licked the midday glow from her upper lip and treaded the water. Thirty seconds? Sixty seconds? Where was Theodora? Or where was her body?

Just when Kate thought it was safe to swim to shore, she saw Theodora's head bob above the water. Theodora gasped for air and flailed her arms above the water.

Theodora Jensen had survived the drop. But could she swim? And if she could, could Kate outlast her?

Kate tore at the waistband of her skirt and pushed the fabric down her legs. Now she was almost as naked as Theodora was, almost as limber and free to race through the water. Kate swam out farther into the gulf, her arms beginning to grow heavy. She sought to swim a path parallel to the beach and toward the safety of the pier. But she could not swim and watch for Theodora at the same time.

The top of Theodora's carpetbag crossed her sight first. Somehow it rode the waves to rest inches from Kate's grasp, although she did not grasp at it. A few seconds later, Theodora floated toward Kate, eyes closed and thick blond braid drifting on the water.

Almost dead? For just as Kate had watched that salesman drown three summers ago, she had also seen him almost dead.

"No—no!" A protest gurgled suddenly from

Theodora's lips and she righted herself in the water. She thrashed for a few seconds before grabbing Kate's shirtwaist and then her throat. She pulled Kate toward her.

Panicked now, Kate tugged at Theodora's fingers and twisted them away from her throat. She clutched Theodora's hands, searching her face for some sanity or recognition, but Theodora's eyes were scrunched closed against the churning water, just like a frightened child taking her first swim. Kate thought suddenly of her own children, all six of them grown, some with children of their own, and all of them dependent upon Kate's bank account. What would happen to them if Kate did not come back from her swim?

Theodora opened her eyes wide and tore her hands free. She grabbed once more for Kate's neck, her fingers slashing at the top of her shirtwaist.

Kate lunged and caught Theodora's thick braid. With braid in hand, Kate dove under the water, pulling Theodora with her. As she held Theodora under the water, Kate thought only of her children and how bereft they would be without their *Maman*.

The women surfaced together—Theodora spitting water and garbling, "N—n—n—"

Kate pulled them both back under. This time she held her breath until she saw Theodora relax entirely.

Then she burst out of the water with the focus of a pelican emerging with its prey. As Kate treaded the water, she took both of Theodora's hands in hers, and once more she searched Theodora's face carefully, frantic to see one more labored breath or hear one more spit of saltwater.

"Was it *no*, Theodora? Or was it *note*?"

Kate scanned the waterline and hunted for signs of anyone else on the beach, anyone else who could stand witness to Theodora's demise. "It was *note*, wasn't it?"

Long after she released Theodora to the sea, Kate reached the shore and stumbled to the safety of the hard sand. As she wiped the saltwater tears from her face, she could not shake the image of Theodora's last shudder and the promise that Kate had made her.

"Yes, I'll type a suicide note for you. It's the very least I could do. And I'll tell your family that I found the note between two stones on the beach. Or that it was in your carpetbag, if that shows up." One of Kate's own black shoes floated ashore and she retrieved it quickly, for she was down to her last pair. "No one should have to blame themselves by wondering if your death was a suicide or an accidental drowning."

A few minutes later Kate saw the indigo-and-crimson carpetbag wash up farther down the beach. She stood up to secure it.

"And certainly, no one should ever, ever suspect that you were murdered."

Fault, blame, and guilt in late nineteenth-century Louisiana.

Although Kate Chopin's novel *The Awakening* is celebrated today as a declaration of female sexual independence, when it was first published in 1899 it was scorned, derided, and deemed vulgar.

What, I wondered, would have happened if author Kate was confronted by one of her early readers? A reader who—like Kate's protagonist Edna—had her life changed forever by her sudden sexual independence? But a reader who—unlike Edna—would stop at nothing to blame Kate for where that independence led her.

Writer or reader, it's not always easy to know who's really at fault.

—Ana Brazil

17 WAYS TO KILL YOUR CO-WORKER

Mariella Krause

Monday

Death by staple gun would be a terrible way to die, Steve thought. But in this case, it would not be undeserved.

It was Monday morning, and Mallory was telling everyone what they'd missed at happy hour the previous Friday. Not that Steve was part of the conversation, but he could hear the whole thing from the next row over. Thanks to the way the cubicles were arranged and the weird acoustics on the fourth floor, the whole department could probably hear her recap of the tiki-bar shenanigans followed by an impromptu karaoke party that sounded like the seventh circle of hell.

Besides, Mallory seldom spoke in what one would describe as an "indoor voice."

Day after day, Steve had to listen to her go on and on

about things he didn't care about. So what if Heather in accounting was having a baby? Who cared if Craig had gotten a job in Ohio? And did the entire world really need to know that Mallory thought Gretchen's shoes were "so cute"?

Steve looked over at Deanna, the art director whose cube was across the aisle from his, but either she hadn't noticed the hubbub or she didn't care. He put on his headphones—a little Green Day would drown Mallory out—and quietly googled *How to know when it's time to find a new job*. A quick scan of the results suggested that that time was now.

Mallory laughed so loud Steve could hear it over the music in his headphones. Who laughed like that? A loud burst like "HA!"—or sometimes more like "Ah-HAA!"—followed by a rolling cackle. To Steve it sounded like a dying cat. It was distracting, and frankly not very professional.

Steve had left an anonymous note for HR, but it didn't seem that anyone had spoken to her about it. None of his anonymous notes ever seemed to lead to any kind of real change. Maybe he should discontinue the practice altogether.

Steve popped a Tums and searched different combinations of the words *Bay Area financial industry marketing jobs*. The listings he found didn't give him much hope. Most of the positions required a commute down to Mountain View or significant digital experience. He could also cross off any listings where they bragged about their perks like free food and use of the onsite gym. That was just code for "We don't expect you to ever leave the building."

No, as tempting as it was to move on, Lending Nation paid him a lot and expected little. Just show up, answer emails, sit through a few meetings, and occasionally write a brochure about the difference between fixed- and adjustable-rate mortgages. That had been his unofficial job description for most of the seventeen years he'd worked for the company, and he was in no mood to start over with a new job and a twenty-six-year-old boss.

Steve took a swig of the Americano he'd brought in from Starbucks—the stuff they served on the fourth floor was swill—and started a new search:

How to kill your co-worker.

Steve scrolled through results, but most of them were cheeky lists like "10 Ways to Kill your Co-Worker with Kindness" or "5 Tips for Dealing with a Difficult Co-worker (So You Don't Have to Kill Them)."

Eh, it's probably for the best, Steve thought as he deleted his browsing history. The company's privacy policy made it very clear that they could and would be monitoring internet usage on work computers. And based on the company's strict nondiscrimination and no-sexual-harassment guidelines, they would take it seriously.

And Steve wasn't serious.

Not really.

Tuesday

Steve was running late. No matter how hard he tried, he could never get to the office before 9:30. Which didn't really matter, because nothing important ever happened before 9:30. But today he was pushing it. It was already 9:43. So he hung a right out of the elevator and took the back way so he didn't have to walk past his coworkers' desks.

As he rounded the corner, he saw Mallory standing in front of the supply cabinet pillaging all the Rollerball pens. He stifled an urge to stuff her inside and lock the door, but she'd never fit. Besides, it was early enough in the day that she'd be rescued as soon as soon as someone came in search of dry-erase markers for a whiteboard session.

Too bad. It would be fun to make her miss the weekly managers' meeting, because she should never have been invited to that meeting in the first place. What could Mallory possibly know about managing a team? As far as Steve could tell, her entire job consisted of writing Twitters, whatever the hell they were.

Jonathan, their boss, had tried to get Steve to take on that particular responsibility himself, but Steve had no interest in social media. He'd felt pretty clever when he'd convinced them to hire an intern to do it. He hadn't even minded when Jonathan had hired Mallory on full-time—although he didn't see why another full-time writer was really necessary. There were weeks when he barely did anything, just watched Netflix on his laptop while waiting around for copy revisions. But if it saved him from having to pretend to care about digital branding, he was all for it.

This manager thing, though—that had come as a surprise. It had taken him twelve years to get promoted to associate creative director. Mallory had done it in three.

Sure, she had written that one Twitter during the Super Bowl that had gotten a lot of attention, but come *on*. From what Steve could tell, her job consisted primarily of looking at Facebook all day long.

Nevertheless, when ten o'clock rolled around, there she was right across the table from him at the managers' meeting, with the exact same job title as his.

"All right," Jonathan said, after they'd gotten the pleasantries out of the way. "What's on everyone's plate this week?"

Deanna's team was heading up the redesign of the landing page, Matt was doing a photo shoot to update their library of stock photography, and Audrey was busy finishing up performance reviews.

When it was Mallory's turn, she walked to the front of the room and pulled down the projection screen. "As most of you know, I've been working on a prototype of our very first Lending Nation app." She clicked some buttons on her laptop and a screenshot appeared overhead as Jonathan smiled approvingly.

Steve couldn't believe how smug she looked. That was it? She hadn't done anything more than superimpose the company logo of a house onto a picture of an iPhone. Any idiot could do that.

She pressed another button and the Lending Nation logo sprang to life. The house grew bigger until it filled the screen, and the front door swung open, rolling out a welcome mat that said *Lending Nation*.

Steve was glad he was sitting in the back of the room because he wasn't able to stop himself from rolling his eyes. Okay, so she knew how to do animation, but still. What a show-off.

"By engaging customers with our app," she said, "we will enhance the customer journey and position ourselves as the premier home-lending partner." She then proceeded to take them through the app screen by screen, saying lots of things that were pretty much bullshit but that had the rest of the room nodding along enthusiastically.

She's like that girl in class who always raises her hand, Steve thought, but worse, because class never ends early, but sometimes meetings do if everyone keeps their mouth shut.

Steve crossed his arms and came close to muttering under his breath. That's what she'd been doing with her time? Building an app? Big freaking whoop-de-doo. Why did Lending Nation even need an app? People had been buying houses for millions of years without apps. Why? Because people need lodging. What could be more basic than that?

Jonathan—who clearly differed on the matter—nodded appreciatively. "Great work, Mallory. Thank you for bringing us into this century."

Steve looked around the room. Why wasn't anyone saying anything? "I don't know," he said finally. "Don't you think it's a little ...?"

No one jumped in with their own objections, so Steve said the first thing that came to mind. "... cutesy? I mean, I know you're trying to appeal to young people, but most of them can't afford to buy a home anyway, so what's the point?"

"Every one of our major competitors has an app," said Jonathan. "We're basically playing catch-up with what's become an industry standard."

Steve plunged ahead. "And have you even thought about privacy issues? What if our app gets hacked?"

Jonathan and Mallory exchanged looks, and Jonathan pinched the bridge of his nose. "That's not how it works."

Steve folded his arms and made a disapproving face. "Well, I just think it's off-brand."

"Actually," Jonathan said, "Mallory has been helping us develop our new brand identity and voice guidelines, and this is the direction I want to see more of our work heading in." He closed his laptop with such an air of finality that he might as well have banged a gavel on the conference room table. "Anyone else have anything they want to share?"

Steve hadn't given his status update for the week, but there wasn't that much to tell. He wasn't all that busy, but he was expecting revisions from the compliance team any day now, so he couldn't afford to have more work loaded on his plate. He stared at his notepad and drew a row of backslashes until the moment passed. "Okay, that's it for this week," Jonathan said as everyone gathered their things. "I really appreciate all the hard work everyone's doing."

Steve went up to the balcony on eight to get some fresh air. He leaned over the railing and looked down, thinking it would be really satisfying to throw Mallory—and her app—over the edge and into the traffic below.

Wednesday

When Steve got in to the office, he found an invite in his inbox for a meeting that had started five minutes earlier. Who scheduled meetings before 10:00 a.m.? Cursing under his breath, he hurried to the conference room.

"Sorry," he whispered as he slid into a chair. Deanna gave him a tight-lipped smile and slid a copy of a creative brief over to him. Great, a new project.

He read the top of the document and groaned inwardly. *Tagline ideation.* The creative department had been trying to sell the executive committee on a new tagline for years, but Steve didn't see anything wrong with the old one. He'd gone through this pointless exercise at least four times already, and there couldn't possibly be any new ideas that no one had thought of yet.

While Jonathan read the brief to them—Steve hated when they did that; why not just email it and let people read it from the privacy of their desks?—Steve started coming up with some initial thoughts:

Lending Nation. My own private hell.

Lending Nation. Where dreams go to die.

Lending Nation. Exploiting the middle class since 1983.

Mallory was busy sucking up to the boss, asking questions with a sincere, engaged look on her face. But Steve saw right through her. She wanted to score brownie points by coming up with a whole bunch of ideas, not realizing none of them would ever get approved. Well, as far as he was concerned, the assignment was all hers. Once she'd been through as many of these as he had, she'd probably throw herself off the eighth-floor balcony and save him the trouble.

"I'd like to see where everyone is next Thursday," said Jonathan. "But since Mallory has a pretty good grasp of where the brand is heading, I encourage you to check in with her before then for feedback."

Steve felt his eyes grow wide and he focused all his efforts on not reacting visibly. There was no way in hell he was going to run things by Jonathan's sycophantic office minion. He'd worked here since Mallory was in middle school. Just because she'd been entrusted with the company Twitter account didn't mean she was qualified to judge his work.

Steve returned to his desk, fuming. He chucked the

creative brief into his recycling bin, then started going through his desk drawers, pondering how many boxes he would need to take home the stuff he'd accumulated over the years.

He would leave the two drawers' worth of files, of course; those were useless. Same with the inflatable palm tree left over from an island-themed office party—back when they used to have those. He considered taking the bottle of Dewar's, but it was more than half empty. He glanced over at Deanna, but she was intently focused on her laptop, so he poured the remainder into his coffee mug and tossed the empty bottle into the recycling bin with the creative brief.

One aisle over, Mallory was holding court. Gretchen of the cute shoes asked if this meant Mallory was getting another promotion—a question that Mallory deflected but didn't outright deny.

Steve managed to tune out their excited chattering—until Mallory's laugh pealed across the floor, causing him and Deanna to look up at the same time and make eye contact. Deanna had a wicked twinkle in her eye. "Someone's having entirely too much fun," she said, and Steve's heart lifted. Deanna felt it, too! See? He wasn't the only one who hated Mallory!

Steve considered asking Deanna if she wanted to go to lunch and talk about the Mallory problem. But he needed to clear his head, so he drained the coffee mug, put some make-believe meetings on his calendar, and headed for the elevators.

An hour and a half and three beers later, he felt a little better. Maybe it was being out in the fresh air along with all the other office drones swarming the streets of downtown to pick up their salads from Mixt Greens. Or maybe it was sitting in a darkened bar with a couple of construction workers and a jabbering homeless man who was trying to pick a fight with the jukebox.

His job wasn't that bad, and Mallory would probably be gone in a year anyway. Was he really willing to ditch it all so he could spend his time day-drinking and wondering why it was so hard to find a job after fifty? No, he'd invested too much time in this job to let her run him off. He'd just have to learn to play the game a little better.

Even if it killed him.

Thursday

After he was done with his morning meetings, Steve took his notepad into one of the creative lounges to do some brainstorming. Might as well get this over with. He plopped down into one of the oversized beanbag chairs that were supposed to make it seem like a cool place to work, took the cap off his pen, and began to write:

Lending Nation. We give you loans.
Lending Nation. Buy a house. It's fun.
Lending Nation. You'd better have good credit.

He doodled a house, then added some flowers and a tree. Feeling inspired, he drew some feet sticking out from under the house wearing ruby slippers. If only a tornado would drop a rustic wooden farmhouse on Mallory and end his suffering.

Lending Nation. We solve all your problems.

Steve turned the page and wrote the words *Lending Nation* at the top. His mind blank, he stared out the window through the dirty glass. A fat pigeon stared at him from a windowsill across the way, and he wondered if Mallory might be susceptible to any deadly bird viruses.

He doodled a picture of Mallory lying on the sidewalk, with Xs where her eyes would normally be and a pigeon perched on her chest. The likeness wasn't bad; maybe he should have been an art director.

He still hadn't come up with a single useable tagline. What was that brainstorming exercise he'd learned during one of those useless Creative Spark meetings they made them all sit through once a month?

Something about mind mapping, but it had been right after lunch and he'd been too sleepy to catch much. Remembering what he could, he wrote the word *Mallory* in the middle of the page and circled it. Then, he began jotting down related thoughts, the words radiating out from the central topic:

Transfer to a different department?
Make her want to quit?
Get her fired?

Some other way to make her go away?

Suddenly inspired, he turned the page and started jotting down ideas as fast as he could come up with them:

- *Find out if she has a peanut allergy.*
- *Bring her a Jamba Juice with peanut butter in it (see above).*
- *Release a rabid weasel when she's working late at the office.*
- *Charter a boat for a department-wide booze cruise and toss her overboard (blame it on her being drunk).*
- *Death by a thousand paper cuts.*
- *Strangle her with the power cord from the overhead projector.*
- *Rig her office chair with tiny poisonous darts.*
- *Tape a note on her that says "basura" and leave her for the cleaning crew.*
- *Clock her with one of those "Primary Mortgage Origination" awards from J.D. Powers and Associates.*
- *Go to happy hour and stage a hit-and-run.*

It felt good to get his brain revved up again, just like in the old days before he'd become a low-level manager. He used to love finding solutions to problems. If only the problems hadn't become so boring. But this list proved that he could still be creative in a pinch.

Paper cuts. He chuckled at the thought of it. It would

take a while, but it would annoy the crap out of her in the meantime.

The booze cruise option would be expensive, but he liked the angle that they would be celebrating her demise while it actually happened.

And just imagine how surprised she'd be if he actually came along on one of those infernal happy hours. He could buy a round of shots, goad her into drinking them, get her defenses down, then who knows what?

He could slip something into one of her drinks, lock her in a walk-in freezer—hell, too bad they didn't still shanghai people like they did back during the Gold Rush. He could just toss her on a boat and let her be someone else's problem.

Steve laughed as he attempted to draw a rabid weasel. He was glad he still had his sense of humor, at least. He felt energized, ready to come up with some new taglines that probably would never sell but at least would get Jonathan off his back for a while.

But first, he thought, tearing the pages out of his notebook, he'd have to go find a paper shredder.

Friday

"Good morning," Steve said to Deanna. He'd gotten there early, only ten after nine, and wanted to make sure someone had noticed his efforts.

"Hey," Deanna answered. "Thank God it's Friday."

"And not a moment too soon," said Steve, but without any bitterness.

He turned on his computer and checked his emails, thinking about his day. Maybe he'd try again to come up with a viable list of taglines for next week's presentation. He still doubted they'd be able to sell one through, but he had to at least have something to show. Yesterday's brainstorming exercise combined with a good night's sleep had given him a new sense of resolve. If all his years' experience were worth anything, it was to show that he understood the company better than the former intern ever would.

"Knock, knock," Jonathan said behind him.

"Hey, what's up?" Steve asked, spinning around in his chair.

"Can I see you in my office?" Jonathan gestured over his shoulder, and Steve nodded mutely and stood. What was this about? He followed Jonathan down the hall, inquiring about his weekend plans, and the polite chitchat got them all the way to his office. They entered, and Jonathan closed the door behind them.

"What's up, boss?"

Jonathan perched on the edge of his desk and gestured for Steve to have a seat.

"So," he began, "I wanted to give you a heads-up that we're going to be doing some restructuring."

"Oh. Yeah ...?"

Jonathan explained how Mallory could use some

backup on some of her projects, framing it as a positive opportunity for growth for everyone involved. "You could learn a lot from her," Jonathan said. "We all could. She's going to help us tap into a whole new demographic, but she'll need someone with your experience to help get us there."

Despite the positive spin Jonathan was putting on it, Steve had been around long enough to read between the lines. Mallory—the shoe-complimenting, karaoke-singing, loud-laughing sycophant—was the future of the company. And Steve was not.

"I want you two to work side by side. It'll be good for both of you. Now, we've redrawn the org chart, and technically, you'll report to her, but don't worry, that's just on paper, something we had to do because of HR."

"So, she's my boss now?" The blood rushed to Steve's head, creating a *whoosh-whoosh* noise with every heartbeat. The sound was almost enough to drown out Jonathan's words.

"She's really into a collaborative work environment, so you shouldn't notice any change at all." Jonathan was watching Steve closely to gauge his response.

"Am I being demoted?"

"No," Jonathan said, flapping his hand with a dismissive wave. "No, no, no, no. We just thought it would be good for the team to shake things up a bit. We value you as an employee, but fresh blood, you know? She's got all these great ideas. And she really follows through on them, too."

"All right," was all Steve said. He stared blankly at Jonathan. There was nothing left to say. Mallory was his new boss. She had great ideas. She could be counted on to follow through. Fresh blood.

Steve left Jonathan's office, his mind spinning. He needed a minute to think, to get some fresh air.

Heading toward the elevator, he ran into Mallory. She must have read something in his face because she slowed to a stop.

"Hey, Steve," she said, shifting a stack of color printouts from her left hip to her right. "You going out for coffee?"

"Um, yeah."

"You mind bringing me back a latte? I have a meeting."

He jabbed the button a few more times, hoping it would make the elevator arrive faster. "No problem."

Mallory was still standing there. Was she going to have him pick up her dry cleaning, too?

"Have you talked to Jonathan?" she asked.

Steve flicked the corners of his mouth up in a tight smile. "I have. He said we're going to be working together."

"Oh, good! I wasn't sure if I should say anything yet. It's going to be great. I have so many cool ideas and I can't wait for you to help me implement them." She kept talking but the roaring in his ears had gotten louder and louder and he couldn't hear anything anymore. She was staring at him expectantly, waiting for him to say something.

"Right," he said, fumbling for a response. A slideshow of images flicked through his brain: Mallory with a pigeon sitting on her chest. Mallory tumbling from the eighth-floor balcony, color printouts raining down around her. Mallory going over the boat's railing and splashing into the bay.

He shook his head and managed to form a response. "No, yeah, I'm super excited."

"Oh, good, I'm relieved to hear it. I wasn't sure if you'd be okay with working with me."

"What?" Steve feigned enthusiasm. "No, it'll be great."

Mallory's face flooded with relief. "Oh, yay. I'll set up a meeting for us to go over everything. In fact, I was thinking we should do our own team status meeting every Monday morning where we can share progress and celebrate each other's successes."

"Really looking forward to it," he said, forcing a smile. "In fact, we should celebrate!"

"Really? That'd be great! We're going to happy hour tonight if you want to join us."

He pictured Mallory at happy hour with a poisoned Appletini in her hand.

"Oh, you'd better believe it," Steve said. He would go to the drugstore at lunchtime. His googling had told him exactly what he'd need. "First round's on me."

One night, having been awakened by the cat, I was trying to come up with an idea for a story and a title randomly popped into my head: "17 Ways to Kill Your Co-Worker." I asked myself, "Why would someone want to kill their co-worker?" Then I thought back fondly on the many people I've met along the way in my day job as an advertising copywriter. There are so many Steves out there, so many Mallorys! The idea took off so quickly, I got out of bed at 4:00 in the morning and had a rough draft written before the sun came up.

—Mariella Krause

THE WATER'S EDGE

Jenny Carless

Wednesday

I like to sit at the water's edge, where the ocean laps gently onto the sand. It calms me down. It's also the only thing that still feels the same between my "before" and "after" lives. Even here in Zanzibar, thousands of miles away from my regular San Francisco beach, the rhythm, the cool water, the briny smell ... it's all very soothing.

It wasn't my idea to come to East Africa. I think my dad just wanted to get out of the house. He didn't want a beach vacation ("We already live by the beach!"), but I did, so we compromised—and when your compromise is one week safari, one week beach, you end up in Zanzibar.

I wish Mom could have come; she'd have loved last week's safari. It made me think of our evenings watching *National Geographic* shows, snuggled together on the sofa under a big, cozy blanket. My dad didn't know about our "sofa safaris." He spent so much time away—a lot of sales meetings or something like that; Mom and I couldn't keep track. If he had known, we probably wouldn't be here now. I don't think even he's that thoughtless.

My dad's been around a lot more lately; unfortunately, so has Dr. X. You'd think my dad would look older, considering everything we've been through. But as I come out of the fog that has been my life for the past year, my sense is that he looks younger. He still has the same jagged eyebrows and crooked teeth in a kind of puffy face. But I think he's dying the salt out of his salt-and-pepper hair, and his wardrobe is actually catching up with the twenty-first century.

Having to be around Dr. X so much these days is what keeps driving me back to the tranquility of the water's edge. I just can't take too much time in her company. Yesterday, we shared a truly cringe-worthy moment when she attempted a badly mistimed and clearly contrived hug. I could tell by the look on my dad's face that he'd known it was coming. I think it's safe to say that if you have to strategize to hug someone, you probably shouldn't do it. Just my two cents.

Dr. X used to be my therapist. Whereas my dad is a big bear of a man, she's the opposite: petite, with an extreme pixie haircut and thick horn-rimmed glasses that make her eyes bug out. Her mouth snarls before it can work its way into a smile. I never noticed this in our therapy sessions, because during all those hours, through all those months, she watched me with an inscrutable expression. No chance of a smile then—not even a twitch across the severe, thin lines of her lips. But now that we're spending all this extra time together, she's trying to smile—a lot.

With my dad's teeth and her snarl, sometimes it feels like I've been adopted by a pack of socially awkward wolves.

• • •

Mom died a year ago yesterday; that's what divides my life into before and after. To mark the occasion, my dad had the brilliant idea to go on a safari. I get that he didn't want to be at home, but going on a major trip? It's like we're celebrating.

Maybe we are—in a sick, insensitive sort of way. It's my first expedition anywhere beyond our house or the hospital, and it's my dad and Dr. X's first trip together since they "came out" as a couple—even though I suspected for a while, thanks to my observant friend Amy from the hospital. Amy gave me the heads-up, but at first I wasn't sure whether to believe her, because she's the absolute queen of conspiracy theorists. That's more or less what landed her in the hospital, I think.

We're staying at an exotic hotel in Stone Town. It's all decorated in an Arab style, and there's a rooftop restaurant with a great view, where you can sometimes catch a soothing cool breeze. From there, you can look out across the other rooftops, a sea of corrugated iron—some silver, some rusted—and red tiles. Stone Town sits on a triangular peninsula, so beyond the roofs we're almost surrounded by the real sea—the Indian Ocean—in varying shades of sparkly turquoise.

I have my own room, but the three of us share a balcony. My room has a soaring ceiling (two stories high!), two large ceiling fans, and soft mosquito netting draped across the large, wood-framed bed. The bed, two sofas, and armoire are all built from dark, intricately carved wood, and the furniture is piled high with bright, sequined pillows. Dark concrete floors help the room stay cool; the overall effect is very cocoon-y. My bathroom is enormous, and the hotel provides light kimono-style robes, nice soaps and lotions, super soft towels, and even little terrycloth bath mitts you can slip on your hands (Step 1) for washing.

Stone Town is a warren of streets and alleys, some so narrow that my dad can reach out and touch the whitewashed walls on both sides of the street at once. Even I can, in some places. Dr. X can't. Tiny shops—no more than closets, really—spill out into the narrow passages. Their doors open like shutters, and the merchants tuck themselves in among the tourist trinkets, canned goods, household supplies, and pungent spices.

Our hotel is close enough to the beach that I can run out the door, go around a couple of corners, and be down at the water's edge whenever I need a break, like when I can't take Dr. X—who now wants me to call her Mary, by the way—anymore. At first, she tried to tell me I couldn't go out by myself. That's new, too: her trying to tell me what I can and cannot do. I asked if she'd feel more comfortable if I carried a knife for protection—my little attempt at humor and quite fitting, I thought, considering. Apart from hissing that I must be feeling better, if I had enough energy to be a smart aleck, she had nothing to say. I continue to go down to the beach by myself.

Yesterday morning, a man with a *dhow*—one of those cool traditional boats with the large sails that glide along the horizon here—offered to take me for a cruise along the coast. So tempting! I sat on the shore and fantasized about sailing away to mainland Tanzania and disappearing—crossing that line on the horizon that looked like it could be a break between my today and my tomorrow. I didn't take him up on it, but since then, I've wondered if I should have gone with him.

After he left, a woman came by and offered to paint my fingers and hands with dark blue henna, which she mixed in a bottle cap. The intricate designs look fantastic; she said they'll last a few weeks. So now I have the henna on the back of my hands as well as the new wristbands I bought in our camp in the Masai Mara.

Our safari guide and most of the people working at camp were from the Maasai tribe. They wore red cloths tied over their shoulders (*shukas*)—which looked really comfortable, especially in this heat, and they made lots of jewelry with tiny, colorful beads. They wore bracelets, or wristbands—some thin and some wide. I especially like the wide ones. The camp sold them in the gift tent; our guide Julius's mother had made the ones I bought. So now I wear them all the time, instead of those small bandanas I used to wrap around my wrists. They stay in place and work better to hide the thin, scarred lines.

Thursday

After lunch today, like every afternoon, we went back to our rooms for a siesta—a custom I've really taken to. It's too hot in the middle of the day to do anything else, and I appreciate the time on my own. I rested on my giant bed, under the ceiling fan, staring at the wall. After a while, I started to notice animal shapes in the plaster patterns next to my bed. An elephant, a giraffe, and then some kind of antelope.

They reminded me of when we came upon a family of lions eating a wildebeest on our first morning on safari. At first, I'd gagged at the sight of all that blood on the lions' faces and the wildebeest's fur, and I'd thought I was going to be sick. I looked down at my hands, and for just an instant, I saw them covered in blood. Images from my sessions with Dr. X rushed into my head and I almost started going through the motions of washing my hands (Step 5). But then I noticed my dad, and the expression on his face pulled me out of the downward spiral. It almost made me laugh, actually: His realization of the absolute inappropriateness of this vacation—out in the wild

African savanna, "kill or be killed" and all that—had come a tad too late.

That wasn't the only awkward moment on our safari. At seventeen, I'm part of the generation that's supposedly glued to our cell phones twenty-four-seven, but with everything to see on our game drives and around camp, I had no interest in getting online. My dad and Dr. X were another story. In fact, on our first day, the camp manager had to tell them to go back to their tent if they wanted to keep using their phones.

What the manager didn't understand is that they didn't need them in their tent; they only needed them around me. They were pretending to check work email or keep track of the many terribly important things in their lives, but in fact they were texting about me. I know this because I snuck a look at my dad's phone later, while they both took a nap. I learned a lot from their exchange right after we saw the lions eating the wildebeest.

But back to the siesta—when I started focusing on the game drive and all that blood, I did what I've been taught: "Change your environment, concentrate your mind on something else." (A year of therapy hasn't been a complete waste.) So I went out to the balcony to take a look down at the street. The latticework that encloses our balcony hid me well; I felt like a secret agent, spying down on the Zanzibaris and tourists.

Voices echoed up through the narrow space between the buildings to our second-floor rooms as people walked by—women and girls with their heads wrapped in colorful cotton scarves, men in skull caps and long white robes, small children laughing and playing, people pulling enormous wooden carts loaded down with construction materials.

When silence descended on the street, in between groups of passersby, I heard softer voices: those of my dad and Dr. X.

Curious, I edged closer, step by step, tiptoeing to try to keep the old wooden boards below me from creaking (Step 3). It turns out that the balcony is custom-made for spying: It held firm and didn't make a sound. I backed up against the wall and slid along to the right until I stood next to their French doors, which hung wide open—like mine, trying to entice any slight breeze into the room. I listened for a while—at first unsure of what I was hearing.

Then, like a giant wave, the full weight of this past year's misery and confusion crashed down on me. My knees almost gave out, and I pressed myself even harder against the wall for support. The gruesome nightmares of Mom, bloody and lifeless, which I'd fought so hard against, rushed back in, leaving me gasping for air. Fearing that I'd pass out and fall, cry, or otherwise give myself away, I inched away and poured myself back into the sanctuary of my bed—badly shaken and determined to look back in my dad's texting history as soon as I could.

• • •

Overhearing that conversation, revisiting the antelope on the wall's plaster: It hit me again how much I wished Mom were with me. This took me back to our sofa safaris, which made me ask myself—for about the hundred millionth time:

How could I have killed her?

Why would I ever have killed her?

Her absence from my life cuts a hole as big as the Ngorongoro Crater in me, and if anyone had told me a year ago that I would kill one of my parents, believe me: I wouldn't have chosen Mom. But everyone said that no one else could have done it. No signs of forced entry, no unusual fingerprints or other evidence.

My dad told the police that he'd found her when he arrived home, her throat slashed and blood all over the bed. All I remember is being woken up in my bed by the sounds of the ambulance and police sirens. At first, the police thought that my dad might have done it, but he had a rock-solid alibi.

I can walk you through the moments leading up her death, step by step—even though I still don't actually remember it myself. There are five steps. I've developed a ritual of sorts, counting them off while tapping the tips of each finger on my right hand in succession. The rhythm is soothing—like the ocean, its waves unfolding in gentle laps onto the sand, over and over again.

So I tap my fingertips incessantly and repeat the steps in my mind; I've walked through them hundreds of thousands of times. I have Dr. X and her particular method of "helping me get over it" to thank for this. The idea, she said, was for me to remember that night, everything about the actual incident; only then could I move on.

In fact, sometimes it felt more like she was training me to kill again. I wonder if that ever occurred to her. I've been over it so many times, talked it through, gone through the motions ... I'm sure I could do it in my sleep now.

Despite all her efforts, though, the scene I always see is my first reenactment, played out under her guidance, within the four claustrophobic walls of her office. I've still never once remembered the actual act of killing my mother.

• • •

After I— After Mom died, I pretty much lost it. That's how I ended up in that hospital. I'm lucky it wasn't prison, I guess.

I have strange, terrifying memories from that time. My earliest impressions are of dark, oppressive spaces, as if I'd lived underground. Probably just the medication. I remember nothing from the first couple of months, and I still have only a vague notion of the two or three months after that. It exhausts me just thinking about that period;

everything seemed to happen in slow motion and to require extra effort, like trudging through deep water.

My dad and Dr. X think I'm still taking my meds. Over time, their hypervigilance has relaxed, and I've been able to take advantage of that in more ways than one. The visits back to the hospital have given me all the reminders I need about how to continue to act muddled: Half of the people there wander around like zombies. I guess I did, too. Also, I've been perfecting my glassy-eyed stare in the mirror.

It feels liberating to be off the drugs. One of the best changes is waking up earlier. On safari, I couldn't leave my tent until daylight because of the wild animals, but since we've been in Stone Town, I walk around in the early morning—or just sit down at the water's edge to look across toward mainland Tanzania and let my mind fly free.

I'm beginning to think more clearly, too. I didn't realize how spaced-out I'd been until I started to come out of the haze, especially over the past ten days or so. My dad has complained for months that he has to ask me everything twice. (But geez: Medicate a person with elephantine doses of drugs, and what do you expect? You can't really have it both ways.) Things are not completely fog-free, but I'm having many more moments of clarity.

In fact, I've almost blown it a couple of times by forgetting to act like a zombie. Take yesterday morning: I stopped to look in one of the closet-sized shops with some beautiful, bright fabrics, and when my dad asked what I thought of a couple of scarves, I answered him right away. I'll have to keep an eye on that.

Of course, thinking more clearly is a mixed blessing. I miss Mom even more, and it has led to an increasing curiosity on my part—to question the picture they've painted for me. Part of me wishes that the old, doped-up me could have just slept through siesta time earlier, instead of going out onto that balcony.

Friday

The afternoon heat does eventually die down, and everyone comes back to life once the sun slips below the horizon. Forodhani Gardens, along the waterfront, is a public square of sorts that metamorphoses at night into a rowdy food-and-crafts market, where locals and tourists hang out, swallowed up by the beat of boomboxes and the shouts of vendors. Strings of tiny lights hang from the trees and across the stalls, adding to the party atmosphere.

Last night, the three of us wandered down there for dinner. The fishermen bring up their fresh catch every afternoon, and the vendors prepare grilled seafood and other local specialties right there in front of you. My dad tried some snapper kebabs and crab claws; I ate spicy vegetable samosas. The chefs used all kinds of knives—long, short, thick, thin. My dad froze when I picked one up (Step 2) from the table of a man who was slitting open the flesh of raw fish, but I was just admiring it.

Okay, I did it on purpose just to freak him out.

After dinner, despite the fun crowd, I started feeling low again, weighed down from the conversation I'd overheard on our balcony. I couldn't focus on anything but my need to check their texts again. I saw my dad's cell phone in his outside jacket pocket, sitting there for all the world to steal. So I slipped it into my purse. Then I told them I wanted to go back to the hotel.

Later I threw the phone on their bed, and he was none the wiser, thinking he'd forgotten to take it in the first place.

But I had become much wiser.

• • •

Sending texts that describe your criminal and moral failings is stupid enough; not deleting them afterward is just asking for trouble. And people say that teenagers are clueless. What I read last night on my dad's phone helped everything slip into place, like the final pieces of a puzzle I'd been slowly constructing for months. How did I not know that Dr. X was his alibi?

When I put those texts together with the ones from last week and the conversation I overheard from the balcony, suddenly my world felt completely different. Strangely, my thoughts went straight to Amy, my conspiracy-theorist friend from the hospital, and how she'll be so pleased when I tell her that her theories have been validated.

I lay on my bed in a daze for a long time—tapping at my fingertips with a fever, unable to stop the five steps from swimming through my mind on an endless, insistent loop. Eventually, all the street sounds died down, except for the occasional dog barking. At that point, it must have been the early hours of this morning. I couldn't keep myself from replaying those steps, as Dr. X taught me so well. The lines blurred between past and present, reality and imagination.

Step 1: I found a pair of gloves and put them on.

Step 2: I selected a knife. We used to have a large, wooden knife block in the kitchen that held a matching set of stainless steel knives: nine different implements in all shapes and sizes—a gift from my dad to Mom a couple of years ago. Back then, they liked to cook together. This morning, I just had the one.

Step 3: I crept quietly, bare feet across wooden floorboards, careful not to cause any creaking. I pushed the door open inch by inch, silent as a ghost.

Step 4: One long, deep slice. Easy with a sharp edge. Seems that both my dad and the fisherman kept their knives sharp. This morning, it was two slices instead of one.

Step 5: I washed my hands and the knife, and I put the knife back where I found it—on the fisherman's table in

Forodhani Gardens, on my way back down here to the beach.

• • •

Sitting here on the sand, I sense that all those times when Dr. X made me go over the steps in my mind are already beginning to dissolve into nothingness, like the lies they represented. Now I finally know, without a doubt, that the reason I could never envision the actual steps of killing Mom is because I didn't do it.

Right now, my mind is flush with new images; they're blurring with Dr. X's invented memories. I'm not quite sure what's real and what's not. But the new ones, if they are real, don't feel so oppressive, so I'm pretty sure I won't struggle under the same tsunami of guilt and devastation that's destroyed me for the past year. In fact, I think I'm going to be able to push back, to strike it all from my mind, once and for all—as soon as I can relax.

That's why I needed to come back here. The sun is just coming up; I'll be able to stop shivering soon. With the lapping of the water, that soothing pulse, I've already stopped tapping my fingertips. Sitting at the water's edge always calms me down.

Images from a visit to Zanzibar during my first trip to East Africa in 2003—the night market in Forodhani Gardens, the atmosphere at Emerson & Greene hotel, *dhows* gliding across the horizon—are still very much alive in my mind. Clearly, the water lapping on the sand left an impression. Dark, shuttered rooms; narrow, winding streets; interesting smells and sounds: Stone Town is an intriguing setting, and before anything else, I knew I wanted to write something based there. This particular story idea began with the notion of a small family traveling together, and something doesn't feel right. But why? It flowed from there.

—Jenny Carless

THE OLD STUDIO

Bette Golden Lamb

Sandy ran as hard as she could down the crumbling Bronx sidewalk. Row after row of ancient apartment buildings rushed by in a blur. She was hot, sweaty; her chest screamed in pain with each breath.

She tossed a quick glance over her shoulder to eye the creeps chasing her.

Damn it! Same punks followed me after school all week.

Each day they get closer, flashing their dirty, mean faces and grungy black jackets with Deadeyes painted across the back.

Key at the ready, she flew up the steps to her apartment building and slipped inside. The heavy glass door slammed shut as the boys reached the stoop. They yelled and shook their fists at her. She turned away and ran to her apartment.

Safe in her room, she dropped her books on the bed and eased out the window onto the fire escape. A fresh gust of spring air caught and swirled her skirt without warning. She grabbed at the flying material, hugging it tight against her body. Why wouldn't her mother let her wear pants to school like most of the other girls? Sandy stomped back and forth on the narrow metal structure—the wind was gone but she still bunched her skirt between clenched fists.

Nothing had been the same since she turned twelve.

Nothing.

When she stood naked in front of her bedroom mirror, the strong boyish lines she'd been so proud of were gone, and getting dressed exposed islands of skin between her blouse buttons where the material no longer met. Hiding under sweaters only made her breasts stick out more. It was disgusting.

She looked stupid. She felt stupid.

Don't want to be a girl. Hate being a girl. Want to be like my big brother—not need anybody, take care of myself like a real Bronx street person. Then nobody will push me around.

She hung over the railing, looked down at the ground three stories below, and thought about her friends. Boys her age from the same block. Boys she used to spend all her extra time with, playing stickball, walking to and from school ... and fighting. Fights where they stood up for each other.

Now those same boys shoved her, jabbed her.

"Sandy's getting tits! Sandy's getting tits!"

She finally understood. There would be no protection

for her anymore. She'd crossed the line and now she was fair game.

She reached through her bedroom window and pulled out a bag of fresh cherries she'd grabbed from the kitchen and balanced it on the railing. As she picked the fruit from the bag, a robin landed close to her fingers.

She tossed a handful of hair over her shoulder. "All right, you." She nudged a cherry close to the bird. "Just one."

The robin snatched the fruit and flew to the eave of the abandoned movie studio next door. Sandy popped a couple more cherries into her mouth, then spat the pits into her hand and threw them as hard as she could into the nearest broken window of the decaying building.

Her gaze wandered along the expanse of the wide red brick wall. There were many broken windows; three of them were opposite her fire escape. Every day she strained to see inside the darkened space, but all its secrets remained in deep shadows.

Ever since she had been old enough to climb out onto the fire escape, she'd talked to the building almost every day. She would babble on and on about her dreams, disappointments—her words floated across to the building and the old studio listened in majestic silence.

All the kids were scared of the place. Even her brother had nothing good to say about it, and he wasn't afraid of anything.

He told her stories that made her shiver—rat packs

rummaging through the rubble, floating ghosts of actors who had been attacked, hanged, or stabbed on the studio grounds.

"They must have been bad people," Sandy said. "They got what they deserved."

"And the building did it to them," her brother said, laughing.

"I don't care. Besides, you just want to scare me."

Instead of being scared, she was dazzled by her own fantasies of beautiful people who had been a part of the studio's past—women with long silky hair and flowing satin gowns, men with hard, strong bodies that defended or defied the world.

Sandy remembered her homework, and then made a point of ignoring it. She spent the rest of the afternoon talking to the old studio. When shadows deepened, street sounds faded, and the sun was gone, she crawled back into her apartment.

• • •

The straps of Sandy's backpack dug into her shoulders, her books poked hard into her ribs as she walked home the next day. It was a long two miles from school to her apartment and she was scared and tired from constantly checking the streets behind her. She knew they were there waiting. She could feel their eyes on her and she picked up the pace. This time when she looked back they were behind her.

She ran full out, wheezing for air as her legs pumped harder, harder.

Can't look back.

Her ears rumbled, exploded with the roar of pounding blood.

"No!"

"Gotcha, bitch." The leader of the Deadeyes yanked her up by the hair, slammed her against the gate of the old studio. The other four boys fanned out, forming a semicircle. They checked the street. All clear. But they knew they were being watched from windows with drawn curtains. Everyone was afraid of the Deadeyes.

"Thought you were gonna get away again, didn't ya? Huh?" The leader gave her hair another vicious yank and wrapped the strands tighter around his fingers. Tears flooded her eyes.

"What happened to all them dudes you used to hang with? Didn't want to play with girls no more? Huh? Well, I like to play with girls." He rubbed his hands roughly over her breasts.

"Don't!" she pleaded. "Please let me go."

"Let you go?" He spat the words in her face. "You'll go when I'm through with you."

"Goddamn!" one of the others yelled. "Look at the ass on her,"

"You see, we all want to play with you." The leader licked her cheek, jammed his lips on hers, and forced his tongue into her mouth.

She squirmed, pushed hard at him.

He shoved his hands between her thighs and bit her cheek.

"Sonuvabitch!" she screamed. She kneed him in the balls and shoved him hard into one of his friends. A scarred eyebrow zigzagged into an ugly twitch. On his beefy arm, tats of cobras crawled between the words: eat or be eaten.

She yanked away and shimmied, barely fitting, through the narrow slats of the old studio's locked, steel fence. Inside the open walkway, she panicked and ran in frenzied circles. She could see the outline of the leader's shaved bullet head bobbing up and down, trying to reach up to the spikes at the top of the fence.

"You bitch! I'll get you good!"

They all screamed, "Bitch! We'll get you!"

Her brother could have protected her if he'd wanted to. But he'd only laughed when she pleaded with him for help. Said what everyone else in the whole world was saying: "Sandy's got tits."

Her ears were ringing; her heart hammered against her ribs. The only way home was through the haunted studio.

Squinting, she narrowed her vision to block out everything except the walkway. The wind whistled mournfully, shattering an eerie silence. Glass crunched underneath her feet with each step.

Ahead was a dark corridor. Her legs were shaking but she forced herself to step inside.

Daylight was sucked away. She groped hand-over-hand along the wall and when she looked back, all that was left of the outside was a pinpoint of light.

Odors of sweet cotton candy startled her; a shimmering white vapor oozed up around her. The misty cloud was warm as it thickened, wrapping her in a pressing silence that crushed her against the wall. Her head rang with a hideous sound that welled into a high-pitched shriek. She screamed in agony as a swirl of diamond-shaped crystals stretched and unfolded out from the framework of the building. They spun around and around her head, evolving into a massive maze of geometric shapes piled one upon another until she could finally see the outline of her friend—the old studio.

The old studio was in her head, telling her its story.

It showed her the long, rectangular building and its walkways when it was new. Then it revealed the inside, with the dressing rooms and stage sets. They glowed and sparkled in the darkness. She knew it had once been a magical place where beautiful people created fantasy.

Her brain hurt, started to explode; she couldn't stand it anymore. She clamped her eyes shut. When she opened them again, she stood alone in the deserted walkway. She looked up at the old studio. It had not only saved her, it had revealed something about *its* world to her.

• • •

The next day they were there again, waiting in the

distance. Legs quivering, Sandy swallowed hard. She knew they would catch her no matter which route she took. If it wasn't today, it would be tomorrow.

Ripping off her book-filled backpack, she wrapped the straps around one hand and bit down into her lip. Then she ran as fast as she could toward the Deadeyes.

She flew with the wind and became a flaming devil, skirt flying, hair spread wide with the strong rush of air, backpack a harnessed weapon. Her ragged cry held them motionless.

"Baasstards!"

But she veered off at the last minute and headed for the old studio.

The leader screamed, "No fucking girl is going to knee me in the balls and get away with it! I'll get her ass if I have to go to hell and back."

She didn't want to look at them. Didn't want to think about what they would do if they caught her. A volcano was burning in her gut; her fists were balled into knots of fear. She was mad. Mad at herself for being in this kind of trouble. Mad that she was a girl.

She ran faster. Cursing, they took after her.

Faster. Faster.

Swinging the heavy backpack over her head like a bolo, she turned and smashed it into the gut of one of them. He went down head first, crashed into the bumper of a parked car. Stayed down in a pool of blood.

The others grabbed for her, but she slipped through

the studio gate. Breathless, she rested her hands on her shaking thighs. When she looked up, the leader was forcing himself through the metal bars.

Panic choked her. She ran through the studio courtyard.

"Help me! Help me!"

"Ain't nobody gonna help you, little bitch!" shouted the leader. "Spread out!" he yelled to the others, who had squeezed through the bars after him.

Sandy ran into the building, down the main stage, flattened herself behind a rotting scenery prop. A gang member grabbed for her but the screeching wood gave way and crushed him to the floor.

"Over there!" yelled the leader.

She shrank deeper into the shadows, climbed onto a sound stage. She was blind in the darkness, but ancient Klieg lights flashed, illuminating two boys closing in from the other end.

"She's here!" they yelled.

One of the Deadeyes followed her into the wings, weaving in and out of a hanging forest of rotting ropes. As he lunged for her, a single rope snapped through the air, coiled around his neck. He was yanked up from the floor; his fingers tore at the decaying strands but soon he hung in motionless suspension.

The leader and the remaining gang member screamed in unison: "Bitch!" They watched their buddy sway back and forth.

Sandy disappeared into a dressing room.

Gesturing for his friend to circle around, the leader yelled, "Get that slut. She's not getting out of here alive."

Sandy peeked around the doorway.

The other boy approached the dressing room, but stopped and looked up. A sudden clap of thunder came from a long row of shattering skylights. Shards of glass spiked him to the floor. His screams were wild with pain.

The leader ran to him, and then jumped back. Dead? He looked dead.

Sandy shivered, but at the same time her body was on fire. She was cornered—there was no way out of the dressing room corridor.

"It's not over," the leader yelled at her. "You're dead meat. Hear me? Dead meat!"

But without his buddies to back him up, he rushed away, heading towards the exit. Every few steps he turned and looked back at her with hatred.

"Dead meat!" he yelled again. "Hear me, girl? Dead meat!"

He stumbled over a large rat. It squealed, twisted around, and dug its teeth into his ankle. He jerked his foot back and forth, trying to toss the rat away.

"Goddamn it, let go, you miserable piece of shit!"

The rat squealed louder, and a pack of rats rushed from the shadows. The Deadeye swatted at them, but more and more kept coming until the ground was covered with their hairy, gray bodies.

One leaped onto his leg and sank its teeth into his calf, drawing blood.

"Leave me alone! Lemme go!"

With the scent of blood, the frenzied rats piled on each other to get at him. His legs dragged the weight of their squirming bodies.

And then he fell.

They swarmed over him, tearing at his clothes, tearing at his flesh.

One rat bit into his neck and a geyser of blood sprayed into the air. The pack grew tighter. They fought to lap up the spreading gore.

Sandy slipped away into the open courtyard. Everything was quiet now.

The spring air was fresh, and she saw a seedling of some kind growing through a crack in the cement. She had survived another day.

She was a real Bronx street person.

———————

"The Old Studio" is fiction, but it's factual enough that it could be a page torn from my autobiography. Growing up in the Bronx in lower-income neighborhoods was dangerous for everyone, but for a girl it was downright treacherous. A lot of my childhood was spent in abject fear. To survive, I became an outstanding runner and strategist. Not every single thing in this story happened to me, but most of it did. As a writer, it was wholly cathartic to do in my tormenters. Payback was sweet.

Writers never forget.

—Bette Golden Lamb

TROUBLE AT TOR HOUSE

Katherine Bolger Hyde

I was surprised when I got the summons to Tor House.
I'm an architectural historian, so I study a lot of old
houses; but usually they're either big and grand, or were
designed by a famous architect, or both. Tor House, the
owner-built stone cottage and tower of the poet Robinson
Jeffers in Carmel, California, is neither of
those—although it is certainly unique. But I got the call to
go there, and I went.

"Una was so insistent," Percy complained from the
passenger seat of my vintage MG as we sped down
Highway 1. "I told her Tor House isn't in our league, but
she would not be gainsaid."

Una Jeffers, the poet's wife, was a noted mystic in her
time. She died in 1950. And lest you think Percy is some
sort of wacky medium, let me explain that he died in 1693.
If there's a wacky medium in this story, I suppose it must
be me.

"Did Una tell you what the trouble was?"

Percy sniffed, pulled a lace-trimmed handkerchief from his embroidered coat cuff, and dabbed at his nose. "No. Frankly, I don't think she knows. Whatever it is, it hasn't actually happened yet."

"Never mind, we'll find out eventually. In the meantime, Tor House will be a nice change of pace from all those overbearing mansions. And Carmel is beautiful this time of year."

Any time of year, really. Carmel is the kind of town the word quaint was invented for. Perched on steep bluffs above a rocky shoreline at the southern end of Monterey Bay, it has narrow streets full of storybook cottages, upscale shops, and art galleries. Petite but luxurious inns nestle among groves of eucalyptus and Monterey pine. It's a prime tourist destination as well as a highly desirable place to live.

When Tor House was built, however, Carmel was little more than a few isolated homesteads dotted along an untamed coast. If the reclusive Jeffers could have foreseen what the town would become in his lifetime, how neighboring trophy mansions would crowd right up to the hand-picked beach stones of his low garden walls, he would no doubt have found some lonelier place to settle.

I left the highway, negotiated the winding streets that led down to the coast, and parked in front of Tor House. The garden gate was locked, and no one was around. I checked my watch.

"I made an appointment," I grumbled to Percy. "Where is everyone?"

Percy waved his handkerchief toward the north. An elderly couple bustled toward us.

"Do forgive our tardiness," the man said breathlessly, pulling a chain of old-fashioned keys from his pocket. "The traffic from Santa Cruz was worse than we expected."

Percy raised an eyebrow at me, no doubt alluding to the fact that we had driven through the same traffic. I pretended to look through him, keeping my face impassive. We've perfected a wordless, even expressionless (on my part) communication style over the years. Percy seems quite solid to me, so at first it was hard to remember that to everyone else he's invisible and inaudible—though he can manifest in that semi-transparent way people expect from ghosts when he wants to terrify someone. A murderer, for example.

The man fumbled the gate open, then turned to greet me. "Arthur Arbuthnot, at your service. And my wife, Hazel."

Arthur was tall, distinguished-looking, with white hair and a thick, well-groomed mustache. Hazel's head didn't reach his shoulder. With her silver beauty-shop hair and plump pink cheeks, she looked like a china grandma doll, if such a thing exists.

I shook their hands. "Julia Wainwright. Thanks for opening the house for me."

Arthur preened his mustache. "Do come in." He led us along a short path to a modern-looking building on the right. This proved to be the gift shop-cum-office. "Do you have a particular reason for visiting today?"

I could hardly blurt out that Una had asked us to come. "I'm an architectural historian. I've read about the house, and it sounds fascinating."

"It certainly is unique. And so much the expression of its owners' personality."

Hazel asked, "Do you know much about the Jeffers family?"

"Hardly anything," I lied. If I was going to find out what Una thought was wrong here, it would help to have this couple talk as much as possible. "But I'd love to learn."

Hazel opened her mouth as if to begin a lecture. Arthur cut her off. "We have another couple scheduled for two o'clock as well. If you don't mind, we'll wait for them and go through everything with the three of you together."

"The *four* of us," Percy muttered in my ear. He never can resist reminding me of his presence when we're around other people. In life he was a gentleman architect—Sir Percival Archibald D'Arcy Wainwright—responsible for many of the Baroque manor houses that dot the English countryside, and he was accustomed to being the center of attention. It's a trial to him that he can now command only the partial attention of one person.

Hazel shot her husband a look that mixed resentment with submission. "In the meantime, feel free to browse our little shop. Here are some pamphlets that explain about the Foundation."

I skimmed a brochure, learning that the Jeffers Literary Heritage Society had taken over the property more than a decade after the poet's death to save it from being sold to developers. By then most of Jeffers' once-extensive holdings had already been sold off piecemeal, leaving only a smallish lot containing Tor House, Hawk Tower, and the garden overlooking the sea.

I'd exhausted the limited charms of the gift shop when the other couple arrived. "Oh, dear," I whispered to Percy. "Typical Santa Cruz."

The couple looked to be in their fifties, both wearing tie-dye (full tiered skirt for her, T-shirt for him), and both with hair to their waists—flowing brown locks for her, a thin gray ponytail for him.

The woman stopped in the doorway, arms extended, blocking the man from entering behind her. "Oh, Byron, can't you just *feel* Robin here? His spirit is embedded in these very walls."

"Tricky, since this wing was built after he died," Percy muttered. He'd gleaned that bit of trivia from one of the books.

"Ms. ... Moonwillow?" Arthur asked, consulting his schedule. "And Mr. Matheson?"

"That's us." Matheson squeezed into the room past the gesticulating arms of his companion. A whiff of a familiar weed drifted into the room with him. I wrinkled my nose.

Percy shook out his lace handkerchief and covered his nostrils.

Ms. Moonwillow clasped her hands before her bosom and exclaimed, "It is *such* a thrill to be here! I've only just moved to this area, or I would have come ages ago. I'm connected to the family, you see. Hamilton Jeffers—Robin's brother, you know—was my great-great-uncle by marriage." She heaved a theatrical sigh. "I'm the only one left of the family now. It's *such* a responsibility."

Hazel bridled. "In what way a responsibility? We at the Jeffers Literary Heritage Society take our responsibility of preserving the Jeffers heritage very seriously, Ms. Moonwillow, I assure you."

"Oh, *do* call me Sybil." She reached out an expressive hand and barely touched Hazel's arm. Hazel flinched. "I'm sure you do your best. But there's nothing quite like being *family*, is there?"

"I should think having actually known Robin and Una would count for something," Hazel said in an acid, stifled voice. "Surely you're too young to have done that."

Sybil drew back with a hurt look. "Well, no, I never *met* dear Robin and Una in the *flesh*. But the flesh, after all, is *nothing* compared to the spirit. And in my spirit, I've known them *forever*." She raised her arms heavenward. "They are kindred souls."

Arthur shot a worried glance at his wife, who looked as if her ears might start steaming any moment. "Shall we begin our tour?" He gestured to include me. "Sybil and—Byron, is it? This is Julia Wainwright. She's interested in the architecture of Tor House. I'll tell you about that aspect while Hazel fills you in on anything you might not know about the family." He smiled at Byron. "Unless, of course, you also consider them kindred spirits."

Byron blinked as if coming awake. "Me? Nah, I'm just the chauffeur." He gave an unmusical haw. "Sybil hates to go anywhere alone."

Percy and I exchanged a look of alarm. Whatever the marijuana equivalent of being over the limit is, Byron was clearly there. "I shall remind you not to follow his car too closely when we leave," Percy said. My thoughts exactly.

I lagged behind the others as we left the gift shop and headed down the path to the original part of the house. "Any word from Una?" I whispered to Percy.

"She's getting extremely agitated. That Sybil woman seems to be the focus of it, though Una still doesn't know quite what's going to happen."

"If I were Una, I'd find Sybil's claims to be a kindred spirit pretty agitating all on their own."

Percy snorted. "She does, rather, but there's more to it than that. She keeps saying 'Danger!'"

"Is Sybil *in* danger, or the source of the danger?"

Percy got that listening look he gets when conversing with his fellow ghosts, then shrugged. "Una doesn't know."

I hurried to catch up to the others. Arthur was

explaining that the original part of the house, which the party was now entering, had been built by a stonemason to Una's specifications. Robinson worked as his apprentice, then built the tower and additions to the house on his own, hauling the stones up from the beach below.

My first impression of the house was that it was tiny, almost a doll's house. I knew Una had been diminutive—her feet were size two—but Robin was quite tall. His head must have barely cleared the ceiling.

The living room was dominated by a grand piano tucked in the windowed seaward corner, leaving only a small fireplace nook for chairs and conversation. Yet, Hazel was saying, the Jeffers entertained extensively here, their frequent visitors being all the artists, writers, and musicians who flocked to Carmel as a creative haven in the early 1900s.

We finished touring the original house without incident, barring Sybil's unceasing gushing commentary on every feature, which Hazel tried unsuccessfully to quash or drown out. The tension came to a head when Arthur stopped us at the roped-off doorway of the added-on dining room, which had been rendered structurally unsound by a recent earthquake.

Sybil remarked, "If I were in charge, I'd make sure the entire property was open to visitors. How can one truly partake of the spirit of the house if one can't see it *all*?"

Hazel turned beet-red and hissed, "Well, you're not in charge. Fortunately the Foundation has more sense than to put its guests in danger because of some 'spiritual' whim."

Sybil muttered obscurely, "That may be about to change."

Hazel's fists clenched. I thought she might slug Sybil or pronounce a curse on her. Arthur stepped between the two women and said, "Let's move on, shall we?"

He shepherded us out of the main house and onto the path that led to Hawk Tower. Hazel stammered something about needing to attend to Foundation business and headed toward the gift-shop-cum-office, while Arthur led us through the tower.

"Robin built this tower for Una," he said. That surprised me, as I assumed a poet would want a tower refuge for himself and his own work. But as it transpired, Robin did use the ground floor as a study, while the second floor, accessed by a steep, narrow outside staircase built into the rock, was Una's place for silent meditation. Above Una's room, the stairs continued to a roof platform on the south side of the tower, while a precarious half-dozen steps that seemed to hang in midair led on to the battlemented top. This last flight of fancy had been a gift to the Jeffers' twin sons. How marvelous to have your very own tower to play on.

"Thus far and no farther," I said when we reached the first platform. I am afflicted with mild acrophobia, and those last narrow steps with nothing but an iron chain on one side for protection were too much for me.

Percy stayed with me. Byron looked as if he'd like to do the same, but Sybil pulled him up after her. His knuckles whitened on the chain as they ascended; then the battlements mostly blocked them from my sight. I turned to take in the glorious panorama of beach, sea, and sky. Only the neighboring modern mansions impinged on the natural beauty with their all-too-human ostentation—in contrast to Tor House itself, which seemed to have grown organically out of the ground.

"Just imagine what it must have been like when Jeffers first built this tower. Not another house in sight—just rocks and beach in both directions, framing that endless sea." Only a ghost could have heard my murmur over the roar of the wind in our ears and the waves below.

Percy turned his brocaded back on the view. "I suppose it's all right if you like that sort of thing."

"Oh, right, I forgot. Nature is to be conquered. Laid out in geometric gardens with tortured topiary and nary a stem out of place."

"Naturally. Man, after all, is the measure of all things."

"Quoting out of context, as—"

A piercing scream rent the sky. "Sybil!" Byron cried. "*Sy-billl!* What have you done?"

● ● ●

I exchanged stares with Percy, then leaned over the edge of the battlements, but the taller portion of the tower projected outward, hiding its base from my view. Byron, then Arthur, raced past us, Arthur on a cell phone calling 911. "A woman fell from Hawk Tower," he shouted as he disappeared around the bend of the stairs.

Percy and I followed as quickly as my acrophobic caution would allow. "I guess we know now what the danger was," I said, panting. Little as I cared for Sybil, I wouldn't wish her apparent fate on anyone.

At the bottom of the stairs I halted, reluctant to round the tower and see what lay at its foot. Percy and I had seen death before—even violent death—but not a body fallen from a forty-foot tower.

"No time to get squeamish, darling," Percy hissed.

I braced myself and took the final step around the corner of the tower. One quick glance assured me that Sybil Moonwillow indeed lay there, prone, her hair spread out in a rapidly darkening cloud around her. Byron and Arthur bent over her.

I looked toward the street, trying to orient myself in the unspoiled garden and relegate the gory sight to its own confined space. Hazel Arbuthnot was bustling down the path from the direction of the office. "What's happened?" she asked me, sounding short of breath. "I heard somebody scream."

"It's Sybil," I said. "She fell from the top of the tower." I didn't voice the other possibilities that leapt to mind: *Or jumped. Or was pushed.*

Hazel stopped short, covering her mouth. "I kept telling them, but nobody would listen. I knew someday some idiot would climb up on those battlements and fall." She broke into a half-run, hurrying to join her husband as he knelt beside the body. I followed, feeling she might need moral or physical support.

"Hazel, stay back!" Arthur called. "This is no sight for a lady. And besides, we mustn't touch anything until the police arrive."

"Police!" Hazel exclaimed. "What for? It was an accident, wasn't it?"

"I—I'm not quite sure, dear. Byron and I were looking at the view, and then suddenly—she was falling."

Hazel wrung her shriveled, arthritic hands. "Oh, dear. The police! Next it will be in the papers! What will happen to Tor House? No one will want to visit where someone has died. And the insurance! What if that man decides to sue?" She pointed a gnarled finger at Byron, whose eyes were glazed. He squatted near the body, rocking and moaning softly.

I patted Hazel on the back. "Don't worry about Tor House. There's no such thing as bad publicity. People will flock here in droves when they hear about this. And I don't think Byron's the type to sue."

In the distance a siren blared. "Come on, Hazel, let's meet the ambulance." I offered her my arm, and she gripped it with surprising strength. I steered her to the office and deposited her on a chair. Then I met the paramedics at the entrance gate and showed them to the body. They confirmed death, then stood aside for the police, who had arrived hot on their heels.

A tall man about my own age—just the wrong side of thirty—emerged from the group. In any other context, I'd have taken him for a surfer with his blond good looks, golden tan, and fit body encased in a leather jacket and jeans. "Detective Tony Smith," he announced. "Who's in charge here?"

His gaze dismissed Byron, then rested a long second on me.

Arthur extended his hand. "Arthur Arbuthnot, president of the Jeffers Literary Heritage Society."

Smith shook his hand. "What happened here?"

"This woman—her name is Sybil Moonwillow—"

"Moonwillow? Seriously? That her real name?"

Arthur gaped in confusion. Byron came to himself enough to say, "She changed it. All legal. See, Jeffers was born on a Monday, and that's the day of the moon and the willow."

Smith gave him a skeptical look. "Right. Go on."

Arthur cleared his throat. "We were on the top of the tower—"

"We?"

"Mr. Matheson, Sybil, and myself. Ms. Wainwright stayed on the level below. My wife, Hazel, had returned to the office."

Smith nodded at each of us as he noted down our names. "Then what happened?"

"We were all looking out to sea. The view is quite spectacular. Then suddenly Sybil screamed, and we realized she had fallen from the battlements."

"She fell? Sure she didn't jump?"

"I—don't know—I just assumed—if she jumped on purpose, why would she scream?"

Smith muttered, "You'd be surprised."

Byron suddenly came to life. "She might have jumped."

"You knew her well?" Smith rounded on him.

"She was my girlfriend."

"Had she been depressed lately? Did you have a fight?"

"No, man, nothing like that. See, she had this thing about Jeffers. Real hung up on him. And Jeffers believed everything was, like, alive, y'know? I mean even rocks and stuff. Sybil said on the way here how she'd like to die where Jeffers died and become one with nature and with him." He dashed his arm across his face. Tear-traces sparkled on the hairs of his forearm. "I guess this would be the way to do it. Become one with the rocks and all." A sob choked off his words.

Smith frowned over his notebook, scribbling fast. "So possible suicide, then." He flipped the notebook shut. "Everybody out of the way, but stay on the premises. Forensics, do your stuff, then get her out of here."

We all walked off in different directions. I was hoping for a private chat with Percy, but Smith followed me to a low stone wall that bordered the walkway. He sat beside me—not touching, but closer than I thought a policeman would normally sit.

"You know any of these people before today?"

I shook my head. "I came alone." Percy coughed in my ear, but I ignored him. "We just happened to be on the same tour."

"You don't know the docents either?"

"No."

"So you've got an objective view of the situation. You look like an intelligent woman." Points for not saying "smart girl," Smith. "What's your take on all this?"

"It's just speculation. You can't see the top platform from the lower one."

"But you must have some impressions."

I sighed. If only I could tell him about Percy and Una. But he'd take back his *intelligent woman* in a hot second if I did that.

"I could imagine it being like Byron said. Sybil certainly seemed obsessed with Jeffers, possibly to the point of being unbalanced." I grimaced. "In a manner of speaking."

Smith blinked, then grunted appreciation of my unintentional pun.

"Also, you couldn't fall off that tower without climbing up on the battlements, and you'd have to be either stupid or suicidal to do that."

He nodded. "So you vote for suicide?"

I made a face. "It looks that way. But—I've seen murder

before. And I have this tiny feeling in the pit of my stomach that this might be murder."

Smith rounded on me, all the friendliness gone from his demeanor. "What do you mean, you've seen murder before?"

"I'm an architectural historian. I visit famous houses, study them, write about them. Once or twice someone has been murdered." I hastened to add, "Purely coincidentally. And certainly not by me."

He gave me a long, searching look, then nodded. "I've met people like that. Seem to have a talent for being in the wrong place at the wrong time." He stared at his notebook. "So. Murder. You think the boyfriend did it?"

"He had the opportunity, but he seems genuinely cut up about it. He was pretty stoned, though, so who knows—maybe he thought she could fly?"

Smith barked a laugh. "I've seen stranger. The postmortem may tell us whether she was pushed or not. How about the other guy, the docent? See any reason for him to want her out of the way?"

"Not really. She claimed to be a distant relative of Jeffers and talked about her responsibility to his legacy. The president of the Jeffers Literary Heritage Society could feel threatened by that, but I didn't see any signs of it. Not in Arthur."

He peered at me. "Not in Arthur. But maybe in his wife? What's her name—Hazel?"

"Hazel did take Sybil's posturing personally. But she was in the office when it happened."

"Right." He tapped his pencil against his notebook. "I better take a look at that tower."

I met his eyes with a little smile. He grinned back.

• • •

Beside me on the wall, Percy crossed his elegant hose-clad legs and drawled, "I do believe Una was wrong. The real danger was for you."

I gave a nervous laugh. I'm never quite sure whether Percy can read my mind, but he can definitely read me like a book. "What danger? He's a cop."

"Nevertheless, I suggest you keep your wits about you, darling. We have a murder to solve."

"It *is* a murder? Is Una sure about that?"

He nodded. "Now that it's actually happened, yes, Una is certain. The danger was to Sybil, not from her, and it was not merely her own stupidity."

"Does Una know who did it?"

"You would expect that, wouldn't you? But she says no. She got distracted by the ghost of her dog Winnie rooting amid the flowerbeds and didn't see."

I huffed. It happens every time. You would think when you are assisted by ghosts in solving murders, one of them would be able to tell you exactly what occurred. But that hasn't been the case. Maybe, with the dead's typical resentment toward the living, they simply don't want to make things too easy.

"Wonderful. Does she at least have a feeling about it?"

"She felt the hostility from Hazel toward Sybil, which you and I witnessed as well. But Hazel wasn't there. I doubt she has sufficient psychic energy to levitate the woman off the tower from a distance of a hundred yards."

"No, I wouldn't think so." A thought flashed across my mind—more of a picture, actually. "Wait a minute. What if Hazel didn't go to the office? What if she only pretended to and then came back?"

"And climbed the stairs behind us? I would have seen her. I wasn't looking at your precious view, remember."

"No, you were flicking a spot of imaginary dust off your immaculate cuff. But it's true you would have seen her if she came up that way."

He frowned in concentration, then a glow of understanding spread across his face. "There's another stairway. Una just reminded me."

"Come on." I raced toward the tower. He glided after me.

Just inside the ground-floor entrance to the tower, inconspicuous behind a wall, was a stairway even steeper, narrower, and twistier than the one outside. Arthur had mentioned in passing that Robin had built this stairway for his twin sons to play secret-passages in. It was just the size for a pair of small boys.

I leaned into the spiraling stairwell and craned my neck. "Does it go all the way to the top?"

Percy made a token gesture of training his monocle upward. "How should I know?"

"You could float up there and find out."

He lowered his monocle and gave me a mocking smile. "Too steep for you, darling? Your poor little acrophobic heart can't handle it?"

I took a deep breath. To rise to his bait would only encourage him. "I could if I had to. But fortunately I don't have to, because I have you." I gave him my most charming smile. "Please, Percy."

He tapped his monocle against his palm. "On one condition."

My heart sank. I knew what the condition would be.

"When—not if—that hunk of a policeman asks you on a date, you will say no."

"Percy!"

He fixed me with his implacable gaze. "No."

I took a minute to ponder. I didn't have to send Percy up the staircase. I didn't even have to climb it myself. I could simply drop a hint to Detective Smith—Tony—and he could figure it out for himself. Let him make the catch and get the glory. Catching killers was his job, after all. To me it was only a sort of involuntary hobby.

But now Percy was looking at me in a different way. No longer implacable. More the way he would have looked at one of the many wenches he seduced while he was alive. But I knew I was more than a wench to him.

"Percy. Please. You are my thousand-times-great-uncle, after all." That's the joke between us, based on the fact that we share a surname.

"No, I think it's more likely I'm a fourteenth cousin two hundred times removed." A twinkle came into his eye. "Not so close as to disbar—other close relationships."

"Maybe not. But there is that one inconvenient little matter of you being dead."

Percy vanished in a puff of wounded feelings. He can do that when he wants to, and he invariably does it whenever I remind him, so coarsely and directly, that he is in fact deceased.

I sighed. I hadn't wanted to offend him. But neither did I want to promise that I would never accept an offer of a date from Detective Tony Smith.

Think of the devil. As I stood gazing up the winding stairs, Tony's sockless black loafers appeared coming down them.

He ducked his head to pass beneath the lintel and saw me. "Oh, hey there. Did you know this stairway goes all the way to the top?"

I smiled. A way bigger smile than the situation called for. And he grinned back.

• • •

Five minutes later, Tony—we were on first-name terms

now—marched up the walk to the office in search of Hazel. He loomed before her where she cowered, tiny in her low chair—he made quite a threatening figure. I was glad not to be in her position.

"Mrs. Arbuthnot. Let's go over your statement again."

She repeated her story of having been in the office while we were on the tower.

"I put it to you that you were not in the office. You only pretended to come here. Once the others were out of sight, you returned to the tower and climbed up the inside stairway to the top, where you hid. When the others' backs were turned, you crept up behind Sybil Moonwillow and pushed her over the battlement. You then ran back down the stairs and toward this room. When Ms. Wainwright looked in this direction after viewing the body, you only appeared to be leaving the office."

Hazel glared at him throughout this recitation, her pink cheeks turning purple. Her breath came thick and fast.

She stood before him, seeming to grow beyond her tiny height. "I had to defend the Jeffers Society from that spurious relative, that harpy who wanted to take Tor House over for herself. I couldn't let her ruin all our work and all our care. I had no choice. It was my sacred duty to silence her!"

Tony signaled a uniformed officer to cuff her as he read Hazel her rights. She screamed incoherently as they put her in the black-and-white.

Poor Arthur broke down as well. I tried to comfort him

to no avail. He followed in the back of Tony's car, unwilling to be parted from his demented wife.

Before Tony got into the front seat, he turned to me. "Dinner tonight?"

I hesitated. "I was planning to drive back to San Francisco."

"I'll make sure you have a place to stay the night."

Oh, that grin. To hell with Percy's jealous caution.

"Dinner tonight." I turned toward my MG as Percy materialized in the passenger seat. "I'm sorry, Percy. I'm not going to let this one get away."

Before I pulled into the street, I glanced at the upper windows of Tor House. A woman's face hovered there. I recognized her from photographs as Una. She gave a little wave and disappeared.

———

"Trouble at Tor House" was born on a visit to Tor House several years ago. As a lover of unique architecture, I found the place deeply intriguing and felt it would make the perfect setting for a mystery. That idea soon grew into a plan for an entire series with an architectural historian and her ghostly sidekick as the protagonists (stay tuned). The Jeffers Literary Heritage Society and its representatives are entirely fictional. In reality, Tor House is capably managed by the Tor House Foundation, whose representatives are conscientious and devoted—but certainly not to the point of murder!

—Katherine Bolger Hyde

TWO HUNDRED MILES

Margaret Lucke

They tell me it's not a long trip. A couple hundred miles. I've never been that far from home. Three and half, maybe four hours. Sounds like forever, I say.

No, they reply, how long you'll stay once you get there—that's forever.

They notch the cuffs in the last position. I can't slide my hands out, but my wrists are so delicate that the cuffs slide up and down my arm. I might like it better if the metal rings clasped my wrists tight, unmovable. The cuffs are joined by a chain fastened to the back of the seat in front of me.

The bus seats are hard. The windows are scratched and smeary. The panes aren't glass, they're plastic, extra thick. On the outside, narrow metal bars run across them.

The other passengers are silent, sunk deep in their thoughts, their fears, their regrets. Except for a frizzy-haired blond chick at the very back, who's screaming about innocence and revenge and how the bastard had it coming.

Maybe he did. Maybe they all do.

The blond girl's using language that would have made my grandma blush and cover her ears. I can almost hear Grandma's voice: Lyssie, I hear you use words like that, I'll whup you good.

She would have, too.

The bus lurches out of the parking lot and lumbers down the main street. This is the town I grew up in, and I'm seeing it for probably the last time. The elementary school. The Baptist church. The Frostee Freeze. People gawk as we go by. A little boy with an ice cream cone points at us, and his mother reaches down and turns his head away.

The Bar and Thrill, where Derek bought me my first drink. The bartender didn't even check to see I was underage. Fairview Park, where Derek gave me my first kiss. The Cottonwood Motel, where he showed me what a woman does to please her man.

The blond girl in the back keeps yelling. Finally they go talk to her. I don't know what they say, but she shuts up.

We roll past the corner of Oak Street. Two blocks down is my grandma's house, where I grew up. A little house, just four rooms. She put me in the attic bedroom, up under the eaves. It was my mother's room when she was a little girl, and at night when I lay awake in the bed Mama had slept in, breathing the air she had breathed, I would make believe she was there with me. I would pretend that she hadn't run away and left me, that in the morning I would open my eyes and she would be there, holding out her arms. I would rush into them and she would hold me and never let me go.

Grandma had this thing about always keeping the inside of the house clean and neat, swept and dusted. Perfect and untouched, as if no one really lived there. Yet it was falling down around us. The roof leaked and the front porch sagged and the yard was full of weeds. One of my chores was to keep the weeds pulled, but I never saw the point. They just grew back again.

Once I met Derek I had no time for chores anyway.

Grandma pretended she didn't have money for repairs but I knew better. One day I was exploring in her bedroom, just trying to figure out what made her so sour and sad. I found the little leather box at the back of her underwear drawer. It had pearls in it, which I'd never seen her wear, and a gold ring, and a huge wad of cash. More than five thousand dollars.

Someone else owns the house now. Maybe it's been mended and painted. Maybe it's surrounded by neat flowerbeds. Maybe a real family lives there. I'll never know.

My grandma never liked Derek. She told me he was a bad influence and I couldn't see him anymore. I said the hell with that, I'm eighteen now and I can do what I damn well want. I said with Derek I'm happy for the first time in my whole life. She slapped me then, harder than usual. My cheek got a bad bruise. I acted like it didn't hurt, the way I always did.

Thinking of Derek makes my body hot. I shift my cuffed hands around so I can touch the magic place between my legs. It's tingling like it's getting an electric shock. I look around to make sure no one is watching. Not that I can do much to pleasure myself when I'm wearing this jumpsuit. It's thick and ugly and way too big for me. If I was going camping with Derek, we wouldn't even need to take a tent.

The bus is on the highway now. I stare through the window bars as the edges of town fade away. The gas station and the mini mart. The tractor dealership and the feed store. Soon there's just flat prairie, dusty and gray, stretching out to touch dark clouds at the horizon. Here and there I see cattle grazing.

I wonder where Derek is now. Is he on his own bus, the men's bus, making a journey like mine? Or is he already at the prison, his cell door slammed shut?

I'm never going to see him again.

That thought squeezes my heart. A sob pushes up through my throat. I try to stop it but I can't. I just hope no one has heard. Tears are burning my eyes, sliding down my cheeks. I don't look at anyone but keep my gaze fixed on a smudge on the window. Outside, the prairie is endless. Nothing but grass and sky, mile after mile.

It'll be so easy, Derek told me. We'll just take the money and go away. Someplace by the ocean. Someplace where we'll be happy forever.

I didn't know my grandma wasn't feeling well that day. I didn't know she would come home early from the church ladies circle meeting. I didn't know Derek was carrying a gun.

Screams, blood, pain, sirens—I didn't expect any of that. I didn't know that afterward I'd feel such grief, such loneliness.

I'm sorry, Grandma, I whispered as they put her in the ground. I wasn't allowed to go to the funeral, but I knew what day it was, the exact hour. I wept the whole time the service was going on. It was almost as if I was hearing the preacher's words, watching the dirt land on her coffin.

Those were the last tears I shed, until today.

Not guilty, I said to the judge. After all, it wasn't me that pulled the trigger. I yelled at Derek not to shoot.

The bus leaves the highway and goes down a narrow road. A few scattered houses appear. Laundry flaps on a clothesline.

Then I see it looming, the place we're headed to. High walls topped with barbed wire. A tower at the corner jabs at the sky.

They make an announcement, and everyone begins to stir. The blond girl in the back starts to wail again. She's carrying on about injustice and self-defense and how she can't survive trapped in a cage like an animal.

With the cuffs on I can't quite reach my hands to my face. I manage to wipe my cheeks dry with the jumpsuit sleeve. I don't want anyone to see I've been crying.

The jury wouldn't look at me when they came back into the courtroom. A bad sign, the public defender said.

The judge read the verdict. Guilty as charged.

All my life I've waited to hear a certain phrase, but that's sure not the one.

Life in prison without parole.

Not that one either.

The words I long to hear, the words no one's ever said to me and no one ever will, are these: *Lyssie, I love you.*

The bus turns in at the gate. The trip is over. Forever is about to begin.

———

Sometimes the muse presents a writer with a gift, and "Two Hundred Miles" is one it gave to me. In my case, the morning journey between sleep and wakefulness is often a long one, and I enjoy lingering in the half-aware state that lies in between. On one such occasion, I was enjoying the warmth of my covers and my random thoughts when a young woman's voice began to speak to me: "They tell me it's not a long trip. A couple hundred miles ..." I lay there and listened. When I got up, I went straight to my computer. Though I fleshed out some details, this story is essentially the tale I'd just been told. Thank you, muse.

—Margaret Lucke

THE LAST WORD

Vinnie Hansen

T he *New York Times* dubbed it "a professional, gang-style execution."

Frank Murphey smirked. *Professional,* he liked that. A single bullet to the back of the head. He rattled the folded paper and tossed back the last of his espresso. But *gang-style?* Murphey shook his head. Gangs these days just sprayed bullets.

He caught the eye of the waitress and nodded at the fiver slipped under the white ceramic saucer, enough to cover the coffee and a nice tip. He wanted her to see it so no slimeball could filch the money. Fair compensation was Murphey's guiding principle in life. The young woman smiled at him.

Murphey rose to his perfect five-foot-eleven, shook out his pressed gray trousers, and slipped on his Ray-Bans. The unidentified victim resembled Murphey—same height, same general appearance, close enough in age.

What gang would target a middle-aged tourist? Of course, the police didn't know yet that the victim was a tourist who hailed from Denmark. Murphey patted the passport in the pocket of his tweed jacket and *tsk*ed aloud as he crossed the street to the Strand Bookstore. The NYPD's misconceptions suited his purposes.

Threading through the jammed bookstore, he arrived at the mystery section. On a table, he spotted a large display of the genre's latest bestseller—*The Hit Man*. Its red-and-black cover taunted him. Here was the reason for everything. This was his book. His book!

His stomach jolted as he flipped to the back of the book jacket and stared at the author photo. T.R. Collins looked different now with his pretentious Hemingwayesque beard.

A poster listing the nominations and awards *The Hit Man* had garnered steeled Murphey's resolve. Tonight he'd be on a red-eye to San Francisco, traveling as the dead tourist, Hans Petersen.

• • •

The hotel resembled every joint Murphey had ever stayed in—overpriced and not as clean as it should be. This was the venue for San Francisco's Mystery of Mysteries Conference.

Usually Murphey selected a secluded top-floor room, but this time, he had Hans Petersen ask for a room one floor up near the elevator. The view was mainly of the street, but if he angled near the window, he could get a glimpse of the water.

Murphey pulled a small cat-urine-detecting flashlight from his jacket pocket to inspect the already existing evidence—fingerprints on the underside of the toilet rim (very common) and fluorescence dribbled across the ottoman. *Probably the proteins of semen.*

In *The Hit Man,* the book that had propelled T.R. Collins from struggling midlist author to keynote speaker for this conference, the protagonist used a PeeDar flashlight just as Murphey had always done. Because *The Hit Man* was his book!

Collins had ripped out his heart. This keynote speaker gig was the final straw.

Fury made Murphey so lightheaded that he had to perch on the corner of the bed, a hand clapped to his chest. He calmed himself by arranging equipment across hotel towels: an automatic transport ventilator and a generic plastic bottle from his shaving kit. The first had given the TSA agent a slight pause. The latter, containing rocuronium, had slid right through with his aftershave. He'd lifted both the ventilator and drug from an EMT vehicle—way too easy for a pro, the doors wide open and all the personnel distracted with the trauma. *The secret is to appear ordinary, to look like you belong on the scene.*

A strangled growl escaped Murphey's lips. *Control yourself, buddy. If every sentence Collins stole gets to you, you won't be able to function.*

His usual gun and silencer would be easier than all this, but those kills had been business. This was personal. When someone stole your life story, what did you have left?

Murphey took a deep breath and placed a bouquet of latex gloves and a hypodermic beside the rocuronium. He spread plastic sheets over and under the desk chair. He hooked up the tubing to the ventilator, easy-peasy. He'd watched a few YouTube videos and had the basics, which was all you needed when you didn't give a rat's ass about the "patient's" comfort.

It had taken him months of trolling travel sites to find Hans Petersen, a plausible look-alike scumbag whose identity he could steal. But at the last minute, there he was, a man whose travel history indicated a penchant for vacations seeking underage flesh.

Murphey flopped back on the bedspread, exhausted from two cross-country flights in as many days—from his home in Vancouver to New York City to San Francisco. It was past time for him to retire.

Anger jolted Murphey upright. T.R. Collins had stolen his retirement too. How could the so-called author live with himself? *The fraud!*

Murphey ran the blade of his new knife along a fingernail. Razor sharp. He set it beside the other equipment.

• • •

Hugging a wall, Murphey slid into the jabbering mass of writers in the hotel bar. At a table squeezed with female authors, Theodore Roosevelt Collins held forth. The man loved to talk. He caressed words with his tongue, words as illicit as Hans Petersen's girls. Collins's large lips glistened from his drink.

Murphey hung back to avoid recognition, a honed skill in his line of work. For years, he'd haunted writing conferences, checking out how the publishing game worked, preparing for the day he'd release his thinly disguised story and take his place at a table like the one now occupied by Collins. All his adult life, he'd remained hidden. He'd lived for the time he could stop lurking in the shadows and be seen. Readers would admire the character he—Frank Murphey—had created, a character of competence and integrity. He'd be recognized, famous even.

Murphey edged forward and clapped a hand on T.R. Collins's shoulder. The man looked up with a smile.

"Big fan," Murphey said.

Collins squinted at him, his gray eyes glassy.

"Of your material," Murphey added coldly. He left his hand in place, the tweed of Collins's jacket rough against his palm.

They'd met at a bar like this one, at a writers' conference like this one. Collins had occupied a stool, moping in his drink, claiming he'd ghostwritten the award-winning novel of that year's guest of honor and wasn't getting the honor he deserved. The man's complaints interested Murphey because at one point, Murphey had employed a ghostwriter. Strictly a business arrangement. It had unnerved him that a ghostwriter could sit on a barstool, claiming ownership. That wasn't right. That wasn't how it worked. The story belonged to the guy who hired him—the one whose idea the book was. The one who had lived the experiences described in those pages.

But Murphey had listened to Collins and held his tongue, because he was nothing if not discreet.

Now, as Collins craned his neck toward Murphey, the dawn of recognition spread across his face. His full beard dropped as his mouth opened.

Murphey's simple disguise consisted of Levi's and cowboy boots, as though he were a Craig Johnson wannabe. The wide brim of his hat was crucial, hiding his face from video cams mounted near the ceiling.

The other authors barely glanced at Murphey. They huddled. One woman threw a collection of bills on the table, and chairs scraped back as though they were happy for the opportunity to escape T.R. Collins's company. Theodore balked under Murphey's tight grip.

Murphey leaned down and whispered in his mark's ear. "In a few minutes, you are going to walk with me to the elevator."

Theodore wildly shook his head. "Are you going to shoot me?"

"If I were going to do that, you'd be dead." Murphey slid into the chair beside Collins and scooped Collins's laptop bag from the floor. The man carried it with him everywhere, distrust being a natural affliction for a thief. "Of course, I'll reconsider if you scream."

Theodore smiled weakly, trying to insinuate it was all a joke. A misunderstanding. "The story was mine."

Murphey snorted. "You used my exact words."

"Here and there." The man raised a shaking glass to his lips and then slammed it onto the table as though insulted by its emptiness. Ice cubes popped out. "There's something you don't under—"

Under the table, Murphey gripped Theodore's leg in a way that made the man's eyes pop.

"Plagiarism." Murphey picked up the cubes and dropped them into the tumbler as punctuation to his words: "The worst." *Ting.* "Offense." *Ting.* "A writer can commit." *Ting.*

Murphey signaled for the cocktail waitress to bring Theodore another. Her eyebrow quirked in question. Murphey shook his head. He never drank while on a job.

Theodore's head swiveled this way and that, searching for rescue, but the writers at other tables were bent toward each other to hear over the noise. At least one person per klatch gesticulated to a rapt audience.

The cocktail waitress slid another drink in front of Theodore. "Bourbon on the rocks."

Without looking up at her, Murphey peeled off a twenty. "Keep the change."

T.R. Collins gulped the alcohol, skimmed trembling fingers over his pate, and met Murphey's eyes. "Really, Frank? The *worst* offense?"

He pinched the nerve in Collins's leg again. "When you steal a person's words, you rip out his soul."

• • •

Collins talked a good game. That's how he'd gotten his dirty mitts on Murphey's manuscript in the first place, back at that other writers' conference, at that other bar. "Sounds like you need help, Bob." Bob Smith had been Frank's alias that time around. "Someone who can spot the holes in your narrative. Now, I don't mean to brag, but I'm expert in this genre. I'd be more than happy to take a look at your WIP."

"My what?"

Theodore had laughed. "Your work-in-progress."

Murphey had bristled. After shelling out thousands to a ghostwriter, it didn't seem like he should need this guy. That ghostwriter—Colin—had been damned good.

On the other hand, no literary agent had snapped up Murphey's manuscript. No publisher had bought it. T.R. Collins was a published author, a man with connections. Maybe he could help.

• • •

Now, at the San Francisco bar table, Theodore tilted drunkenly toward Murphey. "So, when you kill a man, Frank, you don't rip out his soul?"

Frank Murphey hauled the drunk closer. "So you know, the people I kill don't have souls." The Facilitator didn't call him with contracts on Sunday school teachers. Murphey punched the hypodermic through fabric into the meaty part of Theodore's thigh.

"Ow!"

"What's your password, Theodore?"

The man tried to stand, but before he could turn to the nearest bar patron, Murphey tugged him back into his chair.

"Let me guess," Frank said. "*Hitman?*"

"What are you doing, Frank? Did you give me truth serum?"

Murphey chortled. "You wish." He hoisted the laptop bag. Theodore reached clumsily for it, the rocuronium already taking effect. Murphey looped the bag's strap around Theodore's neck and shouldered him up. "Come on, buddy," Murphey said loudly. "You've had one too many."

With the intramuscular shot, Murphey had about ten minutes to get the man up to his room before he'd be dragging a limp body.

Fortunately, the design of the hotel included elevator

doors to the side of the bar. Murphey slumped Collins against the metal wall as they rode up to the next floor.

"You're a hit man," the writer slurred, the drug already paralyzing his muscles.

"At least I'm a real hit man." Murphey pointed an accusing finger at him. "You're a phony writer."

Collins's head lolled side to side as though he were trying to shake it. "I'm yo gothe ..." he lisped, trying to say something.

By the time Murphey plopped him into the plastic-sheeted desk chair, Collins was almost dead weight. But the man's eyes registered terror.

• • •

"Don't worry." Murphey smiled mischievously. "Be happy." He placed the computer on the desk beside the chair and then moved the automatic transport ventilator into position. "I'm going to hook you up so you don't asphyxiate."

If a person cared about the outcome, the "patient" should be lying down. Murphey turned on the machine to warm up.

Collins struggled to move. It was like watching a woman with Botox in her forehead try to lift her brows. Still, the man mustered enough will power and muscle coordination to focus on the gleaming knife.

"Oh, yes," Murphey murmured. "You probably remember this scene from *The Hit Man*. That part was fiction." He tossed a small towel onto Collins's lap. "Much too messy for me." Murphey gloved his hands and picked up the knife. "Until now."

Collins emitted a primal groan from deep in his bowels, like a sleeper caught in a nightmare.

"Appropriate punishment, don't you think, for a liar?" Murphey pulled Collins's tongue from his mouth. "I'm only taking the tip. This thing I'm putting on you is a clip for the lingual artery."

Murphey pitched Collins's body forward so the blood would run outward rather than down the man's throat. With swift motions, he cut the thick muscle, dropped the piece of severed tongue onto the plastic and stuffed the towel in the man's mouth. He peeled off his gloves and released them to the plastic.

Murphey selected a basic setting on the ventilator. Air whooshed in and out, eerily, like a creature breathing, bearing witness.

Did he detect a wiggle in Collins's fingertips? Success had fattened the man like a corn-fed steer, so maybe he had not injected enough. Red soaked the edges of the towel.

Murphey struggled to place the ventilator mask on Collins's face. It wouldn't fit with the ball of fabric in his mouth. Murphey thought quickly. He didn't want Collins to die yet. He concentrated on fixing the mask firmly over just the man's nose and watched in satisfaction as Collins's chest rose and fell in a shallow rhythm.

Awkwardly holding the mask with one hand, Murphey stretched to the laptop. He poked at the keys. The password was not *hitman*. Murphey tried various combinations. He looked at Collins. "Now we've taken care of the lying tongue, maybe we'll do hands next, so you can't plagiarize any more work."

This time Collins's fingers definitely twitched. Murphey wished he'd stolen more rocuronium to keep him immobilized.

He tried adding *the* in front of *hitman* and bingo, the computer unlocked. Murphey scrolled through T.R. Collins's email. The man kept everything! Murphey found his emails to Collins. The first thread contained Collins's response when he received the manuscript: *Wow. This is some fabulous writing.* Murphey read through their exchanges, plumping his justification. Theodore Roosevelt Collins had lied to him at every step: *Still polishing the manuscript,* Collins wrote when he was probably slipping it under his agent's nose.

Polishing! The word twisted a knife in Murphey's back. Even after he'd finished working with the ghostwriter, Murphey had polished and polished and polished his manuscript—still no agent.

His arm ached from clamping the mask.

The last message, before the man had started avoiding him: *The book will be a hit! (Pun intended.)*

Anger flamed through him. He yanked the mask off Collins's nose. "See that!"

As he forced Collins's head toward the screen, Murphey noticed another mailbox. The address was cut off, but familiar. *This can't be.*

He eyed Collins. The man's lids drooped, but he was still conscious. Murphey clamped the mask back over Collins's nose. Murphey clicked the other mailbox icon and scrolled back through years of accumulated messages—back to 2010. And there it was—Murphey's own briefly used email address. The subject on the exchanges was the book's old title: *The Assassin.*

That had seemed sexy to him. Back then he'd been so cocky. *Hey, anybody can write a book.* Then he'd gone to conferences and learned that fiction had all these requirements like *point of view* and *plot structure.* So, he'd hired a professional, the ghostwriter he'd found online. The ghostwriter had insisted on calling the book *The Hit Man.*

Murphey had liked that ghostwriter, the way he took Murphey's scribbled memories and shaped them into a plot. The way he knew how to juice up a scene.

Murphey glanced over to Collins. Blood dripped from the cloth in his mouth onto his shirt, but above the red rag, Collins's eyes hardened to stone.

Murphey's stomach turned. "You're Colin?"

The man in the desk chair, maybe aided by gravity, dipped his bloodied beard in assent.

A strange sensation nearly knocked Murphey back on his keister. "My ghostwriter?"

Collins's head dropped another fraction, the towel dribbling onto his shirt.

Wow. This is some fabulous writing. T.R. Collins's initial response to Murphey's manuscript took on a snarky tone—the aggrieved, injured whine of the man Murphey had met on the bar stool.

He let the mask fall into Collins's lap.

Dizzy as he was, Murphey gloved his hand before poking T.R. Collins's forehead to raise his head. He glared into the man's eyes. "It was still *my* story. My life."

But regret crept in. The man in the desk chair was Colin, the ghostwriter, who had loved his words. They'd shared friendly squabbles about *bullet* vs. *ammo*. They'd been pals, in a way. Colin had encouraged him: "Write. Just write."

T.R. Collins must have been stunned when he received the manuscript from Bob Smith, the man he'd met at the writer's conference, when he saw the title, when he scrolled through the story he'd helped create, when he realized Bob Smith was Frank Murphey, his ghostwriting client. Why hadn't Collins just stolen the book back when he was ghostwriting? Had he been a better person? A less despairing author?

No, Frank concluded, it wasn't that. It was because *The Hit Man* wasn't bestseller material back then. His own two years of rewriting and friggin' *polishing* had made the book.

None of this could change the conclusion, Murphey

thought, the regret now a gut ache. This story could end only one way.

A wiggle. A gurgling. Murphey tugged the wet cloth from Collins's mouth and let it plop onto the plastic.

Like a dental patient, Collins coughed up a garbled word. Even with the R growled up from the throat like a seal's bark, Murphey recognized it.

Murphey undid the tongue clamp and pushed the head back so the blood would run down Collins's windpipe. Circumstances being what they were, the word had to be his last.

Never leave them alive. Murphey switched off the ventilator. Between the blood and the drug, Collins would asphyxiate soon. If Hans Petersen became a suspect, the police would track him to a dead body in New York City. And Murphey would go on living in obscurity in Canada.

T.R. Collins's last word had been a sarcastic *right*, but from Colin, Frank's only friend, hidden inside this traitor, echoed a ghostly *write*.

"The Last Word" has a checkered past.

At the Writers' Police Academy, Nathan Riehl, EMS instructor, taught me to save lives with tourniquets. Little did he know he'd spend the next two years aiding the hit man in my story, helping him to exact his revenge in a most nefarious way.

Originally, Frank, my hit-man protagonist, tried to flee to the Bouchercon anthology in Canada. A computer glitch bounced him back to the states. He bided his time and refined his game.

Finally, with an assist from Nathan, Frank's revenge lust has bled out on the pages of *Fault Lines*.

—Vinnie Hansen

THE CHAMPAGNE GIRL

Susan C. Shea

Winter sunlight blazed into the windows of the office of Horner Global Enterprises on the forty-seventh floor of the Manhattan skyscraper. It bounced off polished leather sofas, glass tabletops, and a score of framed photos covering one wall. The same short man appeared in all of the pictures, staring at the camera as he posed with major politicians, CEOs, a movie producer, a tennis champion, a TV pundit, an actress. In the grip-and-grin pose with George Herbert Walker Bush, he appeared twenty years younger than the forty-first president of the United States. With the new mayor of the city, the short man was wearing a turtleneck and very little hair.

A blond woman, perhaps in her mid-forties, dressed in black slacks and a cashmere twin set, was dusting the pictures, a gold charm bracelet jangling on her outstretched arm. She stopped to walk across the room to the window wall. In the direct light, a web of small lines on her face and neck was visible through her makeup. She pressed a button hidden behind drapes and, with a quiet thrumming, mesh shades descended over the windows. Satisfied, she turned her attention to a low glass table, above which, on a narrow glass shelf, several massive crystal trophies perched. Flicking the duster over the table and the objects, she started to sing.

"For pete's sake, would you shut up? I'm trying to think in here." The voice came from the partially opened door to the inner office.

"*Trying* being the operable word," Angela D'Amato said, raising her voice to be heard from the other room. The phone on her desk rang and she dropped the duster on the table and marched across the Persian rug to her desk.

"Are you going to get the phone or not?" the voice behind the door shouted.

"Ask nicely," Angie yelled. She snatched up the phone. "Mr. Horner's office. Just a minute, please." She put her hand over the receiver and called through the open door, "It's a Mr. Zaborian for you. Want to take it?" She held the phone to her ear and listened for a long minute after Thomas Horner picked it up, then hung up carefully, a small frown tightening her mouth.

When Horner burst out of his office a few minutes later, she was dusting the last of the big crystal pieces. "Did you reach the lawyer yet?" he barked at her as he shrugged on a camelhair coat.

"Which lawyer?" she said. "There's the guy from that

company you're buying, and the one who's suing the contractor in East Hampton for you, and—"

"I asked you to call my personal attorney and get him over here this week. So, that's who."

"I'm just your executive assistant," Angie said, "not a mind reader." She arched perfectly plucked eyebrows and came over to stand in front of him. As she straightened the lapels on his coat, she said, "Better take a scarf. It's freezing out there."

At that moment, the door into the suite opened and a slightly overweight, middle-aged woman entered, raising a tentative hand in greeting to Angie.

"C'mon in, Marie." Angie nodded at her before saying to her boss, "You know I'm right about these things."

Horner pulled away from her. "I'll be back in an hour. Jennifer's coming over. Before that, a courier from Harry Winston is dropping something off. Put the package on my desk. Don't open it."

"What is it?"

"None of your business."

"Why not?" She moved to stand in front of her boss again and brushed some nonexistent lint from his coat collar.

He didn't answer, but looked toward the woman who had just entered. "You waiting for me?"

The woman smiled nervously. "I'm a friend of Angie's. Marie from the thirty-second floor? McKinley, MacIntyre and Weist? I'm new there."

"Ummm," said Horner, losing interest. The woman stood uncertainly for a minute, looking back and forth from Angie to her boss, then sat down gingerly on an upholstered chair in front of the window wall and began flipping through a glossy magazine.

"Where are you going, anyway?" Angie said into the silence.

"It's on my calendar if you'd look once in a while."

She stood motionless for a few seconds, her hand in the air in front of his coat. Then she patted his arm and smiled. "Grumpy today, aren't we?"

"I'm going across town to talk to the guy I met last month about taking a seat on our board, okay? I like him. He's a player and if we don't grab him soon, he'll have too much on his plate."

"Want me to have Anthony bring the car around?" She backed away from him as he pulled on his gloves.

"I already called him. Listen, if Jennifer gets here before I get back, be nice to her. Give her some champagne, talk to her. She's a little shy."

"Sure, I'll do that."

Angie waited until the door had closed behind her boss to snort. "Shy, my ass," she said, spinning on her heel to face Marie. "Sorry to keep you waiting. That was your first time meeting the big man, right? Sorry he was in a rotten mood. You know what? I think we need a little champagne."

With Marie in tow, Angie made for the bar on one wall

of Horner's wood-paneled office, opened the low refrigerator, and took out a bottle of Veuve Clicquot. Opening it expertly, she poured two glasses, waved Marie to the chair in front of her boss's desk, and dropped into the leather chair behind the desk. She lifted her glass.

"Here's to Thomas Horner, who never learns, and to Jennifer, who's ... shy." And she laughed, a loud, unmusical cackle.

"You're something, Angie," said Marie, whose black blouse and slacks were shiny and snug on her body. "I don't know anyone who'd dare treat their boss like that. Aren't you afraid he'll fire you some day?"

"Fire me? Never," Angie said, hooting with laughter.

"I dunno," Marie said. "It seems kinda weird."

Angie jumped up to refill both of their glasses. "Nah. We go way back is all."

"So, who's this Jennifer?" Marie asked.

"Jennifer?" Angie said, squinting at the ceiling. "Who is Jennifer? Well, she's young. Maybe early thirties. She's pretty. She was selling accessories at the Fendi boutique on upper Madison last year."

"Yeah? And?" Marie said. "Don't tell me she caught the richest man in New York by selling him cologne."

"Caught? I'm sure it hasn't gone that far," Angie said, standing up and gathering their champagne flutes. "She just dangles herself and he watches and thinks it over. He gives her presents, but that doesn't mean anything. He can have anyone he wants. She's good looking and she's sexy, but New York's full of girls like her, hanging out at the club parties, working at the designer boutiques, hoping to land a guy with a house in the Hamptons and a fat wallet."

"Has he set her up in an apartment like I heard he did that girl two years ago, the one who died?"

"No, and I'd know if he did since I write the checks. How'd you hear about that?"

"Someone in the office told me about her. Died in a fire. It sounded so sad, her a beautiful model and all. He's probably spooked, poor guy," Marie said. "The other secretaries at McKinley say for someone who can buy anything, he sure has bad luck in the romance department."

"She wasn't right for him, anyway. I could have told him that. A gold digger, not that I want to speak ill of the dead."

"Wasn't there someone else he dated who died?"

"No. He was engaged a few years ago. But she broke it off."

"Was she a model, too?" Marie asked.

"Stephanie?" Angie said with a grimace. "No, a debutante from Greenwich. Ran off with an Argentine polo player. Lives in South America now."

"Wasn't there something odd about it?" Marie said, struggling out of the chair. "The girls at McKinley are big gossips. Your boss is their number-one topic. He's the biggest celebrity in the building, and they love it when they get to ride with him on the elevator."

"I know. Every time he goes to a charity event, his picture's plastered all over the society pages. But he was engaged just that once, and it was ages ago. The only thing I heard—and not from the boss—was that the guy she ran off with denied they eloped."

"Think Mr. Horner will ever get married?" Marie asked.

"Hey, we're close, but not that close. Frankly, I doubt it, though. He's not getting any younger and the girls, well, they're not exactly brain surgeon material. He'd do better to look at someone more his own age, someone who understands how hard he works, you know?"

Angie glanced at the diamond-studded Rolex on her wrist. "Look, I know it's last minute, but I have to beg off lunch. I hate to do it since we're just starting this lunch thing, but you heard the boss. I have to be here to receive a package and entertain Jennifer."

"I don't mind waiting until you're ready. I like having lunch with you—you choose nice places to eat. Otherwise, I'd have a sandwich at my desk," Marie said. "My boss is in court all day, so I can take a longer lunch, the girls say. If it's okay with you, I'll sit here and read."

"Suit yourself. I'm sure he'll be back in an hour."

Marie had excused herself to go to the ladies' room down the hall when the courier arrived from Harry Winston's. Angie signed for the small package and discouraged his attempt at small talk. "Sorry, I have a lot to do before the boss gets back."

"Just make sure this goes straight to him. Strict orders from my boss to me."

"And from mine to me, I assure you," Angie said.

He left then, and glancing at the closed door, she untied the ribbon and lifted the lid of the jewelry box, then stopped abruptly. Slowly she took out a ring so studded with large diamonds that it shot multicolored fire around the reception room, bouncing off the glass table and the crystal ornaments above it.

"Whoa, is this overboard or what?" she said to the empty room. She slipped it on the ring finger of her left hand. "Jennifer, Jennifer, be careful what you wish for," she murmured. "Haven't you noticed? Thomas Horner carries around a little black cloud where girls are concerned."

She wrapped the jewelry box to its original condition and took it into his office. When she returned to her desk, Marie was back on the visitor's chair, reading.

Minutes later, the door to the suite opened and a remarkably beautiful young woman came in. She was almost six feet tall, with high cheekbones, full lips, and glossy brown hair that fell in a straight line down her back. The collar of a floor-length mink coat was turned up and her cheeks were pink from the cold that still clung to her.

"Hi. Angie, right?" she said, peeling off her gloves. "I'm Jennifer. Am I too early? Tommy—Mr. Horner—told me to meet him here so we can go out for a late lunch. Oh," she said, turning and seeing Marie. "I didn't realize someone else was waiting."

"My friend's waiting 'til Mr. Horner gets back. We're going to lunch," Angie said.

Jennifer turned back to Angie. "I had to cut short a fitting at Chanel to get here. They have the sweetest checked suits for spring. Have you seen them?" She smiled, her perfect teeth blindingly white.

Angie looked at her without expression. "No, Jennifer," she said. "I haven't been to Chanel recently, although my guess is they always have checked suits. It's their thing, isn't it?"

Jennifer laughed. "Of course, you're right. Silly me. What do you think of the coat?" she asked, extending her arms and twirling on the rug. "Tommy insisted I have it. It gets so cold when the wind blows along Seventy-Eighth Street I can barely make it from the cab to the apartment."

"It gets colder here than in Tennessee, then?"

"Oh my god, it surely does. We have snow there sometimes, but New York? This is a whole other thing, you know? Where are you from, Angie?"

"New York. Somehow, I've managed to survive the trip to and from Brooklyn all these years, but I don't know how, come to think of it. Want some coffee while you wait? Or a glass of champagne?"

"No caffeine, thanks. It's not good for me. But if there's champagne ...?"

• • •

"Time for the little girls' room," Jennifer said a half hour later, setting her empty wine flute down on the glass table. "This stuff gives me a headache, to tell you the truth. But Tommy's friends drink it practically for breakfast, so I'm developing a taste for it." Her voice had slipped into the remnants of a Tennessee drawl. She struggled a little getting to her feet.

"Tom's private washroom," Angie said, looking up from her computer and sweeping her arm toward his office. "In there on the left."

"Whew, this coat weighs a ton." Jennifer shrugged out of the mink as she stepped away. "I keep thinking I'm going to trip on it or something."

"Very nice," Angie said. "Your birthday?"

"No." Jennifer laughed and swept her hair to one side of her neck. "He just wanted to do something nice for me. Actually," she added, leaning toward Angie and lowering her voice, "I think he's leading up to something. Ever since the week we spent at his house in Vail last month, I've had a feeling."

"You mean marriage?" Angie glanced at the deep ripples of mink that had slipped halfway to the floor. "I would have figured him for a confirmed bachelor by now, not that he talks to me about that kind of thing."

"Oh," Jennifer said as she disappeared into the inner office, "most men, especially very wealthy ones, decide somewhere along the line that they want children. Heirs, you know."

Marie looked up at Angie from her magazine, raising her eyebrows. The phone rang.

"Oh, hi, boss. Yup. She's here. Sure, I'll tell her."

Angie went into the inner office to get another bottle of champagne. She was opening it when Jennifer came back.

"Did Tommy—Mr. Horner—call?" she said. "I'm wondering if I'll have time to go back to the fitting after lunch. I really want to wear that darling suit before anyone else has it, like maybe to the hospital benefit lunch next week."

"He said he'll be back soon. He said to have a little more champagne."

"Actually, I'm a little fuzzyheaded," Jennifer said. "Maybe coffee would be good now, or something to eat if you have anything here."

"Tell you what," Angie said. "I'll run down the block to the place we use when Tom has people in for lunch. Something light like caviar and toast will absorb the champagne without spoiling your appetite."

"Good thinking," Jennifer said, giggling. She snuggled back onto the sofa and into the embrace of her coat.

"That's me," Angie said in a low tone. "Always thinking."

But Jennifer's eyes were closed, and a smile played around her mouth as she ran her fingers through her sleek hair. Angie glanced at the young woman as she pulled her own cloth coat off the rack. "I won't be long."

"Maybe I should go instead," Marie said, looking askance at Jennifer. "Just tell me where it is."

"No, they don't do takeout for anyone else. It's fine. The boss will probably get back before I do." Angie stood still for a few seconds, staring at the wall of photos. Then, straightening her back, she turned to Jennifer. "Sometimes the best thing is to drink a little more." She held up the bottle. "It gets you past the buzzy stage, you know?"

Jennifer opened her eyes, smiled her dazzling smile, and held out her glass. "Oh well, then," she said, "have to get past the buzz."

•••

"NEW TRAGEDY HITS CEO"

The headline spread across all the columns on the front age of the *New York Post*. Gossip columnists eagerly reported the incident: "Young beauty," "Manhattan's wealthiest bachelor," "bizarre accident."

The police department spokesman said the investigation was ongoing, but preliminary results suggested the woman caught her heel in the lining of her fur coat when she tried to stand up from the couch where she was sitting. As she stumbled, she grabbed a nearby shelf, pulling it off the wall. A crystal ornament on the shelf hit her head, and she then fell hard into the corner of a glass table, fracturing her skull.

Mr. Horner was on his way back from a meeting at the time, and his executive assistant was out of the building on an errand. The only other person present, another worker in the building, had gone to get a glass of water for the victim, who had complained of dizziness a few moments before.

Horner Global Enterprises released a statement saying the chairman and CEO was distraught, that he had planned to ask the victim to marry him that very day. "Jennifer was all that is sweet and good, and she will be remembered as a wonderful young woman."

People talked, of course. Poor guy. Remember the Belgian model he dated for a year, the one he took everywhere and seemed to adore? She died in an apartment fire, didn't she? A faulty electrical outlet or something? Others with longer memories recalled a charming girl from a wealthy Greenwich family, an accomplished equestrian who left the billionaire for a polo player. Everyone said it just proved you couldn't buy happiness.

A few people wondered about the coincidences, but kept their questions to themselves. Thomas Horner was perhaps the richest man in a city of rich men, with enough power to make or break the cultural and charitable organizations that lined up at his door every year, and influential friends in virtually every corporate boardroom and social circle. And, anyway, he loved the woman. The manager at Harry Winston, a store known for discretion, even confirmed when detectives interviewed him that their courier had delivered a piece of jewelry to Horner's office that very day.

TV crews camped outside Horner's apartment building and his office for a few days, kept at bay by security guards. He was said to be in seclusion, visited by only a few close friends and dealing only with the most pressing business.

Several weeks later, the police reported that their investigation led them to conclude the young woman's death was indeed accidental, caused in part by drinking too much champagne and an unlucky tangle with her fur coat. Horner's assistant had been very helpful, the report said, although it noted that she blamed herself for letting the victim drink more champagne than was good for her. The case was closed.

Thomas Horner told his board of directors that he had to move his corporate office to another location, and they agreed. His assistant was put in charge of the project and instructed to work with the company's chief financial officer to find and prepare a suitable space somewhere else in midtown Manhattan. In the interim, Horner took a leave of absence. The media moved on to the next scandal.

● ● ●

The only sound was a soft hissing as palm fronds high up brushed into each other, pushed gently by a breeze. The sky was lapis and the sea slightly purple. A few people trailed along the water's edge singly or in pairs, their voices far away and their images distorted by heat waves.

Tom knew that if he turned his head to the left, he would see the long dock where his boat was berthed and perhaps the crew polishing the fittings or loading stores of fresh food. His skin was reddening. He knew he should put on more sunblock, but it was hard to gather enough energy to move from his chaise longue. The boy would be by before long, asking him if he wanted another drink. That would be soon enough.

He squinted at the shoreline. A dumpy woman wearing a wide-brimmed hat was making her way along the water's edge, dabbling her bare feet in the mild surf. As he looked, the breeze tugged the hat and she stopped to tie it under her chin.

He closed his eyes. When he opened them again, she was sitting in the chair next to his. "Hello, Tom," she said mildly. "Watch out you don't get a sunburn."

He grunted in reply. "Took you long enough to get here."

"I wasn't in any hurry." She smiled at him. "Feeling better?"

"Not really," he said, sighing.

She laughed softly. "Anthony warned me you're a sentimental guy."

"It's not funny." He struggled to sit upright and reached

for a shirt. "Don't believe everything my chauffeur tells you. He isn't my best friend, no matter what he says."

"Maybe not," Marie said, the laughter dropping away from her voice. "But he's your most trusted friend, isn't he, Tom? Otherwise, you and I wouldn't have met, and you wouldn't be in mourning, sitting here getting a tan, undisturbed by questions from the cops."

"You came to get paid the rest of your fee," he said. "We don't have anything else to discuss. Just give me your account number and the money will be in your Cayman bank tomorrow."

"Accounts," Marie said, "plural. I like to spread it around. I'll check tomorrow to make sure it's all there." She pulled an envelope out of her beach bag.

"Fine." Tom took the envelope and tucked it in his shirt pocket. "A name on the accounts?"

"Different businesses. I'm sure you know how that works." Marie stood up and looked around casually. There was no one else sitting in the long row of chairs. She leaned down toward Tom. "I know you'll make good. You and your pretty boat won't make it out of the harbor if all of the money's not there. I work alone, but I have associates for times like this."

Tom looked startled, and said, his voice rising a half octave, "You don't need that. I keep my word. You can ask Anthony."

"I did, and that's what he told me. Even when the South

American deal got complicated and it took two attempts, poor girl. I'm just making sure you understand."

"I get it," Tom said sharply. He paused. "Jennifer. Did she ...?"

"No. Surprise, maybe, but no pain. That crystal plaque hit her too hard and too fast for her to feel anything. I'm good at what I do, Tom. That's what you paid me for."

"Enough," Tom said sharply. He leaned back in his chair, but his shoulders shifted uncomfortably. "One more thing," he said, and hesitated. "Angie."

"She doesn't suspect, if that's what you mean."

"She'd never believe anything bad about me," Tom said, sounding sure of himself again.

"She's in love with you."

"Yes, but it's different with her. She doesn't expect me to marry her as long as I give her a big present once in a while, something that tells people in the company how important she is. A fat bonus, a month off, a promotion. These other girls, I don't know."

Tom waved one hand in a wide arc, then dropped it onto the chair again. "They want everything. They're like calculators. The minute I do something nice for them, they start counting up my assets, working their way into a good deal. It shows on their faces, you know?"

Marie made a sound, ambiguous.

"They don't look at me, they look at my money. They aren't even talking to me. They're talking to the money."

Marie sighed and looked at the sea. "If I were you,

though, I'd be careful. Angie's not dumb. Three may be a coincidence, but four? I'm not sure there'll be a present big enough next time."

"It won't happen again. Anyway, it wouldn't be you if there were a next time," Tom said. "That's the secret. That and money."

"Amen," Marie said, and shifted her beach bag from one hand to the other as she turned to go. "Good luck, Tom. It was a pleasure doing business with you."

He watched as she became a smaller and smaller figure in the distance, following the shoreline and kicking at the little waves that broke at her feet until she disappeared around a bend.

"Never again," he murmured, lying back in the chair and patting the pocket where the envelope sat folded in half. "But thank god for money."

I was sitting in the plush reception area of an uber rich, then-bachelor New Yorker's office years ago, waiting with a colleague to discuss a possible million-dollar donation. His well-dressed assistant spun in her chair and yelled—yelled—into the great man's office that we were there. My colleague and I exchanged raised eyebrows, and so this story was born.

—Susan C. Shea

TRUE CULPRIT

C.M. *West*

The coarse ash sifting through my fingers felt like human remains. My suspicions were confirmed when a nugget of bone clunked out of the broken sculpture.

Made by my aunt Imogen, the bulky ceramic crow wore a sly smile, and its exaggerated eyes gave it comical flair, but I'd had no idea of the dark contents it harbored all these years. I shook the shattered vessel, and a man's ring pinged onto the hardwood floor.

Okay, so the ashes dusting my hands were from a human.

"I'm fine, Mom. The quake registered 5.5 magnitude, but the only thing damaged was Aunt Imogen's crow. My bookshelf fell on it, cracked the thing wide open."

"Can you repair it?" The phone buzzed, and her voice sounded faint.

"No. It's totally destroyed."

"What a shame."

I was just a young boy when my aunt died. Like me, she'd been an artist. I'd found her work charming, but now the thing sort of creeped me out. "Mom, did you scatter all her ashes? You didn't hang on to any, did you?"

"That's a weird question. All that's left of Genny is our memories—"

"Well, I don't remember her."

"—and her art. I still have her rooster. She made it after you were born. It was one of her last pieces."

"Does anyone else in the family have more of her big sculptures?" At about four feet high, the crow had easily concealed human ashes. But whose?

"No. My sisters only have her pots."

"And you didn't save any of Grandma's ashes?" I plucked my hardcover copy of The Maltese Falcon out of the rubble and dusted it off. The irony was not lost on me.

"Tru honey, you were there when we released Grandma's ashes into the ocean. You're as cryptic as your father. What's going on?"

I could never forget the texture. "Just that I found something similar inside Aunt Imogen's sculpture." Ash clung to my fingers. I wiped my hands on my jeans.

"Probably just part of the firing process."

"Must be." A puddle of melted gold was sealed to the interior walls and flecked with more bone fragments. A tooth? I held the ring up to the light. A signet ring, platinum. I knew my metals; platinum wouldn't have melted in a kiln, but gold had a lower melting point—so did bodies.

The inside walls had deep red spots, the result of iron oxide and moisture. No one glazes the inside of a sealed sculpture. Clearly, body parts were cremated inside the thing during the firing process, but one ceramic crow wouldn't have held an entire grown man. I remembered seeing a photo of Aunt Genny with a cluster of crow sculptures, enough to do the job.

Inscribed along the base was the potter's insignia. "What's 'Birdland'?" I asked my mother.

"An all-women ceramics collective that was housed in a barn at the bird sanctuary near Bolinas, where your aunt Genny lived on a houseboat. The group went on for a few years, I think."

"The potter's stamp says 1973." Had the ashes been inside the sculpture some forty-five years? Imogen had made the rooster ten years after the crow. "Anyone ring a bell from back then, one of her friends?"

"Imogen was several years older than me. She moved away from home to become a hippie at a beach enclave where she started Birdland. I didn't know any of her new friends. Though I met Karen later on. They were very close and she cared for Genny at the end. Of course, I had my hands full; you were a very busy toddler. Karen could have something of Genny's, I suppose, but I wouldn't know how to contact her."

"An art collective sounds pretty cool. What do you remember about that?"

"Nothing much. I mostly remember my mother's terror that Imogen had joined a cult out in Marin."

"Cult? Like witchcraft?" Momentarily, I imagined human sacrifice and covens.

Mom laughed. "No. Not *occult*. Socialists, feminists. Still, some scary things went on in California back in the seventies. Actual 'Drink the Kool-Aid' cults spread out along the coast. Mother lectured us against hitchhiking in Santa Rosa, where they found young girls strangled and lying naked in ditches. Well, that Zodiac Killer terrified *everyone* off remote roads and trails. All of it so worried your grandma."

I polished the man's signet ring on my shirt and the engraved initials *JA* appeared on the surface. "Sounds dicey. I'm surprised Grandma didn't haul her back home."

"Not likely. You didn't know Imogen."

"And the artists were all women?"

"Decidedly."

"Would Imogen's old boyfriend have some of her work? Wasn't there someone, name with a J?"

"No. You were the only male who ever impressed Genny. We visited her boat sometimes. You were maybe eighteen months when you first saw that crow. It stopped you in your tracks. You stayed there mesmerized, way longer than any baby should."

"I was probably scared shitless."

"No, more like hypnotized. Your reaction did freak Imogen out, and I had to coax you away so she'd calm down. I thought that was the experience that led you to become a sculptor, like her. I made sure you got her crow eventually."

Thanks for that, Mom. So, my mother clearly had no idea what had been inside the sculpture, but Imogen knew. Had my aunt freaked out because she feared I'd somehow reveal her secret?

"Imogen had cancer?"

"Cervical. She died in her early thirties. Can't believe you're that age now."

"There's a photo with a bunch of her crows."

"Yes. They call it a murder, right?"

"That's the term. A murder of crows." Shivers crept down my spine. "What happened to the others?"

"Sold, I suppose. The collective had a regular booth at the Marin flea market. You might be able to track one down, but if it means so much you can have the rooster, honey."

"I'll try to find another crow first. I've got more post-quake cleaning, Mom." After I hung up, I tossed the mess into a heavy-duty trash bag and then sealed it tight.

• • •

The internet was still down. Apparently the tremor had damaged something out there. Restless, I threw my surfboard into the truck and drove away from the close-shouldered density of the East Bay until my lungs expanded wider in the salt-tinged air near the coast. I usually surfed to clear my mind, but today, as I drove, Mom's recollections of brainwashed suicide cults and serial killers cast a dark lens on my view of the remote roads, sharp cliffs, and deep muffling woods of Marin County.

It didn't take much to imagine the reasons a young woman could have for killing a man and hiding the evidence. Considering my own share of skeletons, I had more in common with Imogen than Mom knew. The ring in my pocket felt like an albatross; I wouldn't turn my back on Aunt Imogen's grim legacy. It seemed logical to go where the kilns had been.

The road curved along the shore of the Bolinas Lagoon. At one sharp bend, I pulled into the gravel parking lot of the bird sanctuary. The white clapboard farmhouse and barns were idyllic among the thick green trees and water views, but my goal gave the setting more of a Stephen King vibe.

A man with a faded O'Neill T-shirt and gray hair pulled into a ponytail appeared at the farmhouse door. He limped heavily toward me. "Hey, Quiksilver, nice board. I didn't expect same-day service, but not complaining. We need the foundations and all checked out before we can open to the public. Do it myself except for this bum leg." He slapped his thigh.

I tried to make sense of his welcome. We hadn't talked

on the phone. The door on my truck bore a magnetic sign advertising my business: James Construction. My realization came almost too late; he thought I'd come to inspect his place after the quake. It was my chance to snoop. "I can give it the once-over. My name is Tru James."

We shook hands. "Tru, huh? Don't recall your name but I called plenty of contractors."

"I'm licensed." I retrieved my business card from the glove box.

"Cool. Call me Walt. The Boy Scouts have an overnight scheduled tomorrow, and we have to be careful of aftershocks and instability. I'll show you where to start." He paused at the lawn and slipped into a garden shed full of pruners and saws, then handed me a sharp machete. "That's a True Temper, your namesake. I used 'em in 'Nam; they work great on the poison oak below the boardwalks."

"Can't imagine wielding a machete in combat. You saw a lot of action?" I wondered what else Walt had chopped up with a knife.

Walt's smile faded. "No. Just used 'em for clearing the jungle."

I held up the knife. "This would cut bone though?"

He stepped back a little. "War's no picnic. I only talk about that shit with my group." He rubbed his bad leg.

"Sorry." A bird trilled from the trees overhead. "This is a peaceful spot. Have you worked here long?"

"Off and on. I mowed lawns right here as a young buck. Came back home again 'bout a year ago to retire."

I hoped my inspection would reveal more information than Walt did. The old milking-barn-turned-bunkhouse and the farmhouse had fared well in the quake but I struck out on clues—no hulking ceramic birds on display, nothing related to Imogen's time there.

When I finished, I found Walt in the office. Wiping the dirt off my hands with a bandana, I gave him my report. "The foundation settled long ago in the southeast corner but it's solid enough. There are bolts in the boardwalk so it's fine. Bunkhouse has a fair amount of cracking but it's only surface plaster. Boy Scout field trip is on."

"Great. I've got a form you can fill in, and they'll send a check."

I shook my head. "No, this is a nonprofit. I only want some information in return."

I studied the framed photos on the wall. The pictures were mostly black-and-whites of the old dairy or full-color portraits of raptors. Except for one frame, which held faded Polaroid snapshots of three women in bell-bottom jeans surrounded by substantial bird sculptures posed in front of a barn. The women weren't smiling in the photos. I pointed to the tallest woman, her arms crossed and a kerchief on her head. "I'm related to her. She was part of Birdland."

"Imogen?" Walt squinted at me. "I guess there's some

resemblance, in the height and those eyes. She was a firebrand all right, but you know that."

"No. She died when I was a baby."

"That's right, was a long time ago. Well, Imogen's idealist politics were fierce. Now, I understand she was right, but we got into it way back when I was just a dumb jarhead shipping off to fight the war on Communism."

"Any other guys get into it with her?"

He crossed his arms. "Son, I appreciate your work, but I never called *you* after the quake. So what's your real story—you Imogen's kid looking for long-lost Daddy?"

"You fit the bill, Walt?"

He shook his head. "They were a passionate tribe of women. I had my crushes but never got with any of 'em. Though I heard from the guys that those girls got around. There were constant parties at the docks—Dutch, some European artist, a professor, I think, had import beer kegs delivered right to his sailboat. And some other fella, Shep, had a yacht and cocaine. Seamen, that's your source." His laugh came deep from his belly.

I groaned. Walt's impression of Imogen being a party girl didn't fit with my mom's description. "Not helpful. Anyone with a name starts with J?"

He scratched his head. "Can't mean Jake? A gangly kid went to Santa Rosa Junior College, made ceramic bongs and sold 'em at the flea market. He died in Vietnam."

"What was Jake's last name?"

"Shit, don't recall. All I know is I left for war, missed

the party, and the artist colony experiment here didn't last long after. But Jake and Imogen never got it on."

"Where did the other Birdlanders go?"

Walt touched the image of a woman wearing huge glasses and a grim expression. "Karen lives in a houseboat in Bolinas, but she don't talk much about back then." His finger moved to a closeup of a painfully thin young woman whose face was mostly hidden behind long red hair. "Robin is the famous one. You hear of the tile company Artemis Fire?"

"Sure. My clients can't afford that stuff, though."

He pulled a pipe from his pocket and lit the bowl. "Medicinal." He winked and gestured to me with the pipe. "Wanna get baked and surf the tsunami?"

"Nah, surf's flat. Think I'll go talk to Karen."

"Good luck. She don't like nobody."

• • •

The surfer girl at the general store looked me up and down before telling me Karen lived in the red houseboat on the end. I assumed Karen was the same friend who'd taken care of Imogen in her last days.

The view of the open ocean was plucked from a watercolorist's palette—Gentian blue sky with a Payne's gray sea and Bob Ross magic-white froth at the edge of dull ochre sands— but it would've been better without the stench. The boats that were slumped on the rotting mud of low tide offset my impression of halcyon living.

I surveyed the listing barge on the end. Chalky bird crap covered the deck, and the flaked paint on the siding was sun-bleached to an awkward pink. Somebody had crammed the aft deck with flowering plants in familiar hand-thrown pots.

"Put one foot on board and I'll shoot you for trespassing." Stepping out from a trellis covered in ivy geraniums, a woman with crazed gray hair aimed a flare gun at my chest. "Imogen didn't have any children."

"I'm guessing Walt called ahead. I'm unarmed, Karen." Slowly, I fished the ring out of my pocket and held it up to the light. "What was Jake's last name?"

"You a detective or something?"

"Or something. Tru James. Imogen was my aunt."

"You should keep your story straight." She pulled huge glasses from out of her tangled bird's nest hair and shoved them onto her face with one hand. She scowled at me for a beat then lowered her gun. "You've grown, Tru."

● ● ●

Karen poured more gin over ice then added a splash of tonic. My nostrils stung from the briny potpourri of dead fish, a sharp rusty odor, and wafting clouds of mildew. Shorebirds plucked at the mud alongside the barge.

She sat sluggishly in an off-kilter lounge chair and downed her drink. "Like I told you, it wasn't anything so dramatic as murder." She raised her index finger. "Correction, I mean our government slaughtered Jake when they sent him off to fight. He was a local kid, shipped back in a box like too many others. Shameful waste. I can't even remember his last name. We made the crows as memorials for his ashes. Like a statement on Vietnam, nothing so cloak-and-dagger as whatever you imagined."

"Why didn't Jake's family claim his remains, and why wouldn't they want his ring? And what did Imogen care about Jake? Karen, your story has problems."

She gave a one-shoulder shrug. "Can I see the ring again?" I gave it to her. With a flick of her wrist, she tossed it overboard. "Problem solved. Leave it alone, Frodo."

• • •

At home, the internet worked again, and I searched late into the night. Karen's transparent bluff only convinced me further that she or Imogen (maybe Walt?) had killed someone. But who?

The Vietnam memorial site proved useless without Jake's last name. Shep and Dutch had to be nicknames, and so I struck out again. On the whole, the internet contained sparse information from the seventies. I'd have to go to the library and comb the newspaper archives.

But Walt had given me another clue about Dutch, so I poked around specifically for art professors with that nickname. Eventually, I learned that Delftware was a type of Dutch ceramics from the seventeenth century, with classic designs and a blue-and-white glaze, and that an expert called "Dutch" Anderson had curated a small exhibit of the stuff at the de Young museum in San Francisco back in 1973.

After further trawling in the digital sea of third-hand missing persons sites and bizarre unsolved-mysteries chat rooms, I knew I'd found my man.

Jan "Dutch" Anderson had come to Marin County from the Netherlands as a visiting art professor at some of the local colleges. He'd lived aboard his Islander 36 sailboat and docked it near Sausalito. One summer night the Coast Guard found his boat empty and drifting in the San Francisco Bay. The sheet line had been left loose, and the boom swung back and forth in the wind like an indiscriminate bludgeon. The autopilot showed a course toward the San Francisco Yacht Club. His death was determined to be accidental after they found empty liquor bottles in the cockpit. His body never surfaced.

Locating Robin was simple. A detailed article in *Architectural Digest* featured the mansion of the Artemis Fire Tile Company founder. The photo spread displayed Robin's extensive collection of California Funk ceramics, complete with a murder of crows in the lower gallery. Her home was in the elite peninsula town called Tiburon, the Spanish word for *shark*.

I wanted to talk to the last Birdlander before I faced off with Karen again. The mansion's distinctive rooflines would make it easy to spot, and I headed there at first light.

• • •

The woman who answered the door didn't look like the shy redhead in the faded photograph. She resembled Annie Lennox in a Louise Nevelson costume with elaborate false eyelashes, and her fiercely spiked red hair peeked from under a violet scarf.

"Karen said you had Imogen's eyes."

And I'd hoped to surprise her. "You were close to my aunt?"

Robin held out her manicured hand. "I'm Robin. Genny saved my life."

Past the entry, we walked into an open living room. The terraced house hugged a south-facing downslope that met the shores of the bay. The magazine article had illustrated the unusual layout of the place. The street-level entry was on the top floor and contained the kitchen and an entertaining area with cathedral ceilings and a glass curtain wall. Beneath us were two more floors with bedrooms, private lounges, and, on the lowest level, the gallery and office.

I sat at her exquisitely tiled bar overlooking a room outfitted with white leather couches and featuring a bank of windows with views across the bay of the shining white city of San Francisco. The opulence made a stark contrast to Karen's squalid gypsy barge. Robin quickly cleared two coffee cups off the counter.

Robin opened her fridge. "Want a Bloody Mary?"

"No, too early for me."

She tightened the knot on her scarf. "The doctor told me to cut back on morning cocktails at my age, anyway. Coffee? I have those pod thingies."

"Sure, with milk. Thanks."

While the machine worked its magic, Robin pointed out the significant sculptures dotting her living room. Quite different from my own minimalist steel work, California Funk required a penchant for garish colors, outlandish proportions, and comical figures. The looming statue by Viola Frey reminded me vaguely of my disapproving piano teacher from third grade. None of the artworks in the living room were from Birdland. From the article, I knew the crows were displayed in the gallery on the bottom floor, but only a lower terrace and pier were on view from the windows.

Carefully taking the fine porcelain mug from her, I sipped the coffee. "Tell me about Imogen and the artists' collective."

Robin sat across from me at the bar. Her position precisely blocked my view of the lower terrace and pier. She then wove a story of how Imogen had ignited Robin's ambition and given her the confidence she needed to build her business. She said nothing about life-threatening events and certainly didn't mention Dutch Anderson.

In minute detail, Robin droned on about the production and manufacturing of tiles until I held up my hand to silence her. "Cut to the chase. The three of you killed Dutch Anderson and I want to know why."

She swallowed her remaining sip of coffee. Hiding her expression behind the cup, she said, "Justice. Poetic justice."

I heard a thump outside and, craning my neck, I glimpsed motion on the dock below. Robin stood up suddenly and further blocked my view. Maneuvering around her, I raced to the window.

I watched as Karen awkwardly wrestled a large ceramic crow. Her hair appeared more unruly than yesterday, something I hadn't thought possible. The crow teetered at the edge of the dock, and Karen almost fell into the drink after she rolled the thing off. The splash soaked her shoes. She yanked her tunic down over her belly as she moved out of sight with a determined gait. I faced Robin again.

Robin was pointing a rifle at me.

"What, you keep a gun in the cupboard with the sugar?" I held up my hands. "That's a Winchester lever-action. Not sure it will do the job."

"It'll fire." She fumbled with the lever but managed to cock it.

I crossed my arms. "Why did Dutch deserve it?"

With the gun still trained on me, she took a breath, then spoke in a low voice. "I was a virgin until I awoke, torn up, confused, and sprawled in my own barf on the V-berth of Dutch's sailboat. I had no idea how I got there. He'd gone, of course." Her cheeks flushed pink. "The night before, I'd been drinking at a party on the docks. He was so much older, my professor for effing sake. I'd admired his expertise on Delft Blue glazing techniques and all my classmates saw me hanging on his every word. You understand how it looked."

I remembered Robin's shy young face in the photo. "Jeez. How old were you?"

"Just eighteen, and I'd desperately wanted to be a liberated grownup woman. Lots of guys translated women's lib to mean freely screwing around without consequences. If a woman disagreed, they ridiculed her for not being part of the sexual revolution. A sophisticated older man had chosen me, therefore I rationalized I should've been flattered. Really, I felt traumatized and dirty. I hadn't been beaten or strangled by a random stranger so I blamed myself. I cleaned up my own blood and vomit and kept silent in my humiliation. I saw Dutch a few days later, acted like nothing had happened, and then dropped his course."

Another noise outside interrupted us as Karen appeared pushing a dolly along the dock at a fast clip. She halted it, and the next bird rolled neatly forward into the water.

"Looks like she needs a hand." I didn't think Robin would kill me, so I made a move toward the stairs.

Robin quickly made to block me and took aim at my kneecap. "Don't test me, kid. You'll limp forever, if you don't bleed out before I call the ambulance. Awfully sorry, mistook you for an intruder." Her face paled.

I stood still. "You were absolutely sure Dutch was the true culprit, even though you didn't remember anything?"

Robin's hands trembled as she held the gun. "There's more to the story. I'll tell you while Karen finishes up." She rested the gun barrel on the back of a white leather chair to steady her aim. "Dutch targeted Karen next. Much later she told us how she awoke in the woods—freezing, nearly naked, and bruised without any memory of the studio party or who attacked her. I'd stopped attending parties or I would've warned her. I'd heard I had gained a reputation and knew where the rumor came from. Karen flirted with guys, liked the attention, drank, and did drugs. But, like me, after her rape Karen kept quiet. A few weeks later, Dutch groped Karen and told her she sure knew how to party."

"That's your proof?"

I hadn't meant to sound incredulous. Masses of women calling out influential men as sexual predators was headline news, but every woman I knew had shown no surprise. I wanted to believe abusive behavior toward women came from a distant culture of men from an archaic generation. Still, I'd hoped Imogen had killed Dutch in self-defense and was innocent of furious revenge and murder. And there I stood, the conflicted male outsider.

It would've been child's play to wrestle the rifle from

the old woman. Had she really thought it would protect her? Her story forced me to witness ugly truths, had conscripted me into the role of helpless and judgmental observer—I pondered whether murder was the right punishment for Dutch's crimes. Of course I knew justice would not have been served back then. Maybe not now either? I supposed I might've felt murderous in her shoes.

Playing my absurd part, I asked the obvious sinking question: "Why didn't you go to the cops?"

Her laugh sounded like a seagull's harsh cry. "Proof? Try proving assault months after the fact. Dutch got to Imogen last, but he underestimated her. She tore his boat apart until she found his knockout drugs. Then she brought the three of us together. She knew we had not been ourselves lately and, well, I'd never seen such rage! Genny convinced us Dutch was, besides being a serial rapist, also the murderer of the Santa Rosa hitchhiker girls, and possibly the Zodiac Killer. She planned our revenge carefully. In a terrified and infuriated frenzy, we felt our mission was justified. It was easy enough to lure him to the studio and knock him out with his own drugs. There's your poetic justice. One of us—and I will never say who—strangled him with the clay cutting wire."

I watched Karen work and reimagined the women as a powerful coven. "Did you plan ahead of time to put his body in the sculptures?"

"No. Genny had planned on the kiln but the wire turned out quite effective. His head almost completely separated from his body, which gave us the idea to, uh, continue. That part wasn't so easy. The crows were ready and waiting to be fired, serendipity. Better to contain the body in something than to throw it loose into the kiln, where someone might find the remains on the shelves."

"Messy work."

"You can't imagine." She leaned on the chair, and the gun tipped downward. "That night changed us irrevocably. Using saws was horrible. As we worked, Imogen bolstered us with stories of Eurydice, Artemis, Persephone, and Judith. Her persuasive storytelling made us feel mythical, that we'd slayed a terrible beast. We scored and slipped the greenware back together, leaving vents of course. The kiln burned slowly for days. Then, Imogen applied glaze and the second firing sealed everything up."

"You knew how to handle his boat?"

"I grew up sailing." She carefully peeled off her false eyelashes and muttered, "Karen says only drag queens wear these now."

I sat in an armchair. "Why did you keep the crows?"

"Imogen kept one for sorrow; it's from that old counting crows poem. She was prepared to take the rap. We sold the remaining six at the Marin flea market and went our separate ways. Of course, our secret bound us forever, and I constantly worried about being caught. After I made my fortune, I tracked down and collected them all. It was worth the price."

"What do seven crows mean?"

Robin sang in a soft voice. "One for sorrow. Two for joy. Three for a girl. Four for a boy. Five for silver. Six for gold. Seven for a secret never told."

I wiped my hand across my face. "So was Dutch the hitchhiker murderer?"

Robin blushed deeply. "No. We were wrong. Other girls showed up dead on roadsides after. And I realized he hadn't even arrived in the country when the earliest Zodiac killings happened. You know, those crimes are still unsolved." She blinked tears from her eyes.

I crossed my arms. "You and Karen are close now?"

She shook her head. "Years went by before we saw each other again, not until Imogen got sick. Dutch gave all of us chlamydia. Did you know that increased Imogen's chances to develop the cervical cancer that killed her? Get it? Dutch got her in the end."

I sighed. "I wish I'd known my aunt. Do you regret—"

Karen appeared at the top of the stairwell. "Goddamn it, they're *not* sinking!" She turned her red-faced anger toward me. "I swear, if you weren't related to Imogen ..."

Robin pushed Karen into a chair and faced me again. "We know he was a bad man. Kid, what do you want?"

"I only wanted the truth."

The women were silent. The dark heads of the crows bobbed in the water below. Their rocking motions reminded me of those weird drinking bird toys. Robin laid the weapon against her knee and slumped into a chair.

Karen's breath calmed, and with hands planted over her face, she said, "Sometimes we will never know the truth. Some people are killed, or raped, or tortured, and the psychopaths have no rhyme or reason for choosing those victims except dumb proximity. And, goes without saying, because they were women. Some people get cancer. Others don't." She wiped her brow and then met my eyes. "No one deserves this shit. Again and again there's no justice. That's the truth. But if you want reasons, if you want to know why—well, I gave up on that long ago."

Robin stood again. "Think I'll make those Bloody Marys before you call the cops." She set the rifle down.

I rose from my chair. "Mind if I check out that old gun?"

Karen sputtered, "You're kidding!"

Opening the glass doors to the balcony, I held out my hand for the rifle. "Some secrets will never be told."

Stepping onto the deck overlooking the water, I spotted the crows drifting in the tide. They moved in slow circles, inching toward the shallow shores of the mainland. I took careful aim. Each one popped, then sank with a brief trace of bubbles.

Raised on the tenets of feminism and equal rights, we developed our male sleuth as an artist who possesses emotional sensitivity and a strong moral compass, and whose character is intended as contemporary foil to the unemotional mold of classic male-dominated crime fiction. We populate our stories with strong women and diverse voices as the norm.

The tumultuous events in 1970s Northern California defined an era whose legacy stretches into the fabric of contemporary life. Although fiction, mentioning true crimes and unsolved murders required respectful handling and we hope to illuminate the unresolved justice for those real victims.

— C.M. West

BIRDBRAIN

CJ Verburg

If you were planning a heist anywhere near Mullet
Harbor, you wanted Mandrake. Nobody remembered his
real name. He'd been nicknamed Mandrake the Magician
ages ago, for making objects disappear in one place and
reappear someplace else.

Cosh Pullins swore that Mandrake's fingers really did
move quicker than the eye. There was no lock in the
Tampa Bay area he couldn't pick, no safe he couldn't crack.

Cosh picked up his phone after learning that a small-
time gem trader named Roger Crowell had booked a room
next Tuesday at the Mermaid Beach Hotel.

"Hey, Tommy. We got a mullet coming in for the
Diamond Expo."

"*We* is who? You, me, and ...?"

"Who d'you think?"

"Not Mandrake, man. No way. Not if he's still got that
parrot."

That parrot was a blue-and-orange macaw which Mandrake called Birdbrain. His wife had given it to him as an anniversary present. She left him six months later, claiming he cared more for the bird than her. Mandrake said he cared for her so much, he'd named the bird after her.

"It's a support animal," said Cosh. "He needs it."

"It attacked me! You saw, last time? I reached back to Mandrake for a butt, and *whammo!* Goddamn parrot almost ran us off the road."

"I'm not breaking up this team over a bird, Tommy. Anyhow, we're talking diamonds. One guy, big take, no hassle."

"No parrots on a job, Cosh. You gotta tell him."

Cosh already knew Mandrake's answer. *No parrot, no deal.* "I'm telling you," he said. "He needs the parrot, and we need Mandrake."

• • •

At 9:00 p.m. on Tuesday, Cosh and Mandrake entered the Mermaid Beach Hotel through separate doors. Tommy waited outside in the getaway car with his Nikon binoculars. Birdbrain rode on Mandrake's shoulder.

"Ooh!" said Teri at the front desk. "Pretty birdie! Can you talk? Polly want a cracker?"

"No, thanks, Teri, just a room."

"Oh, now, I wish I could, but ..."

While Teri explained the hotel's policy—service

animals, yes, like seeing-eye dogs, but sorry, no cats or birds or reptiles, even if they were support animals—Cosh let himself into an upstairs service closet. A text from Tommy had confirmed that Roger Crowell was in his room, apparently alone. Now Cosh arranged props: room-service cart, white apron and towels, ice bucket, linen napkin, and cutlery. The plastic cable ties stayed in his pocket; he pressed the stick-on walrus mustache under his nose.

The heist went without a hitch. Mandrake bade Teri a regretful goodnight and nodded to Tommy on his way to the back stairs. Wheeling his cart down the hall, Cosh double-checked his mustache. Roger Crowell looked surprised to hear his doorbell ring, but he took off the chain for this thoughtful welcome from the management. When he fished in his pocket for a tip, Mandrake jumped him from behind, stuffed the napkin into his mouth, and held the steak knife to his throat while Cosh cable-tied his wrists. Together they hefted him onto the bed. Cosh secured Crowell's flailing ankles; Mandrake removed the diamonds from the safe. Birdbrain watched from the top of the TV.

• • •

Tommy had two rules: never drive the same car twice, and never hurry except in emergencies. Until now they'd kept him and his partners off the police radar.

Tonight, red-and-blue lights flashed them to a stop as they approached the Mullet Harbor Bridge.

"Exit the vehicle, please." They did: Tommy and Cosh from the front seats, Mandrake from the back. Birdbrain flapped onto the roof with a threatening squawk.

IDs were checked, pockets emptied. The older cop frowned at Mandrake: "What happened to your hand?"

"Parrot bite. He's a good bird, but sometimes—"

"Right. All those bandages? Let's see what's under there."

He reached for Mandrake. *Whammo!*

Shouting obscenities, hopping, hunching, the cop sucked his shredded fingers.

His partner looked pale. "I'm gonna ask you to confine that bird, sir, or I'll have to charge you with assaulting a police officer."

"I'm so sorry."

"With a deadly weapon!" hollered the bleeding cop.

"He's a support animal. Just doing his job." Mandrake offered Birdbrain a padded wrist. "Sorry, I don't have a cage."

"Into the car then."

The cops cleaned wounds and conferred. So what've we got? Two locals drinking at one of the harbor bars, joined by a stranger with a parrot. No red flags in the database; no links to the Mermaid Beach Hotel or Roger Crowell. Five more vehicles waiting at the checkpoint. "Okay, gentlemen. Get outta here."

Tommy drove down Harbor Boulevard at his customary stately pace. Cosh sang under his breath: *Ya-ta tee-ta!* They wouldn't unwrap the bandages till they got home, because, face it, you never knew with cops.

"Drinks on me." Mandrake raised his lumpy white fist, literally worth its weight in diamonds, and Birdbrain with it.

"Nice work, gentlemen," said Cosh.

The parrot squawked.

Tommy squawked back. "Pretty birdie!"

I'd never heard of flash fiction until last year, and then naturally I had to try it. I'm much more comfortable with novels and novellas, so the question was, What kind of story speaks clearly enough for itself to fit into this nutshell? Spending time in Florida I've met quite a few Elmore Leonard–Carl Hiaasen characters; and living on Telegraph Hill in San Francisco, I've met quite a few parrots. They felt like an obvious match.

—CJ Verburg

PLEASE SEE ME

Deborah Lacy

This paper discusses the problem of increasing crime in the United States in the 1970s, its relationship to society in general and to the victims of a particular deviant act—residential burglary.

The thesis is that crime is not only an individual act but also a social phenomenon. The question that is posed is, "Who takes responsibility for what?" The emphasis is a sociological one.

From everyone else's perspective I went back to my sociology class too soon after Gary was murdered.

Granted, these are the same people who can't understand why I went back to finish my college degree in my thirties anyway. But perhaps they are right this time. I'm weepy, exhausted and irritable. It's a charming combination.

Despite all of this, I returned to class. I had to. No one

else could understand. I had only one more term paper to graduate, and I threw myself into the class to help process the invasion of our home. I wrote my final paper on the growing problem of residential burglary, using interviews with the other victims in my neighborhood as a case study. The topic of the paper is supposed to be the impact of addiction on the human psyche.

This may have been another mistake.

I clutch the graded typewritten pages tightly as I walk across the campus, my macramé purse swinging back and forth. The papers were returned to us in class today. The professor had written the words *Please see me* in red ink on the front page. I've waited until the end of office hours in hopes that no other students will be there to compete for his time.

I know I don't have to go. But even though I'm not ready to talk, I force myself forward because the sooner I meet with him, the sooner it will be over. It's another excruciatingly sunny California day. How can it be sunny when everything is so wrong?

Evidence shows a substantial increase in crime in the United States since 1970. According to the FBI Uniform Crime Report of 1975, serious crimes have increased 39% since 1970. At the same time, population—often correlated to increased crime rates—rose only 5%. This suggests the need to re-examine previous social thinking and treating of crime and its consequences.

As I walk, I can't stop thinking about that night. Someone invaded our home. Our safe little refuge. Stealing what didn't belong to him while *The Rockford Files* ran on the TV, a late dinner of cheese fondue and crusty bread sat ready to be eaten on the table, and our five-year-old daughter put on her Minnie Mouse pj's, just a hallway away. A glimpse of a face that I thought I recognized but couldn't believe. My husband's dead body on the floor. The phone call to the police. Telling my precious daughter that her father had gone away forever.

Refusing to spend another night in that house, I took myself, my daughter, and the cat to my mom's to stay until I can figure out where else we can live. We have a roof over our heads now but no privacy because my mom loves to hover and smother.

While I was writing my now graded paper, I tried to remember what I could about the burglary—faithfully, factually. I tried to type on my mom's IBM Selectric typewriter without emotion.

It was the hardest thing that I had ever done.

Burglary is the prototype of residential crime. It is a crime against property by one stranger to another stranger. Only one burglar in a hundred will knowingly invade occupied premises; even those who do can generally be assumed to have no intention of committing harm.

If my therapist and my mom had their way, I would be

sitting somewhere on a couch with a wet washcloth over my eyes, taking a mild sedative and sleeping ten to fifteen hours a day. But they didn't see the burglar, and I'm pretty sure I did. And it wasn't a stranger.

The thief stole handbags and wallets from every house in our small development, leaving the less desirable contents strewn about our driveways. Then, quickly and quietly, he moved on to the next house.

Burglaries like this have happened to more than thirty houses in our small city in the past six months. As far as the police know, the thief hasn't killed anyone except Gary and no one has been injured. No fingerprints were left and no other evidence of any kind has been found. The cash was gone, of course, and the abandoned credit cards, driver licenses, and empty wallets were completely fingerprint free.

"The thief is unusual," a policeman said about the crimes. He was quoted in the newspaper before the night my husband was killed. "He's smart and agile, but the dollar amounts are small. It's almost as if he's doing this for fun."

I couldn't carry my purse after that night. I threw it away even though it was perfectly good. I specifically asked mom not to fish it out of the garbage, something she totally would do under normal circumstances.

Walking on the concrete sidewalk through campus, the heels of my shoes make slapping sounds with every step. I pass palm trees and dark green juniper bushes covered with spiderwebs. Signs hang on all of the light posts, offering chemistry tutoring, used furniture, and rides home for Thanksgiving. I reach the large stucco building, five stories high, that houses the professor's office and look up. The word sociology is spelled out in big metal letters above the double doors. One office has the shades open, and only one.

I approach one of the big glass doors and open it. Two twenty-something girls with feathered hair like Farrah Fawcett's pass me in the hallway. The names of people who donated money for the building are painted in big gold letters on the walls. It looks awful. If I ever have enough money to donate for a college building, I'm going to ask that my name be left off the wall.

I start climbing the first of three flights of stairs to his office. I've climbed these stairs before, but this time it feels so much different. My steps echo in the empty stairwell.

I think about how our old neighbors come daily to Mom's house with casseroles and cookies, hoping to exchange them for tidbits of gossip about our family that can be used as cul-de-sac currency. I've seen the gossip game being played in our six years in the neighborhood—and have even played it myself—often enough to know that I don't want to be its subject. I decided it would be much easier to listen to the neighbors talk than rehash that night myself, so I began asking them question after question about the burglaries at their own homes:

1. Tell me about the burglary.
2. What did it feel like to have your home invaded?
3. What do you imagine the offender is like?
4. Do you think the burglar will be caught?
5. Under what conditions can you imagine yourself stealing?
6. Do you have friends who take things from their place of work?

Not wanting people to influence other interview subject's answers, I interviewed each neighbor individually. Mom didn't want me to be alone with anyone, so she sat in. If she disapproved of the questions, she didn't say so. She jotted down a few notes here and there as people answered, but she hasn't shared them with me. The answers were as different as our neighbors' houses.

Sabrina, who had been over every single day that week bringing another culinary horror, was the first to be interviewed. "Our back door was unlocked," she said quietly when I asked her to talk about her burglary. "I had been to the grocery store that evening, so I only had twenty dollars in my purse. I'm embarrassed that we lost so little."

"I keep forgetting to lock the doors until we go to bed," Elena said. "It's like if I don't think about it, it never happened."

"I thought our neighborhood was too nice for robbers,"

Janet told me. As if keeping your lawn mowed created an invisible line that kept burglars out.

Patricia fidgeted nervously. "We couldn't find my driver's license in the driveway, so I'm driving without a license until I can get to the DMV."

It was all so trivial.

Everyone I interviewed pictured a different type of person committing the crime, making odd assumptions to make themselves feel safe. But how could they really know anything about this stranger when we don't truly know anyone but ourselves? All but one agreed that the thief must be poor and desperate to take such risks for so little money, and that he, or she, was probably an addict, although Elena thought that an addict might not be so agile.

Sabrina's husband was convinced the culprit was an off-duty cop moonlighting. "Who else would know how to get in and out so quickly without leaving evidence?" Of course, Sabrina's husband also thought it was okay to take things from work. "Everybody does it, so it's not really stealing."

Everyone, even Sabrina's husband, said they couldn't imagine a case where they would commit a crime. Perhaps they weren't being honest with themselves.

I don't want to be winded when I reach the professor's office, so when I reach the second flight of stairs a little out of breath, I slow down my pace.

All of the subjects accepted residential burglary as part of today's societal structure. One indicator of this was that they all carried insurance against burglary. This is a voluntary option of homeowners' policies. All expressed relief at having been "ripped off" for cash as opposed to goods, which they thought harder to replace. Three-fourths of the subjects felt there was a high probability that they would be burglarized again in their lifetime. All reported the burglaries to the police, but their motivation seemed to be insurance, not retribution or protection.

I never realized until this happened how much we forget to protect ourselves. During these interviews my neighbors, our friends, focused on what they lost during the burglary. Once they got talking, they completely forgot about Gary's murder. Until the end of the interview when they'd run out of things to say. I'd see a look cross their face when they realized that I'd lost more than some grocery money. Then the conversations would deteriorate and I found it hard to concentrate.

The questions I've been asking and the lack of gossip haven't stopped my neighbors from coming or stopped my well-meaning mom from letting them in her house.

Every day, Sabrina says, "My God. I feel so violated." But what she really means is, "Thank God, it wasn't my husband."

Others routinely say, "I understand just how you feel, Mary Beth."

But they can't begin to understand when I can barely comprehend it myself.

I will admit that more than once I've wanted to throw one of Sabrina's inedible lime Jell-O mold salads into that smug little face of hers, but I never have.

I keep thanking her and the other nosy neighbors for stopping by, not knowing what else to do. I gently guide them to the door, saying, "We'll be back in the house really soon." Knowing full well that I will never take my daughter into that house or that neighborhood again.

Not one person thinks the burglar will be caught.

The police say my husband surprised the thief. The burglar picked up the Louisville Slugger, signed by Reggie Jackson, to defend himself and wound up killing my husband with it.

My God, Gary loved that bat.

Our future has been stolen. And now I have to make a new one.

I reach the third flight of stairs. I'm almost to the professor's office. What will I say to him? What will he say to me? Did I really see what I thought I saw?

That night, when I started tell the police what I thought I saw, they patted my hand and told me not to worry.

Not to worry.

My child is fatherless and they told me not to worry.

Josie cries at lot, because she doesn't understand. Mom has promised to take her to Disneyland, but I am pretty sure that we don't have the money until I sell the house. I am not ready to sell just yet.

Last night I took Josie to Kmart to buy more clothes and pj's so I won't have to go back to the house. I threw away the bags before Mom could see. She'd think it was a waste of money.

Crime, its prevention, and its consequences have become a national concern. "All members of society are potential victims of a criminal attack of some kind." The FBI UCR for 1975 statistics on victims' risks suggests that "on the average, the likelihood of a serious personal attack for an American in a given year is about 1 in 550." An interesting point on these figures is that they are derived from police reports. Victimization is not always reported. Often a criminal is arrested for one crime and is responsible for others that may never be documented.

How does someone decide that it's okay to go from home to home to take hard-earned money from good people watching TV? How does someone decide to hit another human being with a beloved baseball bat?

I reach the professor's office door and knock. I'm relieved that there is no one else in the hallway.

"Please, come in," the professor says.

I open the door and walk in. He's the only one in his office. The wooden shelves are filled with books that look well read. There are coffee-stained papers on his desk and the room reeks of freshly smoked cigarettes. I wish the window were open so that I wouldn't have to smell the smoke. I don't want to ask him to open the windows.

"Please shut the door, Mrs. Wells, and have a seat." He looks a little like Mr. Rogers sitting there clean shaven in his neat brown sweater. His brow is furrowed.

I do as he says, setting the paper on his desk and my purse on my lap in case I need to make a quick getaway.

"My mother knows I'm here."

"Okay," he says, nodding. He leans forward in his chair, waiting for me to start the discussion.

I stare back at him without blinking.

Maybe he doesn't know where to begin. I'm not sure that I do either. He picks up a pen from his desk and puts it back down.

We look at one another in silence, as we did that night in my house. I don't want to sit there all day staring at him. I want this to be over.

"I don't understand," I say, leaving him room to deny everything, as I had planned. But then I shut the door to denial. I can't help myself . "Why would you rob houses? Taking money from hard-working people. Why risk jail? Are you a drug addict? Did I really see you that night?"

His face shows no expression at the charges that I have leveled at him. "Listing possible answers to your question increases the chances that I will just pick one, and you'll never know the truth. Best to ask me directly why I do it."

"I didn't come here to play games."

"Didn't you? Isn't that why you wrote the paper?"

"Why do you do it? Why do you steal?"

"That is a better question. It started when a friend of mine stole a watch from another friend. It was a family heirloom, and I suspected he stole it, so I stole it back. I was surprised to learn that I make an excellent thief, although with my knowledge of crime, I suppose it isn't so surprising. I restored the watch to one friend, while keeping the other one out of jail."

"But you keep doing it."

He leans back in his chair. "I'm studying people. In their homes. In their handbags. I take advantage of their habits. Their foibles. I don't take much and I give the money to charity."

"That's no excuse."

"I suppose not. Getting away with a crime is intoxicating in its own way. If I'd known it was your house, I never would have gone to that neighborhood. I learned things that night that I didn't want to learn. Saw things that after tonight I will never speak of again." He shudders.

I draw in a breath, "What things?"

"Through the window, I saw your husband lift up your daughter's pajama bottoms and ..."

I freeze.

"I can't hear this." Don't want to hear it.

I didn't imagine it. I'd walked in on him in our daughter's bedroom and saw the same thing. Josie looked like she was bracing herself for something but her face said she wasn't surprised. My intuition screamed that this wasn't the first time.

I should have protected her.

"It's unforgiveable." The professor's head droops and he lifts his hand to his forehead, hiding his eyes. That night I called to my husband. "Can I please talk to you in the hallway, Gary?"

"I think Josie wet the bed," he said with that sheepish grin that made me fall in love with him all those year ago when he hit on me at a baseball game.

I shut the door to the bedroom and led Gary down the hall, and into the living room.

"I was changing her pj's. Don't worry. I'll wash the sheets."

He actually expected me to believe this. That's when I grabbed the Louisville slugger and hit him over the head. On the way down to the floor, his head hit the stone fireplace. I could tell from his eyes that he was dead. He would never touch Josie again.

I looked up from Gary's dead body and saw the professor through the doorway, standing in my kitchen all dressed in black.

"I came in the house to stop him," the professor says to me now. "You beat me to it. I might have done the same thing with that bat, but you beat me to it."

I wring my hands. "I see his head hitting the fireplace every night when I close my eyes. Again, and again, and again."

"Then that is your punishment. Living with the guilt. And that may be the worst punishment of all. But let me be perfectly clear. I will be watching you, Mrs. Wells. If you ever kill another human being, I will turn you in to the police for this crime, no matter what your reason and no matter how it impacts me."

I put my face in my hands but see nothing but Gary in the darkness. I am startled by the feeling of the professor's hand on my back. I lift my head up.

"Now go raise your daughter, and try to heal."

I'm not sure it's possible for me to heal, but for my daughter's sake, I will try.

The question of responsibility has been one of controversy over the years. Victimology is not a new field. The possible relationship between victim and criminal was mentioned by Lombroso. However, little attention was given to this perspective until Hans von Hentig hypothesized that "in a sense, the victim shapes and molds the criminal and his crime and the relationship between the perpetrator and victim may be much more complex than our criminal law."

When I was a kid, a thief snuck into our home and stole my mom's purse and my dad's wallet—while we were all in the house. My parents were still up, so the backdoor was unlocked. Every house in the neighborhood was hit.

My mom was taking sociology classes back then and wrote about the disturbing incident in a term paper. Last Thanksgiving, Mom and I were going through old files and discovered her paper. She stuck it in my backpack and said, "This might be handy for one of your stories." She was right.

—Deborah Lacy

WHOSE FAULT?

Mariah Klein

Charles found the letter shoved under his apartment door when he returned home from the library. He stood in the doorway, holding the envelope up in the afternoon sunlight. A thrill of anticipation shuddered through him. Finally, something out of the ordinary had happened.

He stepped into his studio apartment clutching the white paper offering like a golden ticket. His eyes watered and blinked, adjusting to the dimness. The boredom and frustration of his day at the library were forgotten. His eyes greedily drank in the envelope. Who could the letter be from? What news would it bring?

Canceled stamp on the top right. The letter had been through the post before being slipped under his door. The picture on the stamp was of Paul Newman, the actor. A classic. Charles approved.

His long white fingers flipped the envelope from back to front. No return address. His own address handwritten on the front in a flowing blue script. Personal mail was a rarity in his life. Charles savored the moment.

But wait. Charles looked more closely at the address. Something was wrong. *7170*. He lived at *7710*. The letter had been misaddressed.

He studied the script. The name. *Charles Sutter.* His heart leaped to his throat. His last name was Somers.

The truth hit Charles like a blinding spotlight, harsh and unavoidable. Charles Sutter, at *7170* Hampton Ave.

The letter was not for him.

It must have been delivered in error to someone in his building, and that neighbor, confused by the similar names, had compounded the error by leaving it at his door.

A wave of disappointment washed over him. Then he shook his head. No sense in dwelling on the letdown. He held another man's letter in his hand. For all he knew, this letter was important. His plans for a John Wayne movie marathon forgotten, Charles snatched up his keys and left the apartment.

• • •

Charles Sutter, the intended recipient of the letter now clutched in Charles Somers's hand, must be a rich man. At this end of Hampton Street, the mansions remained intact, not divided into multiple flats like the building Charles called home several blocks away. The estate at *7170* even had a name, The Manor, grandly spelled out in gold letters on the mailbox. Charles hesitated, his hand on the mailbox latch. Sure, he could drop the letter in the box. But maybe Mr. Sutter had already collected his mail for the day. Maybe he wouldn't come back to the mailbox until tomorrow.

Charles looked again at the flowery script decorating the front of the envelope. He looked into Paul Newman's eyes. Newman's baby blues stared back, his gaze obscured by the smudged ink of the postmark. Charles let go of the mailbox latch. He turned and walked up the slate path that led to the front door of The Manor.

The doorbell pealed, long and mournful. Charles licked dry lips and wiped sweaty palms on his slacks. *This letter is for you,* he rehearsed in his mind. *It came to me by accident.* But no one answered the bell. Time for another decision.

There was always the mailbox. Or slipping the letter under the door, as some helpful but mistaken soul had done back at his own apartment. Neither idea appealed to him. Mr. Sutter would never know of his good deed. He would never know how close he came to not receiving the letter at all.

Would it hurt to take a look around the grounds? Maybe Mr. Sutter was enjoying the afternoon in his backyard. How grateful he'd be to have his important letter hand-delivered to him. Charles Sutter, his name so similar to Charles's own, had to be a kindred spirit. Surely, he'd see something in Charles the library staff could not. Charles stepped off the front porch and made his way around the house.

A peek into the first window he came to confirmed that Charles Sutter was not in the kitchen. A peek in the second window confirmed something worse. Charles stood frozen, the letter clutched in his hand, eyes wide and mouth open. Charles Sutter was indeed home. And he was almost certainly dead.

• • •

The fire engine arrived first, sirens wailing. An ambulance followed close behind. How had they arrived so fast? How had they known? Charles stumbled back, away from the window. His stomach churned. There had been so much blood. How could a body have so much blood?

The emergency crews paid him little attention. A man in street clothes opened the front door with a key, then stepped aside as an army of responders trooped inside. Charles remained in the yard outside the window, unsure of what to do next. The scene unfolded like a drama on a movie screen. He couldn't bring himself to look away.

The man who had used the key shot a suspicious glance at Charles. He was wearing slacks and a polo shirt in a turquoise shade. Something about the man scared Charles. He retreated into his usual state of defense. He stared at the grass at his feet and pretended to be invisible.

Footsteps approached. Charles looked up. Polo Man, with someone else. This new man was tall, maybe six-foot-four. His dark hair flowed Clark Kent–style in a perfect wave across the top of his head. Broad shoulders filled out a long tan trench coat. His eyes were as blue as the summer sky. Paul Newman eyes. Charles could almost hear the action-movie theme music playing as the man stood there studying him. Clearly, this was the hero. So, what did that make Charles?

"Who are you?" The deep voice was perfect, Charles thought. Just a hint of gravel to let you know this guy didn't mess around. But a hero would know the other good guys when he saw them. Wouldn't he?

"A neighbor." His own voice cracked at just the wrong moment. "I live down the street."

He gestured in the vague direction of his home. The hero didn't even look. Gum shifted from one corner of the square jaw to the other.

"I'm Detective Stark." Crack, pop of gum against teeth. "Name and address?"

Stark. Perfect movie hero name. His first name was probably something like Ryder or Chance. Charles gulped, then managed to give out his own name and address, conscious the whole time of how unherolike any of it sounded. The detective scribbled it all down in a little notebook.

"What's he doing here?" Polo Man's nose had that distinctive wrinkle, a corner of his mouth slightly raised. A look of disdain. Charles knew that look well. "What're you doing in my father's yard?"

Detective Stark raised one flawless eyebrow. Charles

was impressed but not surprised. Action heroes were capable of perfect timing.

"I came over ..." Charles began.

Just then the front door opened, and the men's attention shifted there. The dead man was carried out on a stretcher, covered head to toe by a white sheet. Polo Man hurried to his father's side. Charles let out a breath. The man hadn't trusted him. Distrust made Charles more nervous than usual.

The detective still watched him. Still waited for an explanation of his presence.

"I had something of his," Charles said. "Wanted to return it. No answer at the door so I—"

"Stark." One of the policemen called out to the detective.

"Wait here."

Stark turned on his heel and stalked away. Charles remained, mouth still open, words of explanation still hovering on his lips. But Stark was off, conferring, barking orders. Charles hadn't mentioned the letter. And it looked like his scene in the movie was over.

• • •

Charles shifted his weight from one foot to the other. He hadn't been told he could leave. The detective kept glaring over at him. Pointing at him. Better stay put.

The letter remained clutched in his sweaty hand. Every nerve in his body felt alive. His part in this movie was *not* over. A man had been murdered. The letter held evidence. He was sure of it. What should he do now?

He couldn't open the letter. Definitely not. That was a federal offense, to open someone else's mail. But still. The letter had come to him. The name and address were so similar. He could be forgiven if he'd opened the letter before realizing it wasn't for him. Anyone would believe it was an honest mistake. Would Stark?

His fingers flipped the envelope over and over. He could say he'd opened the letter by accident, back at his house. Stark was yards away. If Charles was careful, he could open the letter, read it quickly, and find out if it contained important information.

And if it did? Charles would insist that the detective hear his story and he'd hand over the letter. He imagined the respect and admiration in the detective's cinematic blue eyes. *Thank you, sir,* Stark would say, shaking his hand in a real man handshake. *You've been a great help today.*

He closed his eyes. The detective's voice in his mind changed tenor, and he heard Mr. Montague at the library. *Don't waste my time.* Charles trembled and shrank. Montague's voice continued. *Worthless freak.*

Tears stung his eyes. He raked them away with a savage hand. The moment to act slipped through the fingers of his life like so much sand. He clenched a fist. Now or never. Was the letter meaningless? Or did it hold the key? One way to find out. He turned slightly, his back towards Detective Stark.

Charles's fingers tore open the letter.

• • •

Blue, flowing words tumbled and danced over the page like dolphins in a Caribbean sea. Charles struggled to decipher the elaborate script. His pulse pounded in his ears and his hand shook. He'd opened a letter intended for someone else. Could he go to jail for this? Well, it was done now. No undoing the past. Charles spread the letter flat, forced his eyes to focus through the fog of excitement and dread, and began to read.

Dear Charles, he read silently, his lips forming each word.

> *I'll make this quick. I never intended to share this information with you. But I have very little time left, and I don't want to die with this secret on my conscience. You have always believed, despite our marital difficulties, that Bobby was your son. I allowed you to believe that because the alternative was too humiliating to bear. But thirty years have passed, we have both moved on, and it doesn't seem to matter any longer.*
>
> *Bobby is not your son. He is the child of my lover, William Gephardt, who died three years ago. I told Bobby this morning. I am telling you now in this letter.*
>
> *Please do not contact me. I just wanted you to know.*

The letter was signed *Violet Sutter,* with no closing

salutation. Perhaps there was nothing that she felt would be appropriate to the occasion. Charles lowered the letter and let out a breath. His mind raced with possibilities.

Polo Man with the turquoise shirt and the suspicious expression. The son of a rich man. A dead rich man. Who had never received the letter. If this were a movie—Charles closed his eyes. If this were a movie, Bobby would have killed his father to keep him from finding out that Bobby was not really his son. Would he do that in real life?

Charles opened his eyes. He took in the large, immaculate home, the exquisite landscaping. The three-car garage. To protect a substantial inheritance, yes, a man might commit murder for that. And Detective Stark had no idea of Bobby's motive.

A vision rose in Charles's mind. The action hero, confronting and defeating the villain. An admiring woman throwing her arms around him, her long blond locks blowing in the wind as they kissed. A woman who looked very much like Jacki, the research librarian at work.

Charles stuffed the letter back into the envelope. Stark was not the hero of this movie. Charles was the hero. And he had hero's work to do. It was time to meet his destiny.

• • •

Meeting his destiny was not as simple as it had seemed. Charles was barred at the front door by a stern-looking policeman. He was told to wait until the detective became available. Charles bit his lip, feeling anxious. Polo Man—Bobby Sutter—was in there right now. Possibly destroying key evidence. Leading the detective off the trail. Charles had to act. What would Paul Newman do?

Charles hurried around the back of the house. Men tromped about everywhere, scouring the yard, walking in and out of the house. They wore plastic bags over their shoes and gloves over their hands.

Moving up to a bay window on the first floor, Charles strained his neck for a glimpse inside. He thought he saw Detective Stark through the window, but then a large figure loomed before him, blocking his view.

"What do you want?" The officer folded his arms over his massive chest. Charles gulped, then gathered all his courage. He drew himself up to his full five-foot-five and raised his voice.

"I must see the detective in charge," he said loudly. "Immediately. I have evidence that relates to this case."

"Hang on." The officer's growly voice was not encouraging. But at least he was mumbling into a walkie-talkie now.

In a minute, the back door opened, and Stark appeared, followed by Polo Man. Charles swallowed hard. His sweaty hands clutched the envelope even tighter. Polo Man was Bobby, the son of the dead man. Polo Man was the murderer.

Charles stepped closer to Stark's comforting bulk. This was his big scene. The scene where he, Charles Somers, exposed the murderer, right to his face. This would take all his courage. He could not screw this up.

"What is it?" Stark barked. Charles jumped.

"This," he blurted out. He stretched out his hand. "This letter is evidence of motive. I know who killed Charles Sutter. It was his son. You."

Charles's arm swung around, pointing. Accusing. Polo Man's face turned purple. He lunged at Charles.

"You little bastard! How dare you accuse me?" His hand snatched at the envelope but missed. "How dare you say I killed my own father? I'll bury you."

Charles ran. It wasn't how the scene had played out in his mind, but the flight instinct took over and he lost all conscious thought. His feet propelled him across the patio and through the French doors, past a surprised technician kneeling on the floor.

The precious envelope was now a ball crushed in his hands, but at least it was safe from the murderer's grasp. Charles skidded on the shiny wood floors, barely conscious of the shouting and pounding feet behind him. His only thought was to protect the letter. Protect the evidence of Polo's guilt.

Charles swung around a corner into the room where the body had lain on the floor. The body was gone, but blood remained, pooled and spattered. He knew he'd made a mistake coming in here. A big mistake. But Polo Man was right behind him. He had to think. If only he could stop and think.

The floor had become as slick as ice. He took one more step and suddenly he was airborne. His feet flew up into the air, almost kicking his face.

For a moment, time slowed. He could see himself as if from across the room, feet swung out in front of him, face toward the ceiling, lying almost horizontal in midair. Then gravity kicked in, the hard floor met his back, and his head snapped against the wood floorboards. Stars danced in his eyes and everything went silent.

Sound returned quickly as people swarmed around him. Footsteps landed all around him, men shouted. Polo Man, cursing, grabbed at him, trying to pry the letter from his hands. Charles flipped over onto his stomach, hiding the letter under his body where Polo Man couldn't reach it.

Detective Stark pushed Polo Man aside, seized Charles by the shoulders, and yanked him to his feet. Charles's head spun and ached. He stumbled and tried to regain balance.

"What in God's name do you think you're doing?" Stark shouted, his face right up in Charles's face. Tiny specks of spit landed on Charles's cheeks. He blinked.

"He's not Mr. Sutter's son," Charles announced. He pointed at Polo Man, restrained behind the giant, gruff police officer. "He killed Sutter before his father could find out and disinherit him."

"You're crazy!" Polo Man yelled.

"He's the murderer," Charles declared, his voice stronger now. "That's your murderer. Bobby Sutter!"

Silence fell over the group. Polo Man stood slack-jawed. The police officers exchanged glances. Detective Stark sighed heavily and ran his hand through his black curls.

Charles looked from one face to another. This was his big moment. The dénouement. Why was there no triumphant music? Why wasn't Stark arresting Polo Man? What had gone wrong?

"You idiot!" Polo Man burst out.

"Quiet," Stark commanded. He put out a hand toward Charles. "Give me that paper," he said in a voice that was low and stern and would not accept no for an answer. "Now."

Charles obeyed the order. His legs trembled while the detective read. Then Stark folded the letter and slipped it into his pocket.

"There's just one problem with your theory," he said to Charles.

"Just one?" Polo Man shrieked. Stark didn't even look at him.

"This man is not Bobby Sutter," Stark said in an unexpectedly gentle voice. "His name is Gerald Sutter. He's Mr. Sutter's oldest son. The younger son, Bobby, is in the military. He's stationed in Germany. Neither of them killed Mr. Sutter."

Charles felt as if his heart, filled with helium like a carnival balloon, had been pricked with a pin. He deflated before Stark's certainty. His theory lay in pieces shattered on the floor. His dignity had expired long ago, even before the disastrous midair flight in front of half a dozen police officers. There was nothing left for him. The movie was a comedy, not a thriller, and he was the butt of the joke. The only question that remained was how quickly he could retreat to the dark confines of his apartment to lick his wounds in private.

"Hey, boss?" The technician who had been kneeling when Charles barreled into the house stepped toward Stark. "Can I see something?"

Stark nodded. Charles watched as the young woman came forward. She knelt again on the floor where Charles had slipped and fallen. Using a small, pointed tool, she carefully scraped the floor and deposited the contents into a plastic bag. She did this with several other tools, and more evidence, invisible to Charles's eyes, went into bags. Everyone watched in silence, even Polo Man. Finally, the technician stood up.

"I'll need to test this to be sure," she said, addressing Stark. "But I'm ninety percent certain this is the same oily substance we found at the Maple Street murder."

Charles had no idea what this meant. Polo Man, too, was looking from face to face in confusion. An undercurrent of excitement ran through the rest of the officers present. Even Stark flashed a tight smile.

"Get that to the lab ASAP," he said. "If we can make a connection with the other crime scene—"

"Then we've got him." The tech could barely restrain her excitement. "This time, we've got him."

"We don't have him yet," Stark cautioned. "But this could be the last link we need. Take it down to the lab."

The technician hurried away. Polo Man shook off the officer's restraining hands and smoothed his hair. He glared at Charles but made no move to approach him. Charles avoided direct eye contact but kept Polo Man in his sights.

Stark came over to Charles and put a heavy hand on his shoulder. "I'm keeping the letter," he said quietly. "Go home now."

Charles nodded hard, then winced at the pain at the back of his head. He knew he owed Polo Man an apology, but he couldn't bring himself to speak. The best he could do was scurry past the man, head down. He apologized in his mind and prayed it was enough.

• • •

Back at his apartment, Charles collapsed onto his lumpy sofa. What an adventure. And it had all started because a piece of mail had gotten lost. Someone had found it and mistakenly delivered it to him. Without him, would the oil on the floor have been discovered? Was it possible he, Charles Somers, had cracked the case?

A slow smile spread across his face. He didn't have to be at work until ten tomorrow. His hand reached for the remote. There was still time for a movie marathon. And tomorrow, when he recounted the story to Jacki at the library, he knew who would play the starring role.

"Whose Fault?" was inspired by the notion of cascading events, one leading to another, and the unpredictability of what could happen. I also enjoyed playing with the idea of how a person's inner conception of themselves might differ from their outer appearance, and how everyone deserves to be the hero of their own story.

—Mariah Klein

SPED-ING TOWARD SELF-DESTRUCTION

David Hagerty

It's a peculiar ideal that work should be edifying and fulfilling. Teaching special education presents me daily reminders of this paradox—such as the one I face now, a rebellious student named Aaron who stands atop his chair shouting invectives like Captain Ahab in pursuit of the ghostly white whale.

"Sit," I reply.

I use the same tone I do with my dogs, a calm command that defies opposition, but my spaniels cooperate more than my teenagers, for whom the monosyllable proves too much to process. You'd think such a simple word—two consonants surrounding a short vowel—would be easy to interpret. We've practiced The Rules daily, and a banner hangs by the door to reiterate them (*Sit tight! Do your best! Think before you act!*); yet some of these puppies can't pass basic obedience training.

"SIT!" I repeat.

Aaron remains aloft, yelling at Marco for the umpteenth time to give him back his "beastly" pencil, even though five of them lay scattered on the floor around him. They're both skinny boys, the horrormones of adolescence giving them acne and uncontrollable hard-ons but withholding on muscles; yet Marco wears the loose clothes and shaggy hair of a skater while Aaron is bound in the skinny jeans and spiked fauxhawk of a punk, which makes them natural enemies.

They've chafed plenty of times before without violence, but that doesn't mean I'm willing to step between them. I may be twice their age and weight, but I've also got twice their experience with playground brawls, so I know not to leap into scrums like a hockey official.

Instead I triangulate them and promise Aaron "free time" (to wander the halls and disturb other classes) if he'll just "SIT" for another fifteen minutes (the longest he can concentrate, according to our school psych, although I've yet to see him make it that long). From his perch, Aaron looks down at us like a fighter over his insensate foe.

There's no point in disciplining him. My principal, Mr. Sanitone, would rather I act like a referee in pro wrestling, counting to ten and a hundred and a thousand as barbarians commit mayhem on each other. Once, when I asked him to suspend a student for keying my car with the word *SPED*, he claimed there were no inappropriate students, only teachers who didn't know how to manage them correctly. Which leaves me to redirect Aaron's impulses unassisted.

"Follow the rules," I say, but more calmly, "and I'll give you my pencil."

I point to the banner of mottos that governs our classroom (as though a clever saying can rewire a teenager's disconnected brain). For a moment he stares at it uncomprehendingly, yet my change in tone signals a concession of sorts, which stretches Aaron's features into a snarl. He jumps to the floor, shaking our double-wide portable so that the flimsy walls exhale, and sits backward in his chair so he can stare down Marco who, bless him, ignores the taunt.

With all the pound puppies back in their cages, I return to my instructor's manual and resume the lesson. "Can anyone tell me where we use fractions?" I say.

The classroom retains its morning chill, the ticking bomb of a radiator not yet armed, so the kids respond slowly. Finally, Nate says, "Math class." To show his understanding, he snaps a crayon in two and holds it up for my examination. He claims his mom cannot afford another writing implement, despite his array of designer jeans and polos. His whirl of blond hair, pale skin, and light eyes would be pixie-ish if not for his malevolent grin. The school's muckety-mucks are still debating his diagnosis, although I've settled on a hybrid of ADD, ODD, OCD, and PDD. (Every disorder is reducible to its initials; if only fractions simplified so readily.)

"Besides school," I say.

"Weighing drugs," Nate says.

"You mean in a pharmacy," I say. "That's true." Current pedagogy discourages correcting students except on the most egregious errors. So when Nate gives an off-color answer, I honor his reply while suggesting a more appropriate one. "Anywhere else?"

I scan the other faces, but Tiara slumps in her pillow posture, collapsing in upon herself, while Ben faces the wall, rigid and fixed. This doesn't mean they're off task, according to our psych, since Ben is autistic and unable to make eye contact, while Tiara is so heavily medicated she can't attend a "static" teaching modality like a lecture; it merely means they have other ways of expressing their engagement. Such as daydreaming, or sleeping.

"Marco?" I say.

"Huh?" His hand involuntarily mashes a pencil into the desk, breaking the tip and leaving a graphite scar I'll have to bleach out. Leadless, he walks to the sharpener, taunting Aaron with his stylus, and grinds it to a point so fine it would make inmates quiver.

Though he's unaware of it, and it's forbidden for me to say, Marco is my favorite of the stray dogs and the only one I can imagine maturing to adulthood. If I can insulate him from the others. At present this seems unlikely as he tests the pencil point on his fingertip, then parades past Aaron with a sidelong glance.

"What about shopping?" I say. "Has anyone seen fractions in a store?"

"Like half off?" Marco says.

"Exactly," I say. "What does half off mean?"

Nate raises a finger of truth and says, "My mom can buy twice as much."

"Let's see why that is." I stride to the board and retrieve two dry-erase markers (both of which are simply dry but still effective as props).

"If I give one pen to Ben," I say, and extend him a dead felt-tip, only to have him fixate on it like it's dynamite. "Or Tiara." As I place the pen upright on her desk, her eyelids flutter, fighting the inevitable. "And I give one pen to Marco, then Tiara has what fraction of the total pens?"

In the silence that follows, Aaron's boot heel jackhammers off the linoleum while Tiara wheezes so slowly I worry she's deflating.

"Roll the ball down the middle and knock over as many pins as you can," my master teacher once told me. She neglected to mention that the pins sit misaligned, making it impossible to hit more than two at a time without a lucky ricochet.

"How many?" I repeat. To answer my own question would concede defeat, so I wait like a failing comic searching for the one-liner that will save the show.

"One out of two?" Matt says.

"And what fraction is that?" I say.

The students' creaks and whines continue while I wait, silent.

"*Half!*" Nate yells, and stands to emphasize the point. "Are you all mental?"

He glares at the others with disgust, but Ben is still staring at the wall, Aaron is busy gyrating, and Tiara is teetering off her chair at such an angle I worry she'll fall.

"Wake *up!*" Nate yells and pounds Tiara's desk, which finally rouses her.

"Time to go?" she says, eyelids half open.

• • •

My only reprieve comes during gym, when state law mandates that my kids mix with the mainstream ones so they can learn their place in the pack order. *Prep* is what the union calls my break, but I call it time out for teachers. Often I sit silently and count my breaths, one to ten and back again, as I learned in meditation, ignoring the heater's malevolent ticking. My guru claims the exercise calms him, but its primary effect on me is slowing time before the bell for class change.

However, today I'm looking after Tiara, who fell asleep on her feet last week during volleyball and got pelted in the head; she hasn't yet been cleared to return to physical exertion (though she's incapable of it). For once I'd rejoice if she just slept, but instead she's driftwood, floating around the classroom, rubbing against the boy's backpacks, and finally lodging herself beside my desk, where she watches me tallying grades.

"You like us?" she says. She sits half on the desktop, like a sorority girl in a pickup bar, so that her dress hikes up her pillowy thigh.

"Some days."

"No, you don't." Her tone and baby-doll expression suggest coquetry.

"I just wish you all would follow the rules."

"Why you still here if you don't like us?"

It's a fair question and one I've often asked myself without an adequate reply. I never chose special ed; it chose me. After graduating with honors in American Lit, I planned to wow students with my insights into Gatsby and Moby, but the state government was experiencing one of its budget paroxysms, and new staff were being dropped like last year's curricula. When my principal offered me a long-term sub job with special needs kids, it was SPED or unemployment—never mind that I was unqualified. Five years have passed since, but not the state's deficit, and while my status has shifted from temp to tenured, I still think of the job as transitional.

"I want to help you move on," I say to Tiara.

"I'll never leave you."

From her tone I can't tell if she's feeling flirtatious or resigned. Then she laughs once— like a hiccup—and turns away, sashaying to our one window so she can watch the boys trip each other in soccer.

Of course, she's right: there is no escape from this dog pound, no rescuer waiting to adopt these strays; the only way out for these kids is age. So we endure our incarceration together. Perhaps someday I'll get my honors English class, but until then I'm an underpaid tabulator of Aaron's misconduct.

Yet after phys ed, Aaron is oddly subdued, seated, hunched, hands buried in his lap. Perhaps Mr. Wrickrack finally took my advice and made him run all period. Like my spaniels, the hyper kids need to vent their animal aggressions. If I owned a school for ADHD boys, I'd enforce eight hours a day of aerobic exertion. Before class, I'd ride in a golf cart as my students jogged until they couldn't support their own weight; then I'd repeat the drill after lunch and dinner so that no one could claim I hadn't taught them impulse control. Until I acquire that autonomy, though, I can only follow my lesson plans.

We're reading *Lord of the Flies*, a state standard (albeit in middle school, not high), and a book I hope my runts and mutts can relate to. First, we need to get through chapter one, and since few of my kids understand that homework must be completed at home, I'm "wasting" valuable class time reading aloud to them (so says my principal).

During the long pauses I use between sentences (to let the slower ones process), I check their engagement: Nate is drawing curlicues in the margins of his text (a good multimodality learning strategy), Ben is studying the water stains on the ceiling like they're predictive, Aaron remains engrossed in his palms, Tiara is (of course) sleeping, and Marco is mouthing the words to himself. I've spent many hours after school teaching him the phonics patterns of English, which has taught me how our language torments those for whom it's not intuitive.

How many ways can one pronounce -*ough*? I've counted eleven, although my survey hasn't been exhaustive. How many spellings exist for the long *A* sound? I'm confident it's five, although even I can't explain why -*ei* is one of them other than the perversity of our German forbearers. And why -*tion* makes the same sound as *shun* is one question that forced me to answer "because" like the exasperated parent of a toddler insistently asking "why." Still, Marco persists, mumbling the words in the misguided belief (encouraged by me) that kinesthetic practice will cure his dyslexia. If all students acted so determined, our school's graduation rate would be perfect.

"Are we almost *done?*" Nate says.

"Almost," I say.

I let them finish the last page on their own. In the silence that follows, even I am distracted by the buzzing and flickering of the fluorescents overhead, which I've read can trigger migraines and eyestrain in the autistic. For the moment, Ben appears calm if disengaged, but I'm so convinced of their ill effects that I've petitioned our PTA to fund incandescents. The parents refused, saying these lightning rods were state standards, so I often extinguish them; but with only one small window offering daylight, reading is tough.

Once Ben raises his head, I begin a comprehension check.

"Describe Piggy," I say.

"He's fat like a PIG," Nate says.

"Good," I say. "Is that the only reason he's called Piggy?"

I look to Marco, but he's still masticating the words.

"He wears glasses," Ben says.

Although he won't look at me, Ben is fingering his own frames, an encouraging sign of identification.

"That's true too," I say. "But pigs don't wear glasses, do they?"

Suddenly, everyone is studious.

"So why is he called Piggy?" I repeat.

As the radiators tick out time's passage, a trickle of sweat descends my lower back. By afternoon the heaters reach full boil just as the sun warms our asphalt roof, slow roasting us all, yet somehow retaining the smell of dampness and mildew. I'd crack the door except then my ADD kids would be distracted by every cricket's chirp and squirrel's skitter.

"Is it because he's a pig?" I say.

While I await an answer, something clatters to the floor by Aaron's desk, drawing even my attention. He's too quick, though—before I can see it, he pockets the trinket, leaving me an untenable choice: do I a) punish him without knowing what he's done, b) risk a search that he'll resist (which could result in an excessive-force complaint), or c) ignore it, knowing he'll repeat the mistake within minutes? I opt for the last.

"What about Ralph?" I say. "What's he like?"

"He's a pig too," Nate says.

"Is that in the text?" I say. "Remember, our opinions have to be supported."

Aaron creaks, Tiara snores, Ben stares. I'm about to violate the social prohibition on talking to oneself when Marco looks up.

"He's a leader," Marco says. "He keeps the other guys in check."

"That's right," I say. "He's a norming force."

Before I can explain what *norming* means, there's another clatter by Aaron. This time he steps on the gadget and draws it back to him with his foot, making a metallic scrape and leaving a gash in the floor that cannot be polished away.

"What's that?" I say.

"What?" Aaron says.

"Under your shoe."

"What?"

He stops moving but keeps his combat boot firm so I can't see beneath it.

"Whatever that is, put it away," I say.

"*What?*"

Aaron uses a mask of incredulity to appeal for support. One day this act will impress his cellmate, but none of this gang are backing him now. Even Nate keeps a silent resistance to Aaron's insurrection.

"Quit goofing," Marco finally says, "I want to understand this."

And with that the rebellion is quashed.

• • •

We pass three-quarters of an hour with a film about the atrocities of the Civil War, which Nate contemptuously notes does not include disembowelments or amputations. Then we slide into our final half hour, an evaluation of the day and goal setting for the next. Even I'm counting the minutes, subdividing them in my head to make them feel shorter: thirty minutes out of six hours makes 30/ 360 or 1/12 when reduced (note to self: explain fractions tomorrow using time). During my adolescence, teachers evaluated us as a solo act, but these days everyone tries to teach kids—especially SPED kids—metacognition, so I perform it as a group activity.

"What did we learn today?" I say.

"*Nothing!*" Nate says.

I look to the others for support: Tiara still has her head down in the book though we finished with it an hour before; Ben has found a new fixation out the window; Marco is looking through his illegible notes; and Aaron is leaned back, his chair on two legs, hands pocketed, probably fingering himself.

"Anyone?" I say.

Aaron's chair squeaks as he tilts back more, engrossed in his grab bag. Whatever he's got, he doesn't want to let it go. If it'll keep him subdued like this, I should ask him to play with it every day.

"I'm starting to get fractions," Marco says.

I nod and note Aaron's lack of outbursts, a true measure of progress. To reassure me, he inclines farther still, planking his body so he can stroke his prize unrestricted.

"Anyone else?"

Aaron goes rigid as if on the verge of ecstasy, then teeters past the tipping point and crashes backward. Whatever he was holding skitters across the floor like a mouse: something white and polished but with glints of metal along the spine. Once it ricochets off the baseboard, it disappears from my view, but my intuition dictates I can't ignore it any longer.

"What *is* that?" I say.

I stand and scan, but the mystery critter hides under a desk.

"A knife," Marco says.

From where he's sitting, Marco could see it. By my brief glimpse I judge he may be right, the white body being some sort of handle.

"For real?" Nate says and squats toward it.

"Back *off!*" Aaron says.

Faster than any of us, he's off the floor and across the room to pocket the mouse blade.

"Is that a weapon?" I say.

I walk toward him but stop with two desks separating us. I don't need an administrative protocol to know better than to confront an impulsive kid with a knife. If Aaron's capable of forethought, I haven't seen it.

We've got him cornered, though, with Marco seated to his right, Nate rising to his left, and me in between, so the hyper one makes like a vole, curling in on himself as he withdraws the loaded hand from his pocket. The knife winks at me as only metal can, and his eyes pinball between the three of us as he fingers it open.

Calmly, I say, "You're violating the rules."

I don't bother pointing to our banner, since it neglects to prohibit acts of violence (which exceed an administrator's purview). Instead, against my instincts, I reach out far enough that I can almost touch Aaron's thin chest. His jittery gaze stops on me, and the rest of him freezes as well. Either he can't decide what to do or his overloaded brain has seized.

"Fol-low-the-rules," I repeat, giving each syllable the weight of a sentence.

The fluorescents flicker and the heaters tick, but Aaron stands unmoved except for his itchy trigger finger, which ratchets the blade wider. I stand as still as he, arm outstretched, unsure what to do if he won't comply.

The blade clicks into its lock with the finality of a door closing. Aaron's narrow pupils suggest intoxication, and I wonder if he's snorting his medication again.

I leave my hand extended, palm up, as I would to an

unfamiliar dog, hoping Aaron can't sniff the fear in me. He responds by tightening his grip until the tendons in his forearm quiver.

He's paralyzed, the blade gleaming as it trembles in his hand, so I swipe at it. The sucker punch connects, but his grip holds and the knife remains. A moment later, my palm shows a gash two inches long, but the blood lines it slowly, telling me the wound is shallow.

Seconds pass at the pace of weeks. I'm about to make another grab for his wrist when a wrecking ball wipes away all of it.

Next thing I know, Aaron is screaming and Marco is straddling him and the knife is spinning away from both of them.

Faster than I, Nate leaps for the weapon. He holds it up so we can all see its scythe of a blade.

"Murderous," he says. "It's got blood on it."

Mentally I rank him as the lesser threat, since Aaron is still wailing like a trapped puppy and Marco has a death grip on his hand. When I stoop to pull them apart, I see the butt of a pencil impaling Aaron's palm and his blood speckling Marco's T-shirt.

I know that my protector is about to be prosecuted. Even though Aaron violated school rules by bringing a weapon and should be expelled, my principal punishes actual violence more severely than threatened, and he will surely suspend Marco for the rest of the semester at least. Before my class is further diminished by a third or a half,

I separate the combatants to opposite corners, retrieve the knife from Nate, and send him to the office for help.

While we wait, Aaron holds his bleeding hand like it's destined for amputation. Marco rubs at a crimson smear on his wipe out! T-shirt. My own cut pulses out a thread of blood in time with my heart. Somehow we have all lost this fight.

I vainly seek an explanation for this tableau until Tiara awakes with a snort and asks, "What I missed?"

She sounds alert, though I'm skeptical. If she witnessed any part of the fracas and could testify, I'd offer her an A for the semester, but I know better than to hope for leniency. No matter what the kids say, I'll be blamed for the aftermath. Not even my war wound will be enough to elicit anything but condescension from my principal, the prig, who will interpret my injury as a failure in damage control. At best I'll get off with a reprimand, but probably it will go to a fair hearing, as though such a thing exists.

"Nothing happened," I say. "Go back to sleep."

As I'm tallying my losses, Ben distracts me by saying, "Norming."

"What?" I say.

He still won't look me in the eye, but he's no longer fixated on the window. "The boys"—he nods to his warring classmates—"they were norming."

And with that I know my career hasn't been a waste after all.

Every teacher, if they stay in the profession long enough, has a class like this: one where instead of supporting each other, students chafe; one where the jokes that never failed before fall flat, and the motivational tricks assembled throughout a career prove ineffective. Typically, our only revenge is report cards. I prefer fiction. And wine.

—David Hagerty

TRIP TO PARADISE

Diana Chambers

They say the Mission is part of San Francisco's sunbelt, but that's a poetic stretch. It certainly wasn't sunny today, one of those damp spring afternoons when you know summer is only going to get worse. The clouds hung over Dolores Park like a black eye as Jack Bridges squeezed his trusty Honda between a driveway and a red zone too shiny to ignore. The fact was, even plainclothes cops had to pay parking tickets—at least in his department.

It was a litany of regulations, all the thou-shalts and shalt-nots that had been wearing him down. That, and everything else.

Slamming the door of his SFPD Crown Vic, his partner, Sam Russell, crossed the street. "Why the hell you don't want gas and insurance on the City's dime, I'll never know."

"One less form to fill out. One less vehicle on the scene that doesn't shout *cop*."

"You're a good guy, Jack, but too damn ornery."

"Luckily, I got you to run herd on me." Jack winked. They'd had this conversation before, but Sam never quit trying to put him on the straight-arrow path. "Should have watched the weather report last night," he said, buttoning his plaid flannel Pendleton.

A wiser man in every regard, Sam was wearing his rain-or-shine Eddie Bauer parka. As they moved down Dolores Street, Jack surveyed the grassy park slopes—a few bundled-up dog walkers, the joggers in watch caps and mittens.

But the in-your-bones chill didn't deter anyone from ice cream. Bi-Rite Creamery was thronged as usual, people lounging out front with their cones, chatting or texting. Or both. The line flowed around the corner.

Shouldering through the crowd, Sam growled, "Doesn't anybody work these days?"

Jack edged past a guy entering a stock order on his phone. "It's the New Economy, man."

"Now you tell me. What the hell am I doing in this job?"

"Beats me." Jack glanced away from the young lovers sampling each other's flavors in a doorway. Ice cream was not on their menu today.

Nor was it on Jack's. The plan was to go in quiet, no action on the street, no vehicles to tip off the bad guys. He saw the determined set to Sam's shoulders. Today's bust would be Sam's first since losing his nephew to a lethal cocktail of crystal meth and opioids. The kid was an Advanced Placement high school student and star basketball player, but one Saturday night two months ago he'd partied with the wrong folks—the punks Jack and Sam were about to "visit."

Sam was prematurely gray, like Steve Martin with darker skin. But not as funny. In fact, he rarely smiled. It hurt him, Jack knew, how there were fewer and fewer brothers and sisters in the city, no more jazz clubs or AME churches. Good kids being brought down by drugs. Sam's culture was dying in San Francisco, so sure he was serious. But he was a man you could learn from. Rely on. Jack and he protected each other—from the brass as much as the bad guys.

Even so, the job extracted its pound of flesh, and all twenty-one grams of soul.

When things got too much, Jack took his old board to Ocean Beach and let the vicious surf beat it out of him. Sam handled his stress by nervous eating. His jacket had been getting progressively smaller over the past few years. It was now at the zipper-at-risk point. Jack always bitched at him to cool it with the pork ribs and jelly doughnuts, and Sam always protested it was his life, so back off. You could not ask for a better partner, though.

A block from the dealers' apartment, they passed some kids cutting class. Jack caught a whiff of that familiar skunk scent. But pot was Boy Scout stuff compared to the nasty shit being peddled these days. It was like pushing a damn boulder up Filbert or Jones—and he was getting weary.

Maybe he should have stayed in Racine, been a cop there, ice fishing and swatting mosquitoes. Or moved to Half Moon Bay, combatting pumpkin theft and illegal beach fireworks. Or another beach town, an ocean away, and maybe even a century—Hilo, a bit of tropical heaven that had turned his head around on a recent surfing trip.

He glanced at the purple-gray clouds getting ready to cut loose. It rained in Hawaii, too, but it was a nurturing rain, warm—like her. A lithe, focused surfer he'd met, a math teacher whose class you'd never cut. Lani had ignited something in him, a sense of hope. Which had taken shape with the Hilo PD job offer. It could be more than a one-week vacation and sunburn. It could be a life. A family. One thing he knew for sure, he preferred green and blue to gray and blood-red.

He and Sam rounded the next corner, pausing to eyeball the faded Victorian midway down the street, one of the few untouched by gentrification. The houses were quiet, the curbs lined with late-model cars, no junkers. Still, Jack's nerves were on high alert; he had a bad feeling—despite the no-knock warrant in his pocket.

They stopped outside the narrow building, two stories with dingy white trim, three drawn window shades upstairs, two on the bottom. Eight steps up to the brown door on the right. He brushed off a raindrop, exchanging a hard look with Sam.

Jack was first inside. He and Sam had cased the place one day while the two punks were out, seen the peeling wallpaper and five scratched brass mailboxes. Smelled the mildew. The light was dim, and they took it quiet and easy to the stairway.

The men hit the first step with a loud creak that froze them to the spot. They waited in dead silence. The only sound was a woman accompanying the Beatles in a melancholy rendition of "Yesterday." Following the music and an odor of sizzling garlic, they made for the second floor.

The hall was lit by a bare bulb hanging from the water-marked ceiling. Approaching the door at the end, they slowed and drew their weapons, moving lightly on rubber soles. Jack's gut tightened.

It wasn't so much the fear. It was more this world he was stuck in, the rules and fools and lowlifes. Dealers in shit dreams to kids. Poison for the masses. Then—flash forward—there they were, smirking as they strutted out the courthouse's revolving door, grinning in disdain. It was discouraging, depressing, all the budget cuts, the lack of respect.

Jack slammed his foot below the knob—flimsy wood and no resistance. He and Sam burst in, their weapons drawn.

"Freeze!" Sam ordered the two track-suited punks at the card table—which suddenly tipped over in a burst of white pills and plastic baggies.

"On the floor." Jack pointed his gun at the pair, one pimply, the other weasel-faced and cross-eyed. "Hands behind your heads."

They raised their hands and hit the floor. With a quick scan, Jack noted the sleeping bags jumbled on a couch, pizza cartons on the rear counter—and next to the counter, a closed door. The john.

While Sam covered him and the dealers, Jack crossed the room in about two strides ... reached for the knob ...

A heavyset, long-haired Latino burst from the bathroom firing a pistol.

Concealed by the door, Jack saw Sam drop behind the couch and return fire. The thug staggered back against the bathtub, his weapon falling with a clatter. He slid onto his butt, blood oozing through his tight maroon shirt. His open black eyes staring sightlessly.

The dealers were already pounding down the stairs. After a quick check of the dead man—two rounds in the chest and a third in the forehead—Jack and Sam dashed after them.

Under a heavy rain, they pursued their targets, racing toward an alley.

"Stop!" Jack commanded.

Stumbling and weaving and bumping into each other, probably high, they kept running.

Sam fired two rounds in the air.

At the alley, the pair halted, hands up, at a chain-link fence. Weapons ready, the officers moved in for the collar.

Jack grabbed the back of a soggy, sweaty jacket and flipped Weasel Face against the fence. Sam pushed the other punk next to him, covering the men as Jack patted them down.

"Clean." Jack reached for his cell to call for backup.

Sam cuffed them, reading their rights. "You have the right to remain silent ..."

"Yeah, yeah, eat it, man," the pimply one said. "We know all that."

"Anything you say ..." Sam continued, looking impassive even to the downpour.

"Holy shit. You're bleeding," Jack said, interrupting his call. He opened Sam's parka, seeing the trail of blood down the left side of his shirt. Into the phone he barked, "Send an ambulance and the meat wagon. We have an injured officer here and one dead *pistolero*."

After the Mirandizing was done, Sam found the nasty wound below his armpit.

Jack took his right arm. "Sit down, man."

"Yeah. Think I will. Feeling a little dizzy." Sam brushed off his damp brow and lurched toward the front stoop next to the fence.

Relieved to hear the siren, Jack re-cuffed the punks to the chain-link, pulled a bandanna from one of their pockets, and hurried to Sam. "That asshole in the john." He pressed the cloth against his partner's flesh. "Hold this."

With a wince, Sam put his right hand over the

bandanna. "Adrenaline rush. Never felt a thing … until now." A gray cast over his brown skin, he looked at Jack. "I'm the last cop that fucker's ever gonna shoot."

Jack delivered a grin, masking his concern. "The understatement of the year, partner."

A red-and-white ambulance skidded to a stop, double-parking in the street. Two San Francisco Fire Department paramedics hopped out, hurrying to the injured cop on the stoop.

"I'll do the paperwork on this one, buddy," Jack said. His Pendleton heavy and water-logged, he paced the slick sidewalk while they examined Sam. Another siren shrilled closer.

"Missed your lungs. Lucky," the female medic said, her freckled face screwed into a frown. "Doc just needs to cut the lead out and stitch you up."

After the other medic returned with a stretcher, they rolled Sam to the ambulance.

Walking alongside, Jack wiped off Sam's forehead. "Sounds like you'll make it, old man."

"You sure?" Sam tried to smile.

"If you don't, I'm gonna kick your ass all over the Mission."

Sam patted his left ribs. "I knew this padding was good for something," he said before the paramedics shut the door.

The red-and-white drove off with a splash of rainwater

that left Jack drenched from the knees down. He closed his eyes, but still saw gray concrete running with blood.

• • •

Jack's Levis were sodden, but at least the rain had stopped, and the sun peeked out with what Jack knew was false cheer. Finished at the crime scene, the lab boys and medical examiner emerged from the Victorian, moving back to their vehicles scattered around the steaming street.

As the dead Latino was carried out on a stretcher, the driver of the medical examiner's van crushed a cigarette underfoot, then opened the door.

"Burn that piece of shit," Jack said. "Don't waste space in the good earth on him."

"Anything you say, Bridges." The driver winked. "You need a ride?"

"Thanks, but I've got my own wheels."

As bad as it was for Sam, it could have been a lot worse, Jack realized, heading back through the Mission to his car. Their informant had told them there'd be two guys; they hadn't expected a third. The shooting troubled him. Too many close calls.

Customers had returned to Bi-Rite, or hadn't left—rain or not, it was the best ice cream in town. In the old days you could show your badge and jump the line, but no more. Besides, Jack had left his appetite back in that apartment. If he made time, he might avoid a ticket.

He was lucky there, too, for as he approached his blue

Accord, the windshield appeared empty. He only wanted to get to the station, finish the g-d paperwork, deal with the suits and protocol shit. Then check on Sam. Pulling out his remote ignition starter, he punched the button.

An explosion of sound and orange flames knocked him backward onto the wet pavement. Shards of glass and hot metal debris fell around him. Arm over his face, he rolled into a ball.

Squinting open his eyes, Jack watched the fire engulf what was left of his faithful Honda. Some poor kid's bike ate it, too.

As the smoke cleared, and somebody yelled into a phone at her front door, Jack lay there. Dazed, unhurt, and pissed. "Shit, man. I loved that car."

• • •

Jack erupted into his boss's office, slamming the door so hard it rattled the glass panel. Lieutenant Evans,, standing at the window, spun around.

"Somebody tried to kill me—put a bomb in my car."

About fifty years old, tall and thin, with a Marine's brush cut and a spit-and-polished demeanor, Evans stepped forward. "You must be kidding."

"When I hit my remote, the sonuvabitch blew all over the street. Luckily I was parked between a red zone and driveway, so no other vehicles got hit. No bystanders." Grabbing a straight-backed wooden chair, Jack banged it down in front of the desk and sat.

"I heard about Sam," Evans said, pained. "His prognosis is good, but it's tough. You want a cup of coffee? Some water?"

"What I want is a double shot of vodka and a beer chaser. And to know who in the department set me up!"

"Set you up? Get out of here." Evans lowered himself into his chair, shaking his head.

"Lieutenant, Sam and I had been working the case on need to know. Nobody on the outside knew we were hitting the target and when and where. Which leaves someone on the inside to have planted it or farmed it out."

"Really, Bridges? You're a little paranoid there. Don't you think? Why would any cop in this unit, the department for that matter, do such a thing? And why not Sam's car?"

"Sam keeps it bottled up. I'm the mouthy one, going on about all the shit around here. I pissed off the wrong person—and everyone has a price. That's the premise we work under when we want the bad guys to roll over. It's a two-way street."

"Maybe some pissed-off person—on the *outside*—tailed you. That damn Honda makes you stand out like a sore thumb. But, hey, you want an excuse to quit—just do it. We'll even throw you a farewell party."

"Save your money. I doubt anyone would show up. And hell if I care ... a fellow officer trying to cream my ass." Jack got up. Done.

"You're all wrong, Bridges," Evans said with a disgusted

look. "I'm placing you on administrative leave. Take that time to think about what you're saying."

Jack smiled coldly. "Sure thing, Lieutenant. But first, I am going to hit the hospital, look in on my partner, then head over to the Hang-Up for a vodka and beer chaser."

"Your second home, huh?"

"Truth is, I've broken many a case in that dive. The kind of people I need you don't meet in the library."

"You've got a good gut for the street. Get it together and you're up for a promotion, Bridges. Give it some serious thought."

"Exactly. While me and my gut are warming up that stool, I plan to give my life some very serious thought." Jack turned and made for the door.

"If I read you right—you're considering that offer from Hilo PD. Or the woman you met there got under your skin. Just come out and say it. Don't use all this 'somebody set me up' bullshit as an excuse. You taking that job or what?"

"Paradise is looking a lot better than the Mission." Jack looked back from the doorway. "And I hear the surf's up." Then he was gone.

• • •

Even at four in the afternoon, the Hang-Up was loud and smoky, Johnny Cash on the proud old jukebox and greasy burgers on the grill. Thinking about Sam, who swore he'd be back on the street in under a week, Jack watched the entrance from his booth.

"Thanks, Sid," he said as the barman served his second vodka and beer chaser.

The door opened. A short overweight man in an open gray raincoat crossed the room and squeezed in next to Jack, pushing him against the wall. The guy reeked of cigar smoke.

Jack eyed him, then knocked back the vodka. "Hello, Chub."

"You get my message?" Chub asked.

"The phone call ..." Jack slammed the glass on the table. "Or the other one?" *Sonuvabitch.* The lieutenant was right. "Why'd they have to junk my wheels? I was very fond of that car."

"Man says you're taking too much interest in his Mission enterprises. So, he makes a statement."

"It's my job ... was my job ... to bust the bad guys. Right?"

"Was?"

"Too close today. I thought somebody in the department got paid to set me up. You proved I was right to be paranoid. Only it was *your* gig. Mind telling me who?"

"You got to be kidding."

"No." Jack took a swig of beer. Glanced at Chub and smiled. "Just thought I'd ask. For old times' sake."

"For old times' sake is why I'm talking to your ass."

"Message received. Both of them. I'm out of here. Off to the land they call paradise."

"Good move, Jack. I knew about your remote starter from the time you and I took a ride. I owed you this one warning. Next time, you won't see it coming."

"What about my partner?"

"He needs to get assigned to Pacific Heights. Wounded in the line of duty—that shouldn't be hard."

Jack shook his head. "He's a tough nut, Chub. But I'll see what I can do."

"I like you, kid. Today was for the helping hands you sent my way. Go to paradise on your own before somebody sends you there."

Chub moved out of the booth and started away, then turned back. "For what it's worth—the guy who paid would never soil a finger in your lousy department." He buttoned his coat and headed for the exit.

Jack yelled after him, "Thanks for nothing, pal."

Chub raised a hand and waved him off.

Jack watched him go, wondering if there was any way you could relocate that twenty-one grams of soul. Maybe you could. Maybe it would be waiting in Hilo.

• • •

For the second time today, Jack burst into the boss's office. He pulled a wire and recorder from under his shirt, tossed it on a stack of papers.

Evans looked up, angry. "What the hell?"

"This is for my partner. And his crazy dream to clean up the streets." Jack stared him down. "Get Chubby London in front of a grand jury and twist him a little. Get him to talk, and you'll have the SOB who paid him to blow up my wheels. And controls the Mission drug trade. I'll call you from my new desk in Hilo."

"You're going to let your pension go down the drain?"

Jack gave him a pitying glance, then tipped his chin at the wire. "My parting gift to you, Lieutenant: The department wasn't involved in planting the bomb. You guys are clean as a whistle." He walked out, looked down the gray corridor.

With a grin, Jack picked up his pace. He had places to go.

Several years ago, my husband, Everett Chambers, and I worked on a script set on the Big Island of Hawaii. *A Very Romantic Death* is about a Japanese ritual double suicide, the investigating cop, with a subplot about the Hawaiian sovereignty movement.

We wondered how the San Francisco cop, Jack Bridges, ended up in Hilo, and the result is "Trip to Paradise."

—Diana Chambers

About the Authors

Ana Brazil (anabrazil.com) is the author of the historical mystery *Fanny Newcomb and the Irish Channel Ripper* (Sand Hill Review Press) and the winner of the Independent Book Publishers Association 2018 Gold Medal for Historical Fiction.

Ana earned her master's degree in American history from Florida State University, has worked as an architectural historian, and is now writing fiction full-time. Her heroines are the independent American women of the late nineteenth and early twentieth centuries who worked smart, fought hard, and persisted always.

Ana's ventures into short story writing include "Miss Evelyn Nesbit Presents," which appears in *Me Too: Crimes Against Women, Retribution, And Healing* (Level Best Books, September 2019).

Jenny Carless (jennycarless.com) began her writing career in environmental nonfiction and moved into corporate communications for Silicon Valley clients before tackling fiction. She loves international travel, wildlife, and photography. A safari addict, she spends as much time as possible in the African bush—which (along with a side trip to Zanzibar, in this case), is the inspiration for her fiction.

Diana Chambers (dianarchambers.com) was born with a book in one hand and a passport in the other. She began her explorations in the local library. From Paris cobblestones and Asian bazaars, she landed in Hollywood, where costume design led to scriptwriting. Then her characters demanded their own novels. The first was *Stinger*, an espionage thriller set in Pakistan and Afghanistan. Her latest, *Conspiracy of Lies*, takes place during the final days of Soviet Russia. She is working on a World War Two spy novel set in Asia and Europe. Diana lives in Sonoma County and is president of Sisters in Crime NorCal.

David Hagerty (davidhagerty.net) is the author of the Duncan Cochrane mystery series, which chronicles crime and dirty politics in Chicago during his childhood. Real events inspired all three novels, including the murder of a politician's daughter six weeks before election day (*They Tell Me You Are Wicked*), a series of sniper killings in the city's most notorious housing project (*They Tell Me You Are Crooked*), and the Tylenol poisonings (*They Tell Me You*

Are Brutal). The fourth book in the quartet, due for release in Spring 2019, derives from the false convictions of ten men on Illinois's death row. Like all of his books, David is inspired by efforts to right criminal injustice.

Vinnie Hansen (vinniehansen.com) fled the howling winds of South Dakota and headed for the California coast the day after high school graduation. She's now the author of numerous short stories, the Carol Sabala mystery series, and *Lostart Street,* a cross-genre novel of mystery, murder, and moonbeams. Still sane(ish) after twenty-seven years of teaching high school English, Vinnie has retired. She plays keyboards with ukulele bands in Santa Cruz, California, where she lives with her husband and the requisite cat.

Katherine Bolger Hyde (bhyde.com) is the author of the traditional mystery series Crime with the Classics (most recently *Cyanide with Christie,* Severn House, March 2019) as well as several books for children. Katherine lives in the mountains above Santa Cruz, where she shares a home with her husband, the youngest of her four children, and two obstreperous cats. When not reading, writing, or editing for her day job, she can generally be found knitting while watching British mystery series or singing in the choir at St. Lawrence Orthodox Church.

Judith Janeway's (judithjaneway.com) lifelong love of mystery and suspense infuses her recent works, *The*

Magician's Daughter and *Odds of Dying*. She won the Orlando Prize for "The Street Artist," which was published in *The Los Angeles Review*.

Judith holds a master's degree in Comparative Literature and a doctorate in Health Psychology. She worked as a social science researcher at the University of California, San Francisco, studying people coping with life-threatening illnesses and their caregivers.

She now writes full time. When she's not writing, she hangs out with family and friends, walks along the bay wetlands, and follows the varying fortunes of the Oakland Athletics.

Mariah Klein (mariahklein.com) lives in the San Francisco Bay Area with her husband, two daughters, and one son. A former public school teacher, she now works as a credential analyst for a university teacher education program. Mariah secretly aspires to be Jessica Fletcher, who managed to be a best-selling mystery writer while traveling the world and solving mysteries.

Mariella Krause (marla-cooper.com; mightybigideas.com) is a mystery author, travel guidebook writer, and freelance copywriter whose day job is coming up with ideas for other people. Writing as Marla Cooper, Mariella pens the Kelsey McKenna Destination Wedding Mysteries, currently being developed for television. Her debut novel, *Terror in Taffeta*, was a 2017 Agatha and Lefty award finalist for Best First Mystery Novel, and *Dying on the Vine* was a 2018 Lefty nominee for Best Humorous Mystery. Her goal in life is to be one of those people who splits her time between two different cities.

After a mix of odd jobs—exercise demonstrator, go-go dancer, office temp, house painter—it was probably inevitable that **Susan Kuchinskas** (kuchinskas.com) became a writer. As a journalist, she's covered a wide variety of technology and science topics, with a focus on automotive tech. She's the author of *The Chemistry of Connection: How the Oxytocin Response Can Help You Find Trust, Intimacy and Love* and the science fiction/detective novel *Chimera Catalyst*. The sequel to the novel will be published in 2019. She lives in El Cerrito with her mate, their socially challenged dog and super-chill cat, and some 50,000 honeybees.

Deborah Lacy's (deborahlacy.com) short mystery fiction has appeared in numerous magazines and anthologies, including *Alfred Hitchcock Mystery Magazine*, the anthology for the world's largest mystery convention. and *Mystery Weekly* magazine. She writes for Macmillan Publishing's Criminal Element (criminalelement.com) and runs the Mystery Playground blog (mysteryplayground.net).

Bette Golden Lamb (twoblacksheep.us) is an RN, three-dimensional artist, and writer. Unmistakably from the Bronx, she says that growing up in New York City and being an RN are clues as to why she loves to write dark and gritty medical thrillers. The Gina Mazzio RN thriller series, co-authored with J.J. Lamb, features a gutsy nurse who can't ignore life-threatening situations.

Bette also writes in other genres. Her science fiction novels, *The Organ Harvesters I* and *II,* will make your hair stand on end. *The Russian Girl* is a historical novel based on the true story of a woman lost in the New Mexico desert on the year's hottest day. Her delirium reveals her story: As a young girl she is forced to emigrate from Russia to America, where her life becomes one of upheaval, lost love, and activism in a turbulent twentieth century journey.

J.J. Lamb (twoblacksheep.us) started his writing career as a newspaper photojournalist, then an Associated Press staff writer. The US Army grabbed him, gave him a top-secret clearance, a locked room with file cabinet, a table, a chair, a typewriter ... and time to write fiction. His PI series, featuring Las Vegas–based Zachariah Tobias Rolfe III, got its beginnings in Virginia City, Nevada, and was further developed poolside at a nudist resort in Southern California. The most recent, *No Pat Hands,* was a Shamus Award nominee. A highlight of his writing career has been collaboration with wife Bette Golden Lamb to produce eight medical thrillers and three other crime novels.

Margaret Lucke (margaretlucke.com) flings words around as a writer and editor in the San Francisco Bay Area. She is fascinated by the power of stories and the magic of creativity. Margaret writes tales of love, ghosts, and murder, sometimes all three in one book. Two of her novels (*Snow Angel* and *A Relative Stranger*) feature artist/private eye Jess Randolph, and two others (*House of Whispers* and *House of Desire*) star Claire Scanlan, a real estate agent who specializes in haunted houses.

Margaret has published more than 60 short stories and feature articles, and is the editor of *Fault Lines*. She teaches fiction writing classes and has authored several how-to books on writing. She takes great pleasure in sharing her love of writing with others.

Susan C. Shea (susancshea.com) has five critically praised mysteries in print, all also in ebook formats, and several of them in audiobook formats. There are three Dani O'Rourke novels and two Burgundian mysteries so far, with two new manuscripts bubbling on the stove in 2019. She is amazed at this, since her dream when she quit her day job was to see one book published. She is on the national Sisters in Crime board and a proud member of the NorCal chapter.

Robin C. Stuart (robincstuart.com) is a veteran cyber crime investigator and author. Her nonfiction work includes contributing to *Handbook for Information Security*

(John Wiley & Sons, 2006). She consults on all things cyber security for Fortune 100 companies, series television, and media outlets including BBC and NowThis News. Robin was a significant contributor to the Tech Museum of Innovation's acclaimed Cyber Detectives interactive installation, one of the museum's most popular permanent exhibits, which opened in 2015 and earned praise from the Obama Administration. She lives in the San Francisco Bay Area.

Rich in the art, culture, and politics of Southeast Asia, **Nancy Tingley's** (nancytingley.com) art whodunits—*A Head in Cambodia* and *A Death in Bali*—feature a museum curator turned detective. Nancy, formerly a museum curator and art consultant, is a specialist in South and Southeast Asia. Her nonfiction includes *The Art of Ancient Vietnam: From River Plain to Open Sea*. Her flash fiction has been published in *Panoply, Moon Review, New Flash Fiction Review, 3Elements Review*, and *River and South Review*.

CJ Verburg's (carolverburg.com) hopscotch career—academic editor, award-winning playwright, director, author, traveler—is a passionate exploration of voices and places. Her Cory Goodwin mystery series (*Silent Night Violent Night, Another Number for the Road*) stars the international journalist daughter of New York detective Archie Goodwin. Her Edgar Rowdey Cape Cod mystery series (*Croaked, Zapped, Disarmed*), like her biography *Edward Gorey on Stage: A Multimedia Memoir,* honors the artist who was her long-time friend, neighbor, theatrical collaborator, and fellow Agatha Christie fan. In 2019 look for a longer story from CJ in *Sherlock Holmes Mystery Magazine* #30, and (fingers crossed) a new novel.

C.M. West (partnersincrimefiction.wordpress.com) is the pseudonym for co-authors Carol Elkovich and Mark Butler. As authors, visual artists, a college professor, a building contractor, and life partners—Carol and Mark draw on their collective experiences and keen imaginations to write dark-hearted stories sprinkled with ironic humor and eccentric characters. They live together in the East Bay with their brilliant teenaged son and two ridiculously entertaining Boston terriers. Their stories have been published in mystery periodicals and they are currently at work on a series of novels featuring artist sleuth Tru James and written against the backdrop of the avant-garde in Northern California.

Acknowledgments

To paraphrase a familiar adage, it takes a village to make a book. And as another old saying puts it, many hands make light work. *Fault Lines* is the product of the many hands—and the energy, time, and great ideas—of the members of the Northern California Chapter of Sisters in Crime.

We wish to acknowledge the guidance of president Diana Chambers and past president Terry Shames, who believed in the possibility of the project.

Highest honors go to Margaret Lucke who embraced the project wholeheartedly, researching the work of other chapters who have produced anthologies, guiding a committee to make decisions from the general to the specific, and finally to edit the stories. Her work has been exemplary.

Ana Manwaring, as our submissions coordinator, oversaw the collection and anonymous distribution of the manuscripts to the selection panel, who worked diligently

ACKNOWLEDGMENTS

to select the best from a fine group of submissions. The panel members included Mysti Berry, Margie Bunting, Pat Dusenbury, Heather Haven, Thonie Hevron, Mariella Krause, Rita Lakin, and Terry Shames.

Throughout the process of planning, producing, and publicizing the anthology, we had willing volunteers who contributed their work and their valuable ideas: Margie Bunting, Leann Connell, Vinnie Hansen, Mariella Krause, Deborah Lacy, Terry Shames, Nancy Tingley, and CJ Verburg. Sue Trowbridge designed the interior of the book, and Miguel Ortuno of PR Chicago/Cover Story Design created the cover.

Our thanks to one and all.

About Sisters in Crime, NorCal

The Northern California Chapter of Sisters in Crime brings together women and men who share a common passion for mysteries and crime fiction and who support the goals of Sisters in Crime. Known familiarly as SinC NorCal, our organization is affiliated with the national Sisters of Crime organization (www.sistersincrime.org).

The chapter's motto is "Quaking in Our Books." Founded in 1992 and guided by a volunteer executive committee, SinC NorCal counts both writers and readers among our 150 members. We offer opportunities for:

- Networking with fans, authors, agents, publishers, booksellers, and librarians.

- Learning from experts about mystery literature, the craft of the writing, and related fields like law enforcement, forensic anthropology, and medicine.

- Promoting members' work through events, publications, and an active speakers bureau.

SinC NorCal activities include monthly meetings and field trips to local sites of interest to readers and writers of crime fiction. The quarterly newsletter, *Stiletta*, features interesting articles on a variety of mystery and crime topics and keeps members up to date about their favorite local authors' books and events.

We invite you to join us. Please check out our website for details.

www.sincnorcal.org

Made in the USA
Columbia, SC
20 April 2019